G-MAN

Learning to Fly

by Chris Giarrusso

Learning to Fly

created, written & illustrated by
CHRIS GIARRUSSO

THE MIGHTY SKULLBOY ARMY appearances co-written & illustrated by
JACOB CHABOT

web design, book design & color assists by
DAVE GIARRUSSO

edited by
BRANWYN BIGGLESTONE

www.chrisGcomics.com

IMAGE COMICS, INC.
Robert Kirkman - Chief Operating Officer
Erik Larsen - Chief Financial Officer
Todd McFarlane - President
Marc Silvestri - Chief Executive Officer
Jim Valentino - Vice President

Eric Stephenson - Publisher
Todd Martinez - Sales & Licensing Coordinator
Jennifer de Guzman - PR & Marketing Director
Branwyn Bigglestone - Accounts Manager
Emily Miller - Administrative Assistant
Jamie Parreno - Marketing Assistant
Sarah deLaine - Events Coordinator
Kevin Yuen - Digital Rights Coordinator
Jonathan Chan - Production Manager
Drew Gill - Art Director
Monica Garcia- Production Artist
Vincent Kukua - Production Artist
Jana Cook - Production Artist

www.imagecomics.com

For International Rights contact - foreignlicensing@imagecomics.com

G-MAN, VOL 1: LEARNING TO FLY. Third Printing. October 2012.
Published by Image Comics, Inc.
Office of publication: 2134 Allston Way, 2nd Floor, Berkeley, CA 94704.

ISBN: 978-1-60706-270-7

CHAPTER ONE
STAY OFF THE ROOF!

An all too common misconception among beginner flyers is the notion that jumping from high places such as cliffs, tree branches, or rooftops will aid in or result in flight. In actuality, such behavior is not only ineffective, but also highly dangerous and will almost always result in serious injury or death. The authors and publishers of this book do not condone such behavior and will not be held responsible or liable for the consequences resulting from such behavior.

The purpose of this book is to teach the safest methods and techniques for super-human flight, which always begin on the ground.

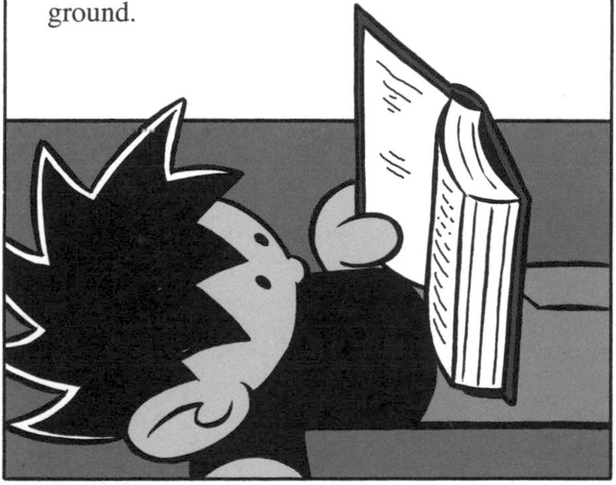

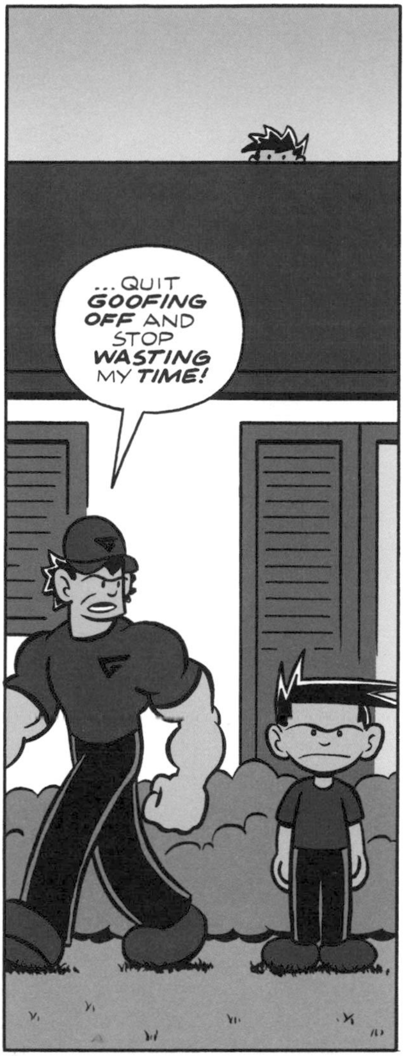
...QUIT *GOOFING OFF* AND STOP *WASTING* MY *TIME!*

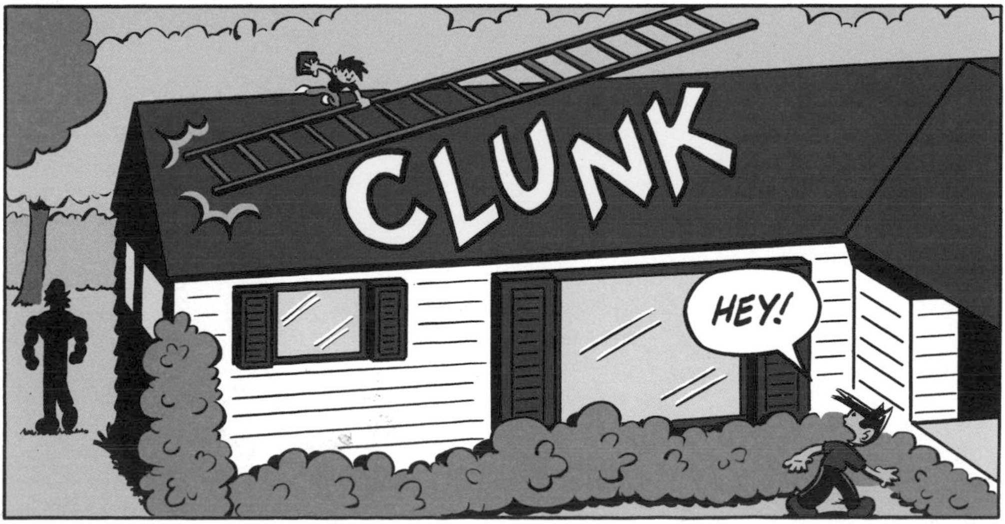
CLUNK
HEY!

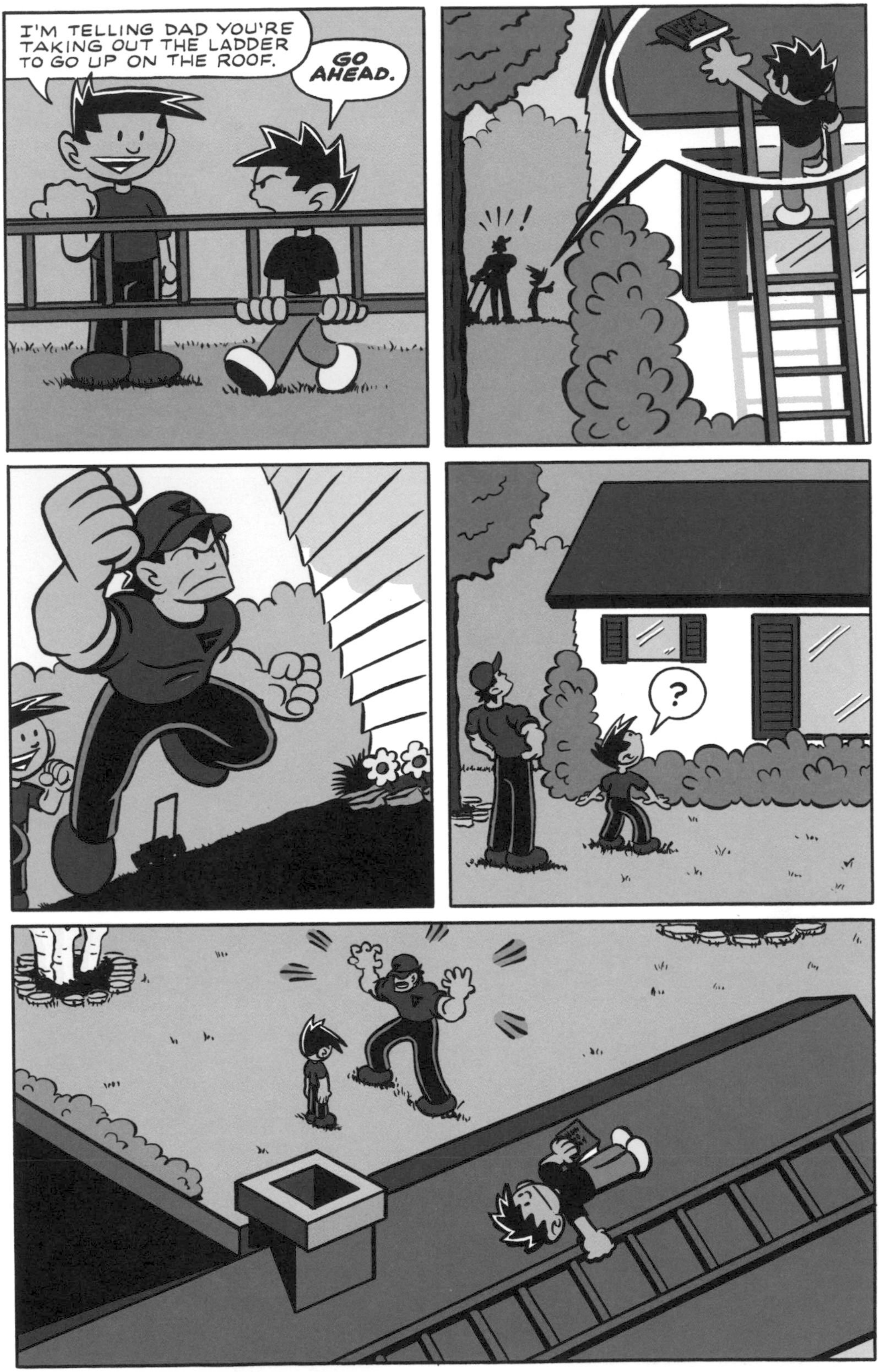
I'M TELLING DAD YOU'RE TAKING OUT THE LADDER TO GO UP ON THE ROOF.
GO AHEAD.
!!!!
?

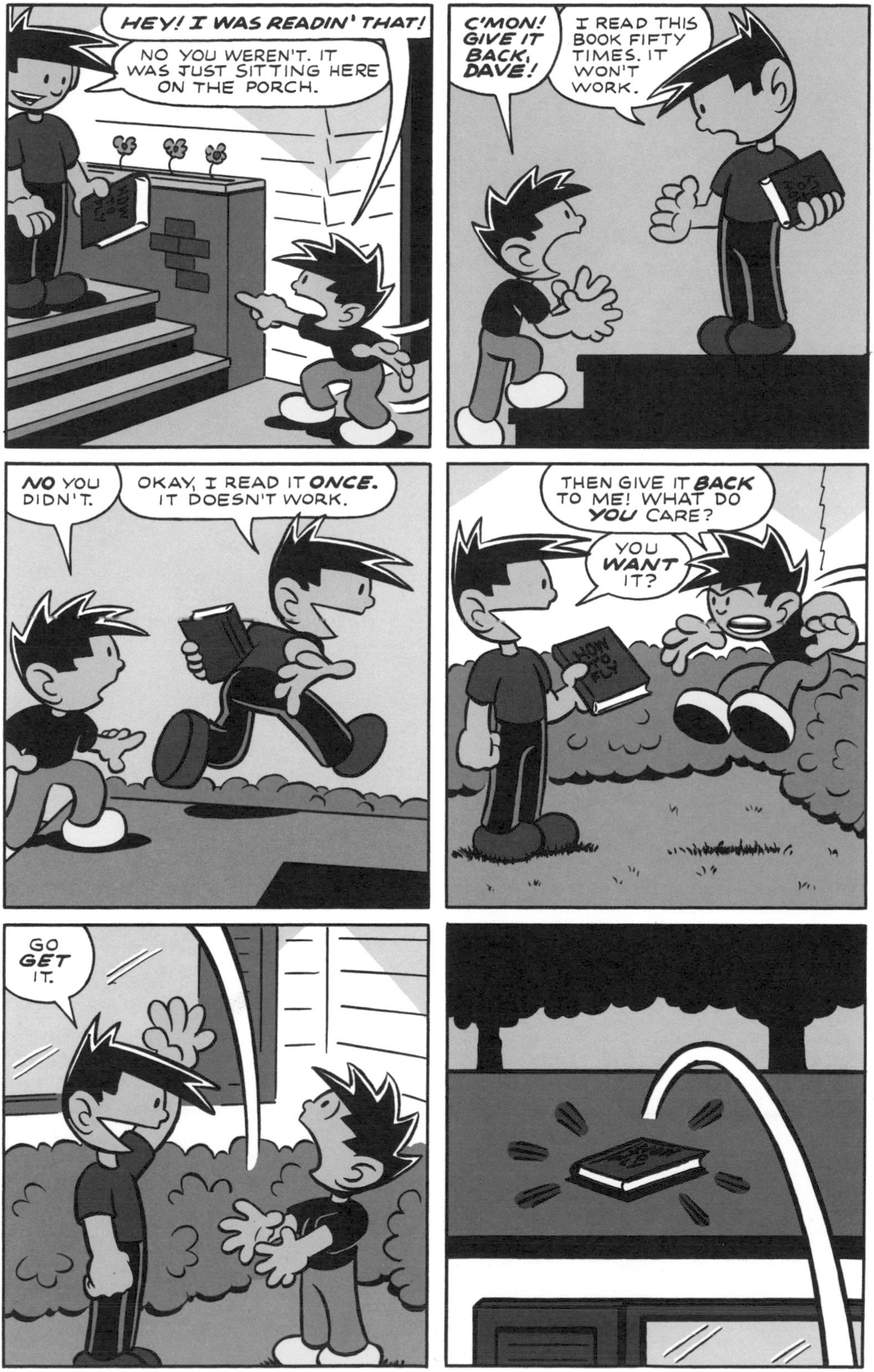
HEY! I WAS READIN' THAT!
NO YOU WEREN'T. IT WAS JUST SITTING HERE ON THE PORCH.
HOW TO FLY
C'MON! GIVE IT BACK, DAVE!
I READ THIS BOOK FIFTY TIMES. IT WON'T WORK.
NO YOU DIDN'T.
OKAY, I READ IT ONCE. IT DOESN'T WORK.
THEN GIVE IT BACK TO ME! WHAT DO YOU CARE?
YOU WANT IT?
HOW TO FLY
GO GET IT.

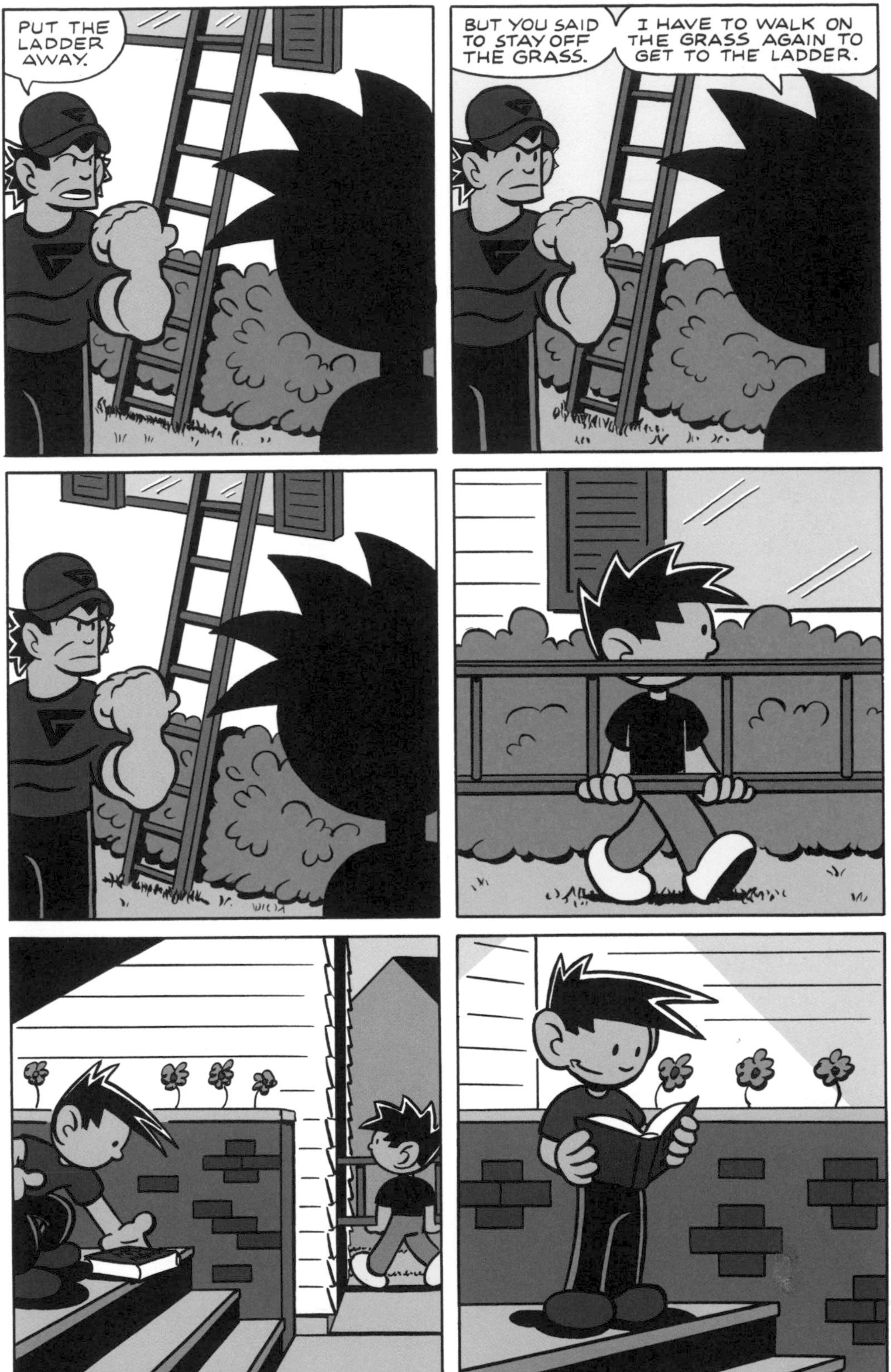
PUT THE LADDER AWAY.
BUT YOU SAID TO STAY OFF THE GRASS.
I HAVE TO WALK ON THE GRASS AGAIN TO GET TO THE LADDER.

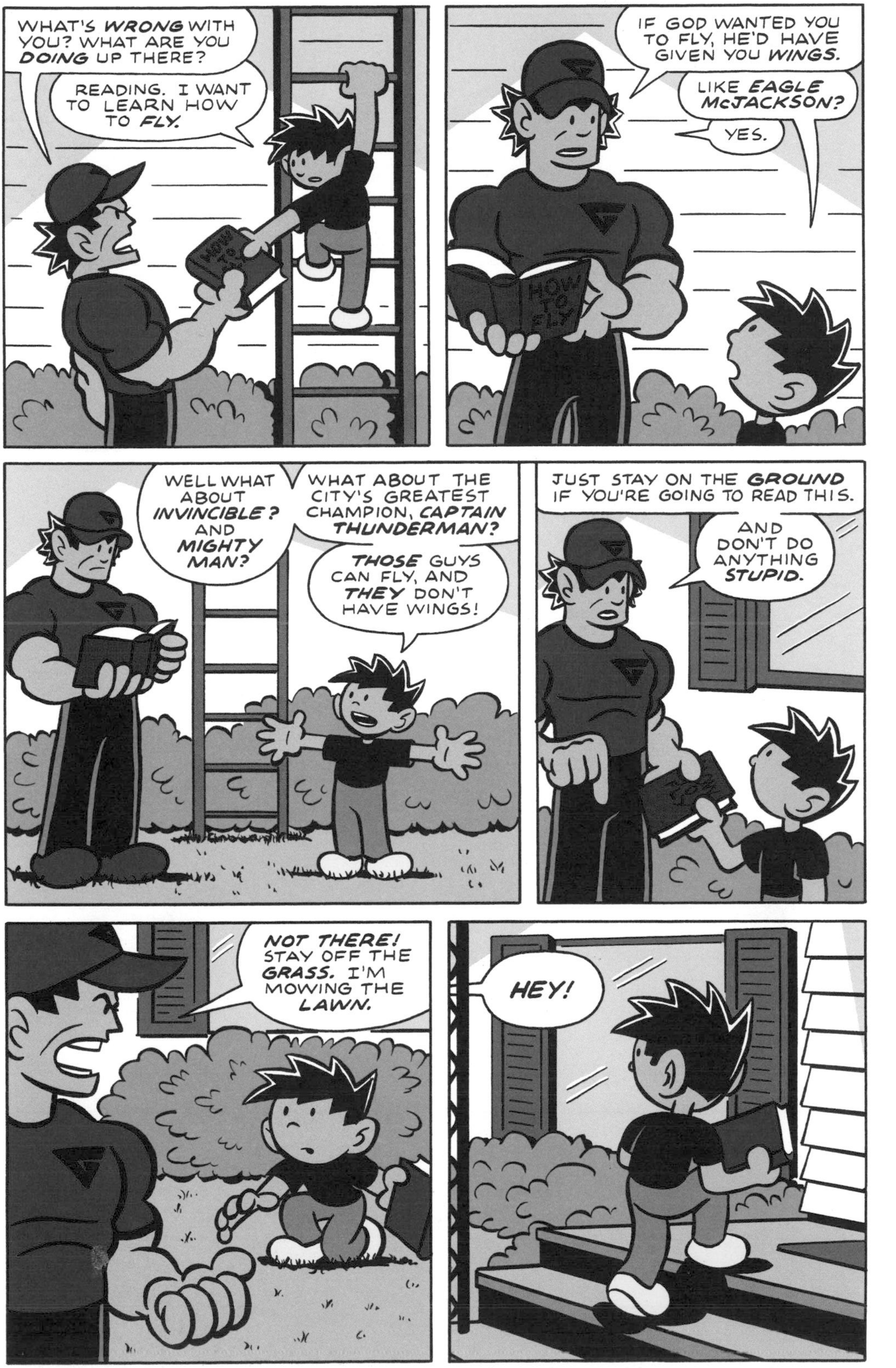
WHAT'S WRONG WITH YOU? WHAT ARE YOU DOING UP THERE?
READING. I WANT TO LEARN HOW TO FLY.
HOW TO FLY
IF GOD WANTED YOU TO FLY, HE'D HAVE GIVEN YOU WINGS.
LIKE EAGLE McJACKSON?
YES.
HOW TO FLY
WELL WHAT ABOUT INVINCIBLE? AND MIGHTY MAN?
WHAT ABOUT THE CITY'S GREATEST CHAMPION, CAPTAIN THUNDERMAN?
THOSE GUYS CAN FLY, AND THEY DON'T HAVE WINGS!
JUST STAY ON THE GROUND IF YOU'RE GOING TO READ THIS.
AND DON'T DO ANYTHING STUPID.
NOT THERE! STAY OFF THE GRASS. I'M MOWING THE LAWN.
HEY!

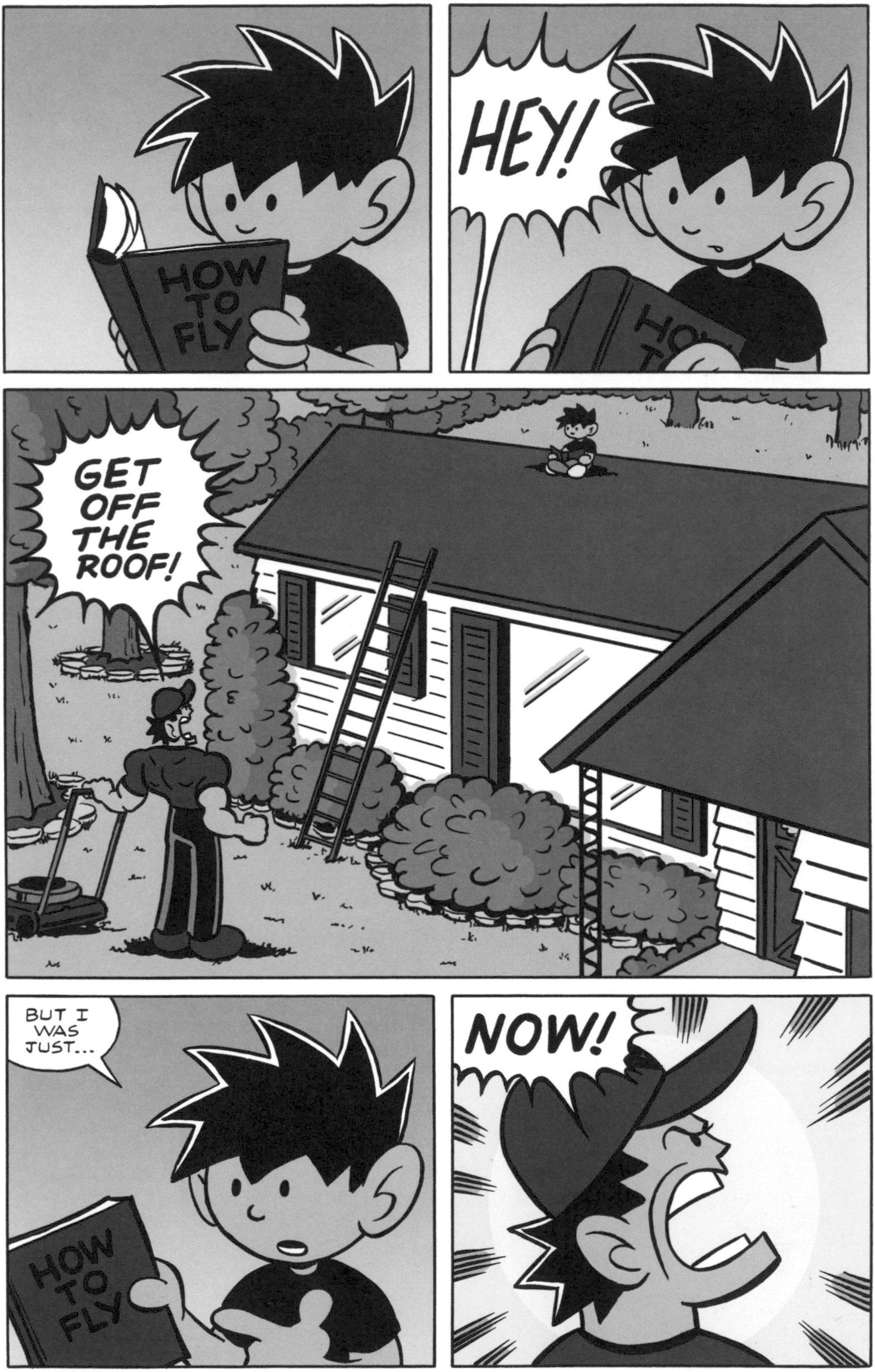

HOW TO FLY
HEY!
GET OFF THE ROOF!
BUT I WAS JUST...
HOW TO FLY
NOW!

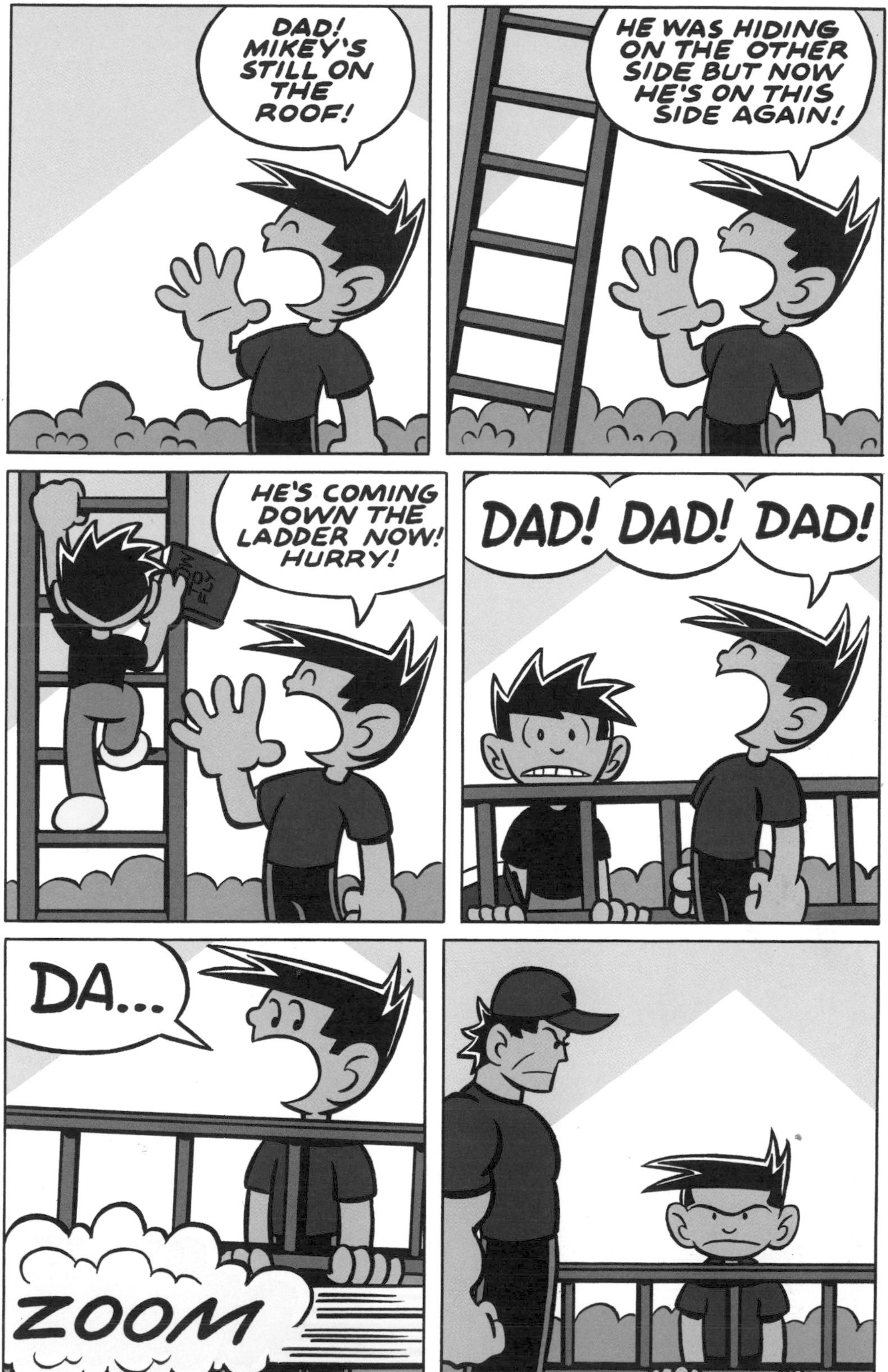
DAD! MIKEY'S STILL ON THE ROOF!
HE WAS HIDING ON THE OTHER SIDE BUT NOW HE'S ON THIS SIDE AGAIN!
HE'S COMING DOWN THE LADDER NOW! HURRY!
DAD! DAD! DAD!
DA...
ZOOM

CHAPTER THREE
LEVITATION

Levitation, or floating, is the first step towards achieving flight. If you are warmed up, in your proper attire, and on solid ground, you are ready to levitate.

To begin, get in your levitation stance and concentrate on supernaturally overcoming the forces of gravity. It is important to resist jumping, as jumping involves a state of mind that acknowledges the laws of physics -- the very laws we seek to ignore!

Through meditation, simply open a dialogue between the cells of your body and the molecules of the surrounding air, and you'll be levitating in no time!

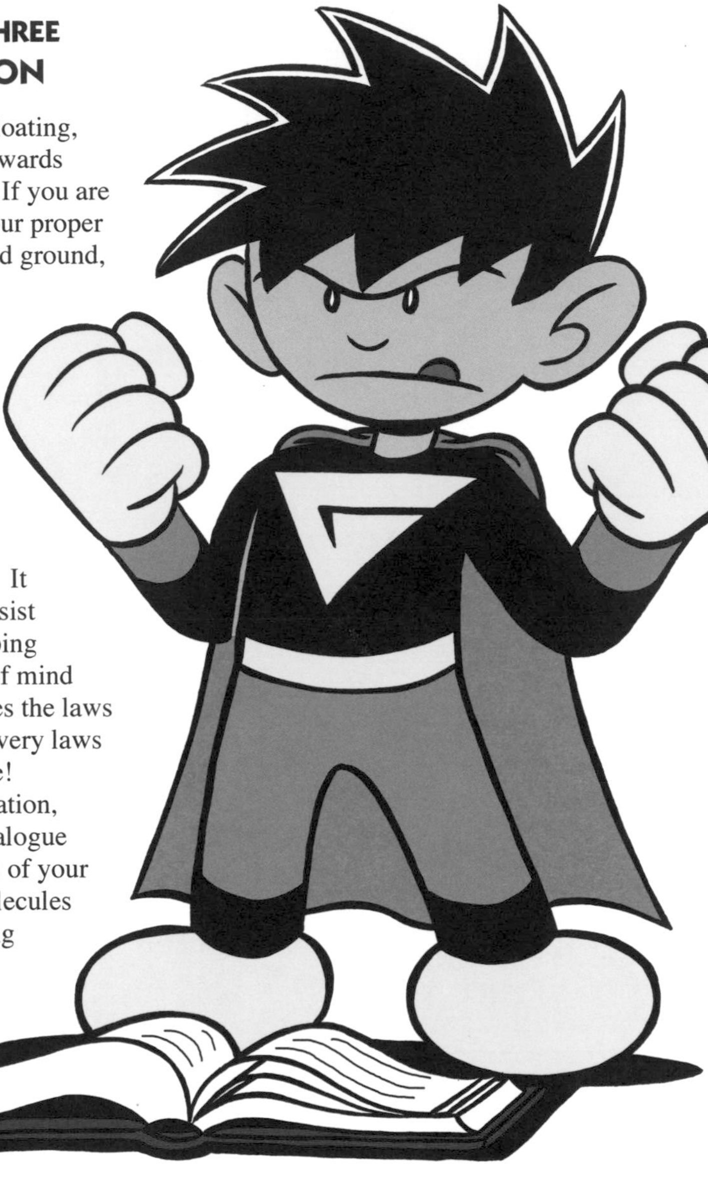

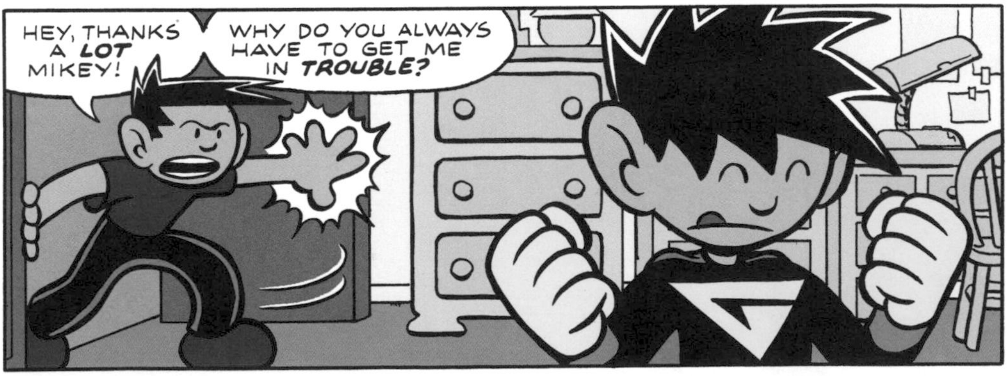
HEY, THANKS A ***LOT*** MIKEY!
WHY DO YOU ALWAYS HAVE TO GET ME IN ***TROUBLE?***

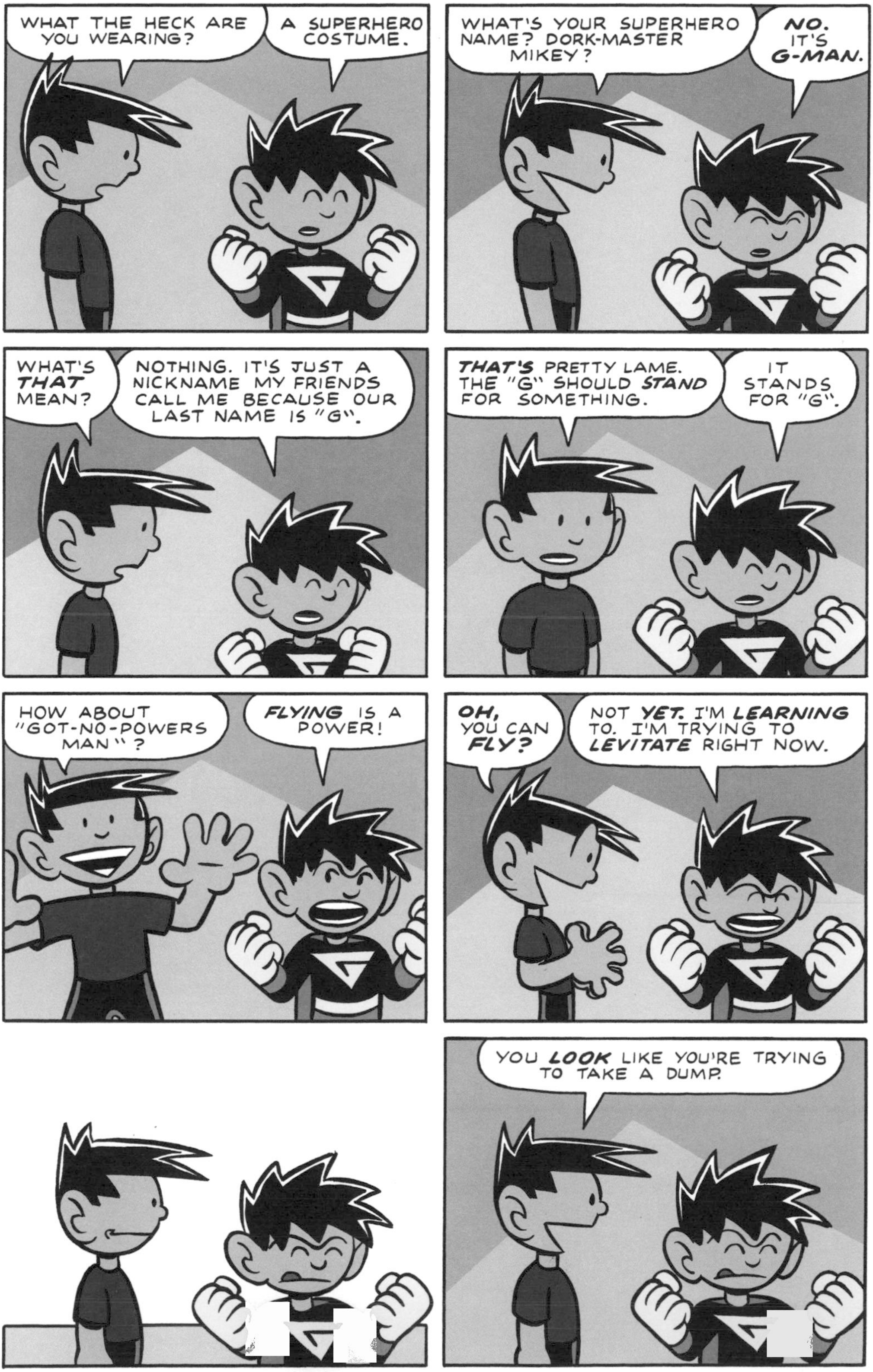
WHAT THE HECK ARE YOU WEARING?
A SUPERHERO COSTUME.
WHAT'S YOUR SUPERHERO NAME? DORK-MASTER MIKEY?
NO. IT'S G-MAN.
WHAT'S THAT MEAN?
NOTHING. IT'S JUST A NICKNAME MY FRIENDS CALL ME BECAUSE OUR LAST NAME IS "G".
THAT'S PRETTY LAME. THE "G" SHOULD STAND FOR SOMETHING.
IT STANDS FOR "G".
HOW ABOUT "GOT-NO-POWERS MAN"?
FLYING IS A POWER!
OH, YOU CAN FLY?
NOT YET. I'M LEARNING TO. I'M TRYING TO LEVITATE RIGHT NOW.
YOU LOOK LIKE YOU'RE TRYING TO TAKE A DUMP.

YOU SHOULD GET RID OF THIS CAPE. IT LOOKS STUPID.

LET GO! THE CAPE'S THE MOST IMPORTANT PART!

SEE?!

IT SAYS SO RIGHT HERE!

The cape* is considered by many to be the most important part of the flight uniform because wearing a cape helps to convince your environment that gravity holds no power over you.

Wind resistance is not a factor in flight, nor are most laws of science

YEAH, WHATEVER. I ALREADY READ THAT BOOK.

I TOLD YOU IT DOESN'T WORK.

WHAT THE--?

MISSED THAT PART BEFORE!

considered to be the most part of the because we helps to con environme gravity ho no power over you.

*Magic capes work best.

...LAST NIGHT WHEN CAPTAIN THUNDERMAN ENDED MISTER MENTAL'S CRIMINAL RAMPAGE BY TOSSING HIM INTO THE CITY VOLCANO. IN OTHER NEWS...

HEY MOM, WHERE'S OUR MAGIC BLANKET?

CHECK THE HALL CLOSET.

SNIP SNIP

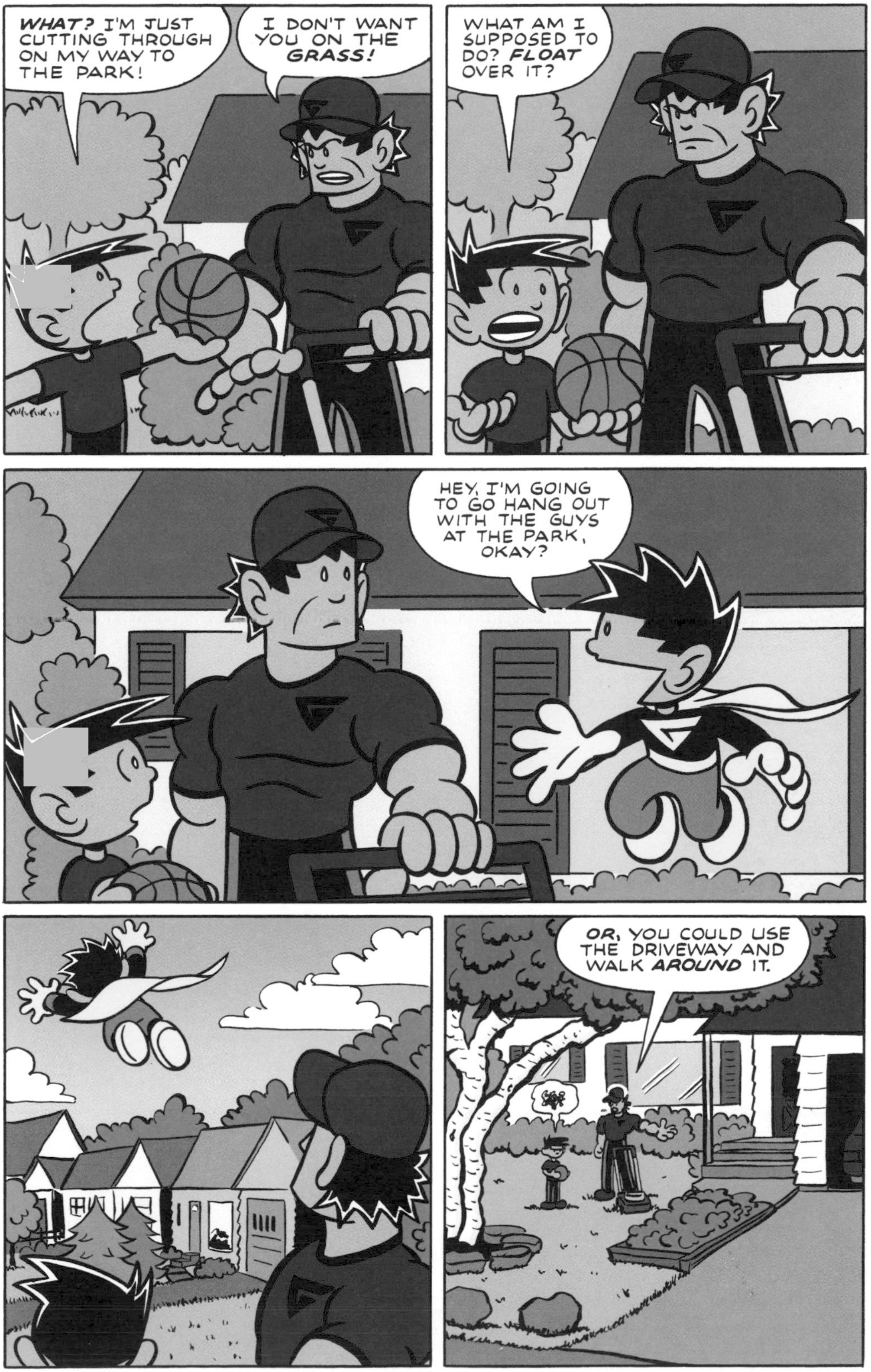
WHAT? I'M JUST CUTTING THROUGH ON MY WAY TO THE PARK!
I DON'T WANT YOU ON THE GRASS!
WHAT AM I SUPPOSED TO DO? FLOAT OVER IT?
HEY, I'M GOING TO GO HANG OUT WITH THE GUYS AT THE PARK, OKAY?
OR, YOU COULD USE THE DRIVEWAY AND WALK AROUND IT.

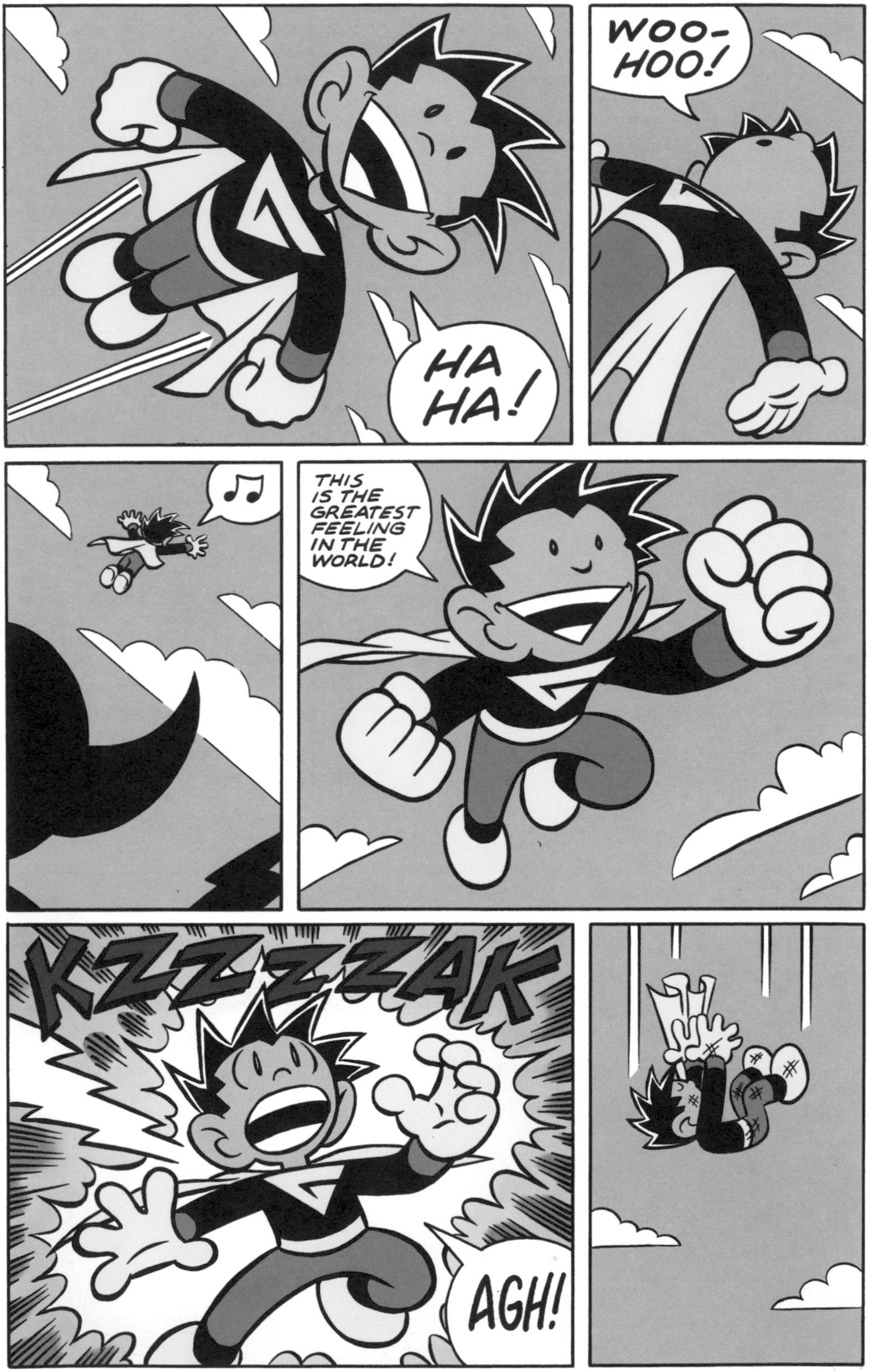
HA HA!
WOO-HOO!
♫
THIS IS THE GREATEST FEELING IN THE WORLD!
KZZZZZAK
AGH!

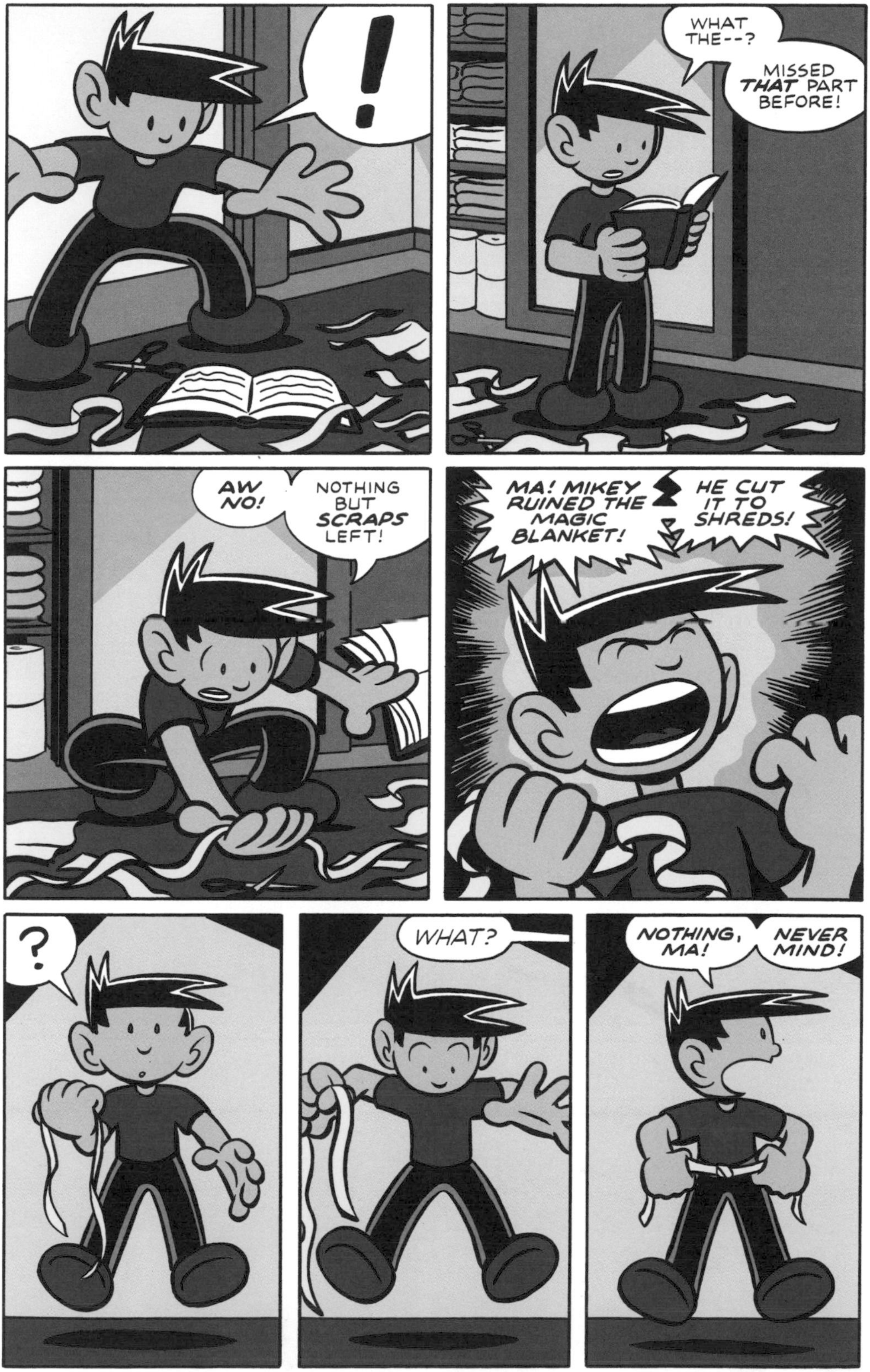
!
WHAT THE--?
MISSED THAT PART BEFORE!
AW NO!
NOTHING BUT SCRAPS LEFT!
MA! MIKEY RUINED THE MAGIC BLANKET!
HE CUT IT TO SHREDS!
?
WHAT?
NOTHING, MA!
NEVER MIND!

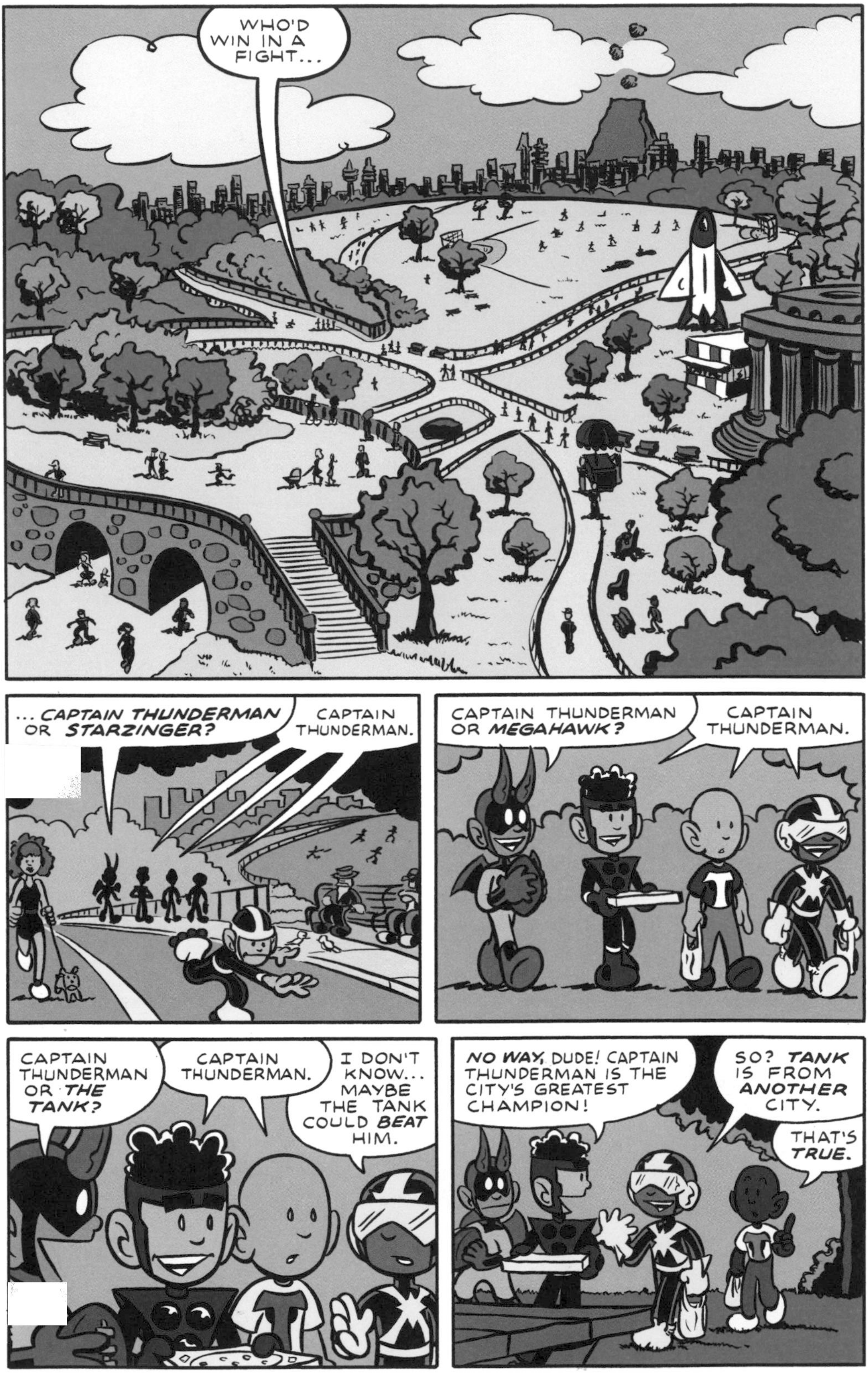
WHO'D WIN IN A FIGHT...
...CAPTAIN THUNDERMAN OR STARZINGER?
CAPTAIN THUNDERMAN.
CAPTAIN THUNDERMAN OR MEGAHAWK?
CAPTAIN THUNDERMAN.
CAPTAIN THUNDERMAN OR THE TANK?
CAPTAIN THUNDERMAN.
I DON'T KNOW... MAYBE THE TANK COULD BEAT HIM.
NO WAY, DUDE! CAPTAIN THUNDERMAN IS THE CITY'S GREATEST CHAMPION!
SO? TANK IS FROM ANOTHER CITY.
THAT'S TRUE.

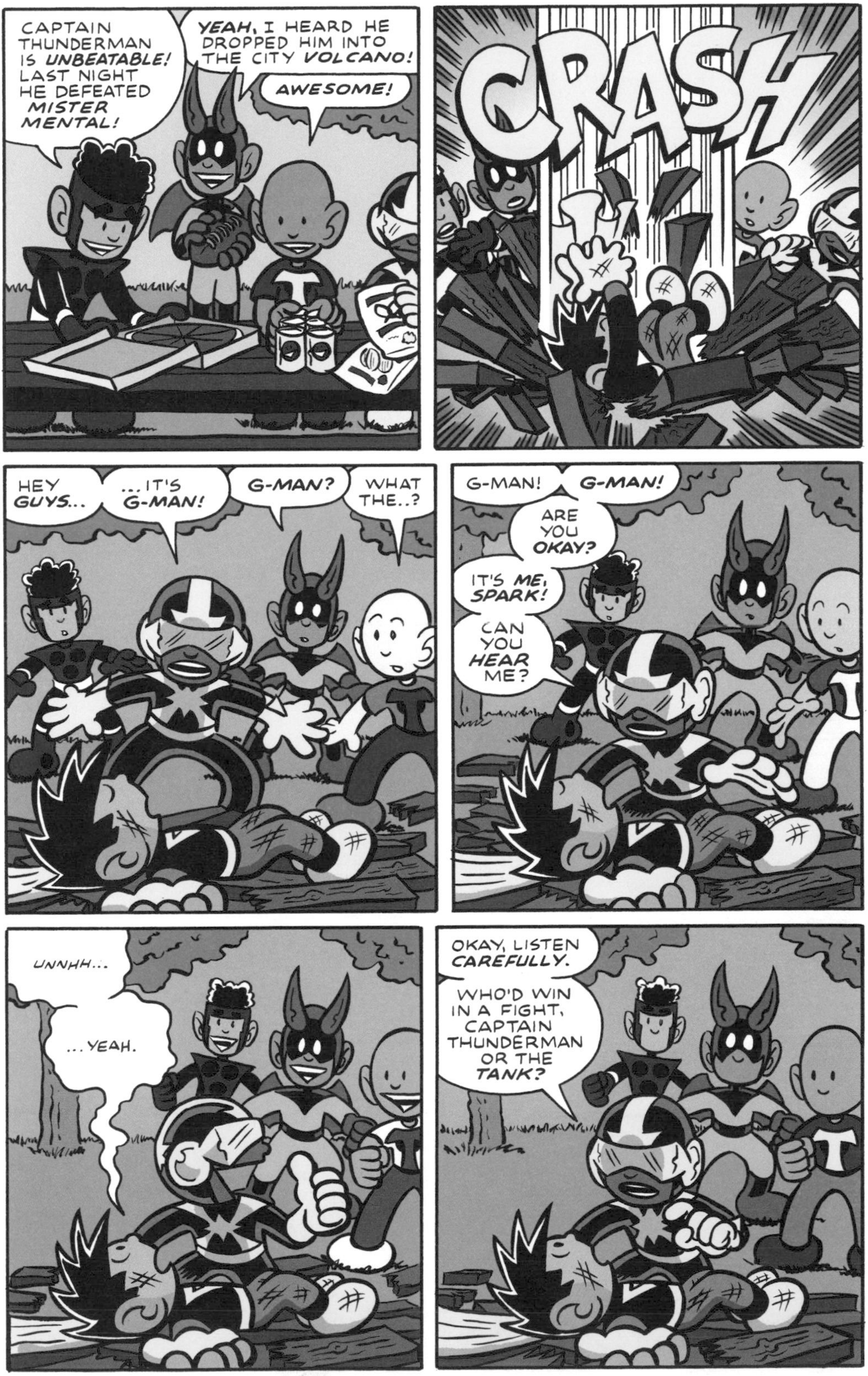
CAPTAIN THUNDERMAN IS UNBEATABLE! LAST NIGHT HE DEFEATED MISTER MENTAL!
YEAH, I HEARD HE DROPPED HIM INTO THE CITY VOLCANO!
AWESOME!
CRASH
HEY GUYS...
...IT'S G-MAN!
G-MAN?
WHAT THE..?
G-MAN!
G-MAN!
ARE YOU OKAY?
IT'S ME, SPARK!
CAN YOU HEAR ME?
UNNHH...
...YEAH.
OKAY, LISTEN CAREFULLY.
WHO'D WIN IN A FIGHT, CAPTAIN THUNDERMAN OR THE TANK?

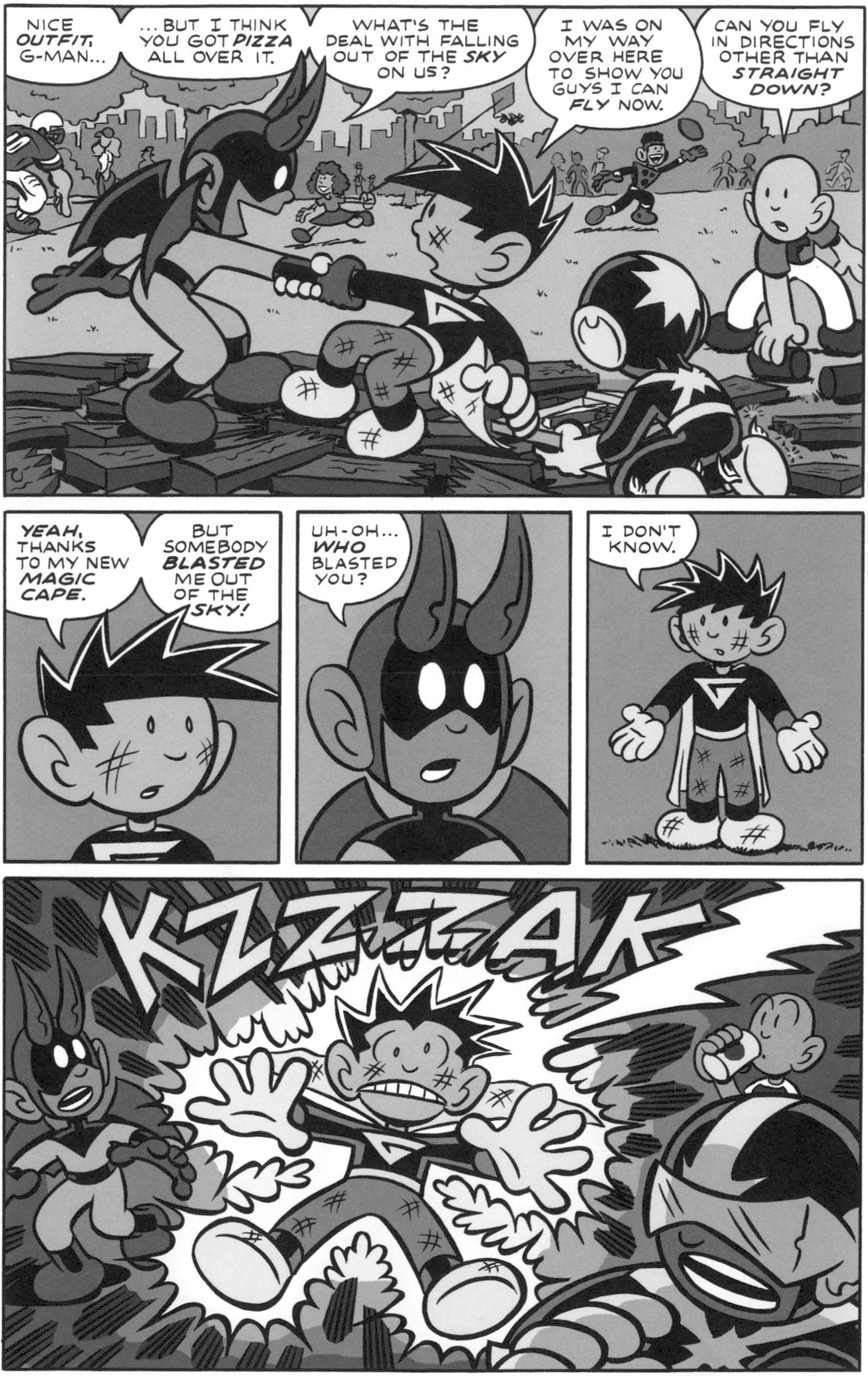
NICE OUTFIT, G-MAN...
... BUT I THINK YOU GOT PIZZA ALL OVER IT.
WHAT'S THE DEAL WITH FALLING OUT OF THE SKY ON US?
I WAS ON MY WAY OVER HERE TO SHOW YOU GUYS I CAN FLY NOW.
CAN YOU FLY IN DIRECTIONS OTHER THAN STRAIGHT DOWN?
YEAH, THANKS TO MY NEW MAGIC CAPE.
BUT SOMEBODY BLASTED ME OUT OF THE SKY!
UH-OH... WHO BLASTED YOU?
I DON'T KNOW.
KZZZAK

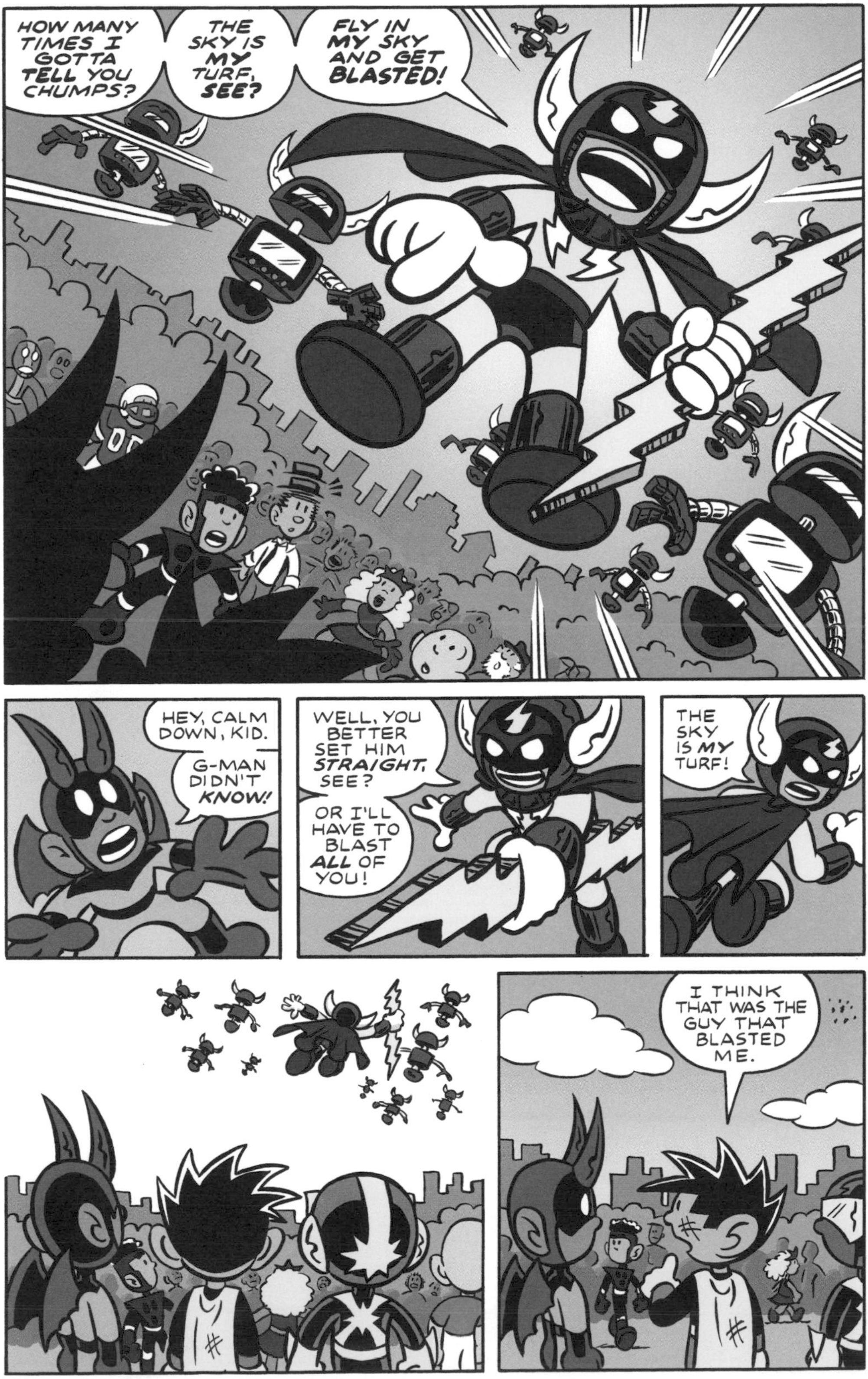
HOW MANY TIMES I GOTTA TELL YOU CHUMPS?
THE SKY IS MY TURF, SEE?
FLY IN MY SKY AND GET BLASTED!
HEY, CALM DOWN, KID.
G-MAN DIDN'T KNOW!
WELL, YOU BETTER SET HIM STRAIGHT, SEE?
OR I'LL HAVE TO BLAST ALL OF YOU!
THE SKY IS MY TURF!
I THINK THAT WAS THE GUY THAT BLASTED ME.

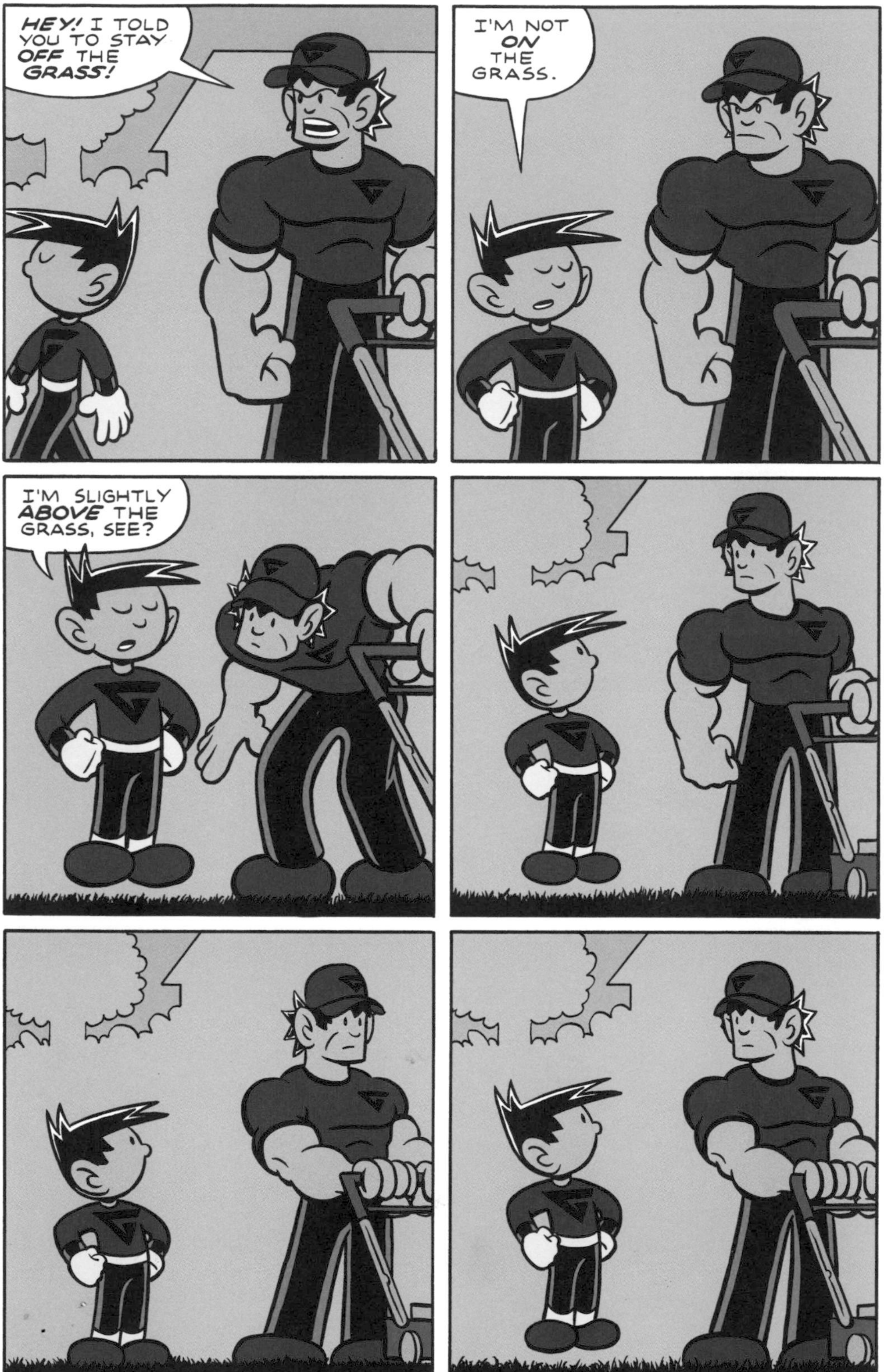
HEY! I TOLD YOU TO STAY OFF THE GRASS!
I'M NOT ON THE GRASS.
I'M SLIGHTLY ABOVE THE GRASS, SEE?

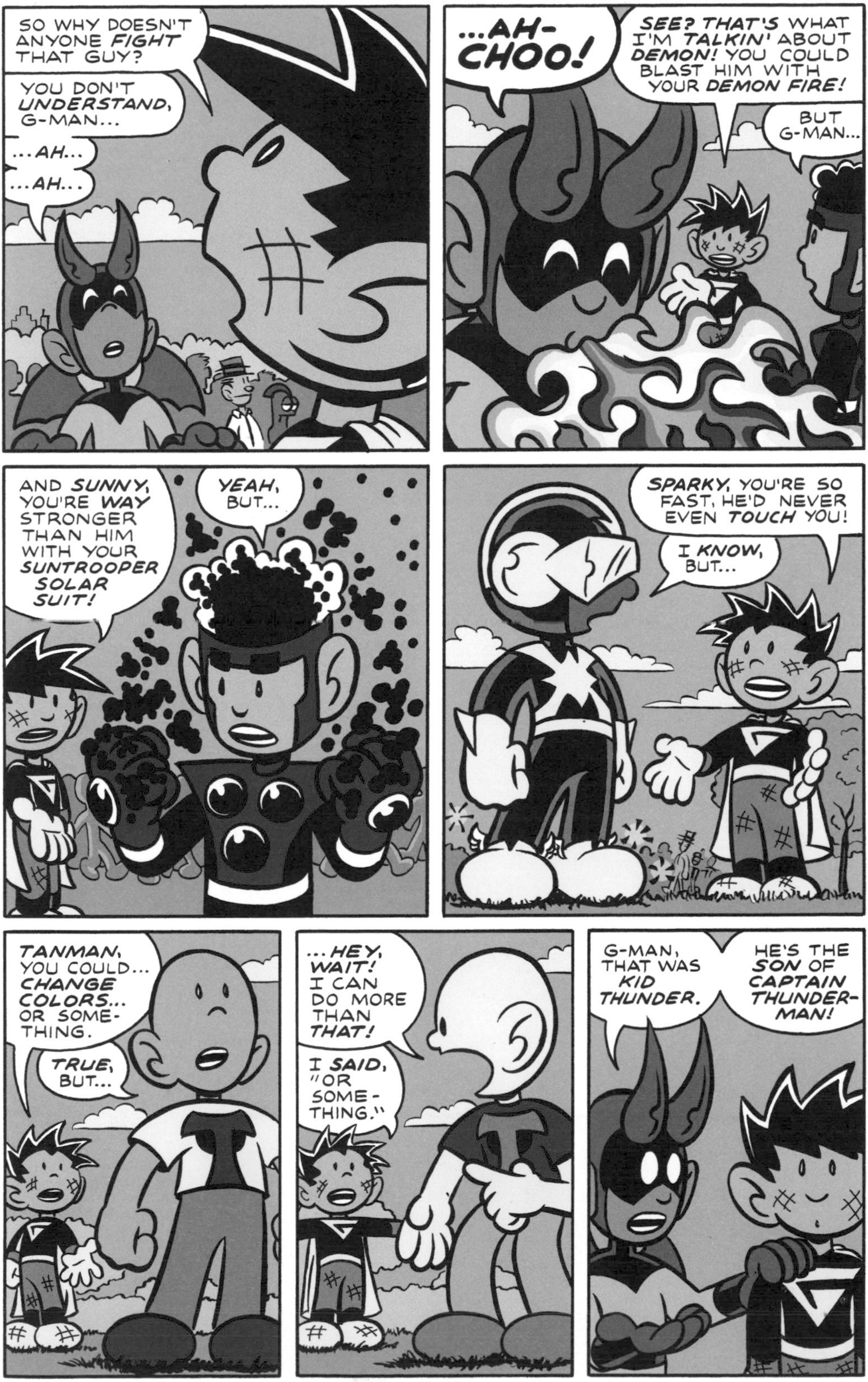
SO WHY DOESN'T ANYONE FIGHT THAT GUY?
YOU DON'T UNDERSTAND, G-MAN...
...AH...
...AH...
...AH-CHOO!
SEE? THAT'S WHAT I'M TALKIN' ABOUT DEMON! YOU COULD BLAST HIM WITH YOUR DEMON FIRE!
BUT G-MAN...
AND SUNNY, YOU'RE WAY STRONGER THAN HIM WITH YOUR SUNTROOPER SOLAR SUIT!
YEAH, BUT...
SPARKY, YOU'RE SO FAST, HE'D NEVER EVEN TOUCH YOU!
I KNOW, BUT...
TANMAN, YOU COULD... CHANGE COLORS... OR SOMETHING.
TRUE, BUT...
...HEY, WAIT! I CAN DO MORE THAN THAT!
I SAID, "OR SOMETHING."
G-MAN, THAT WAS KID THUNDER.
HE'S THE SON OF CAPTAIN THUNDERMAN!

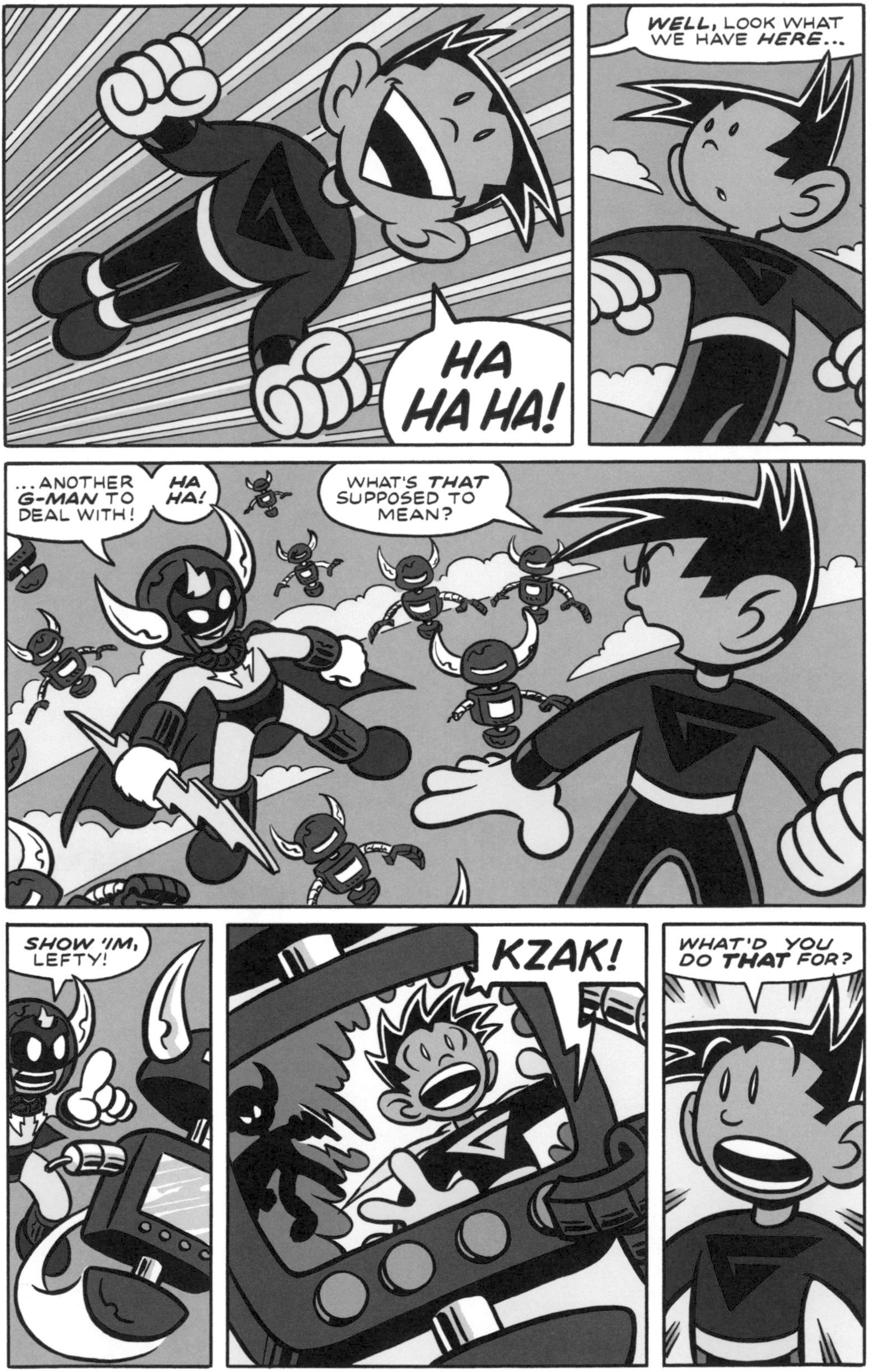
HA HA HA!
WELL, LOOK WHAT WE HAVE HERE...
...ANOTHER G-MAN TO DEAL WITH!
HA HA!
WHAT'S THAT SUPPOSED TO MEAN?
SHOW 'IM, LEFTY!
KZAK!
WHAT'D YOU DO THAT FOR?

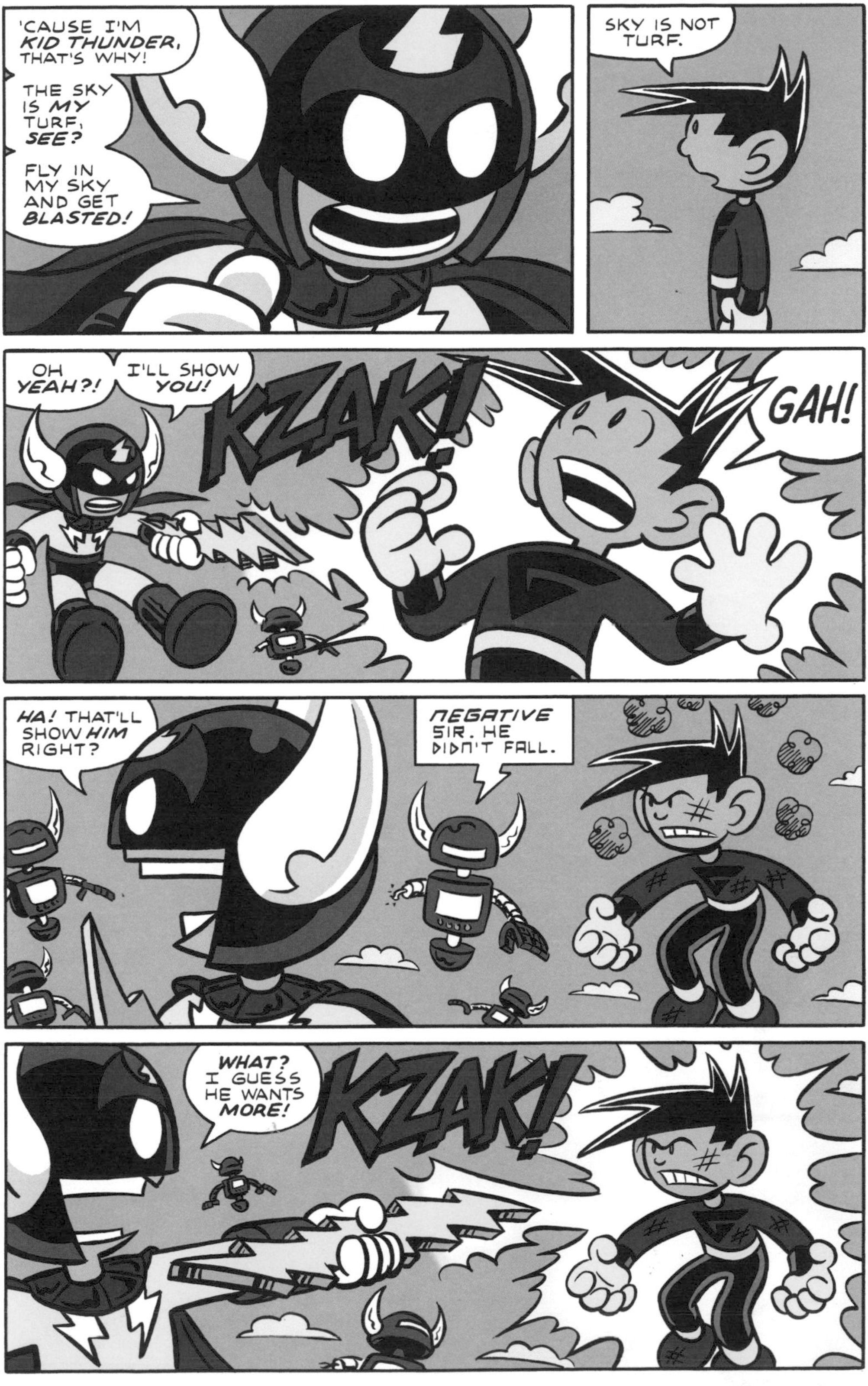
'CAUSE I'M KID THUNDER, THAT'S WHY!
THE SKY IS MY TURF, SEE?
FLY IN MY SKY AND GET BLASTED!
SKY IS NOT TURF.
OH YEAH?!
I'LL SHOW YOU!
KZAK!
GAH!
HA! THAT'LL SHOW HIM RIGHT?
NEGATIVE SIR. HE DIDN'T FALL.
WHAT? I GUESS HE WANTS MORE!
KZAK!

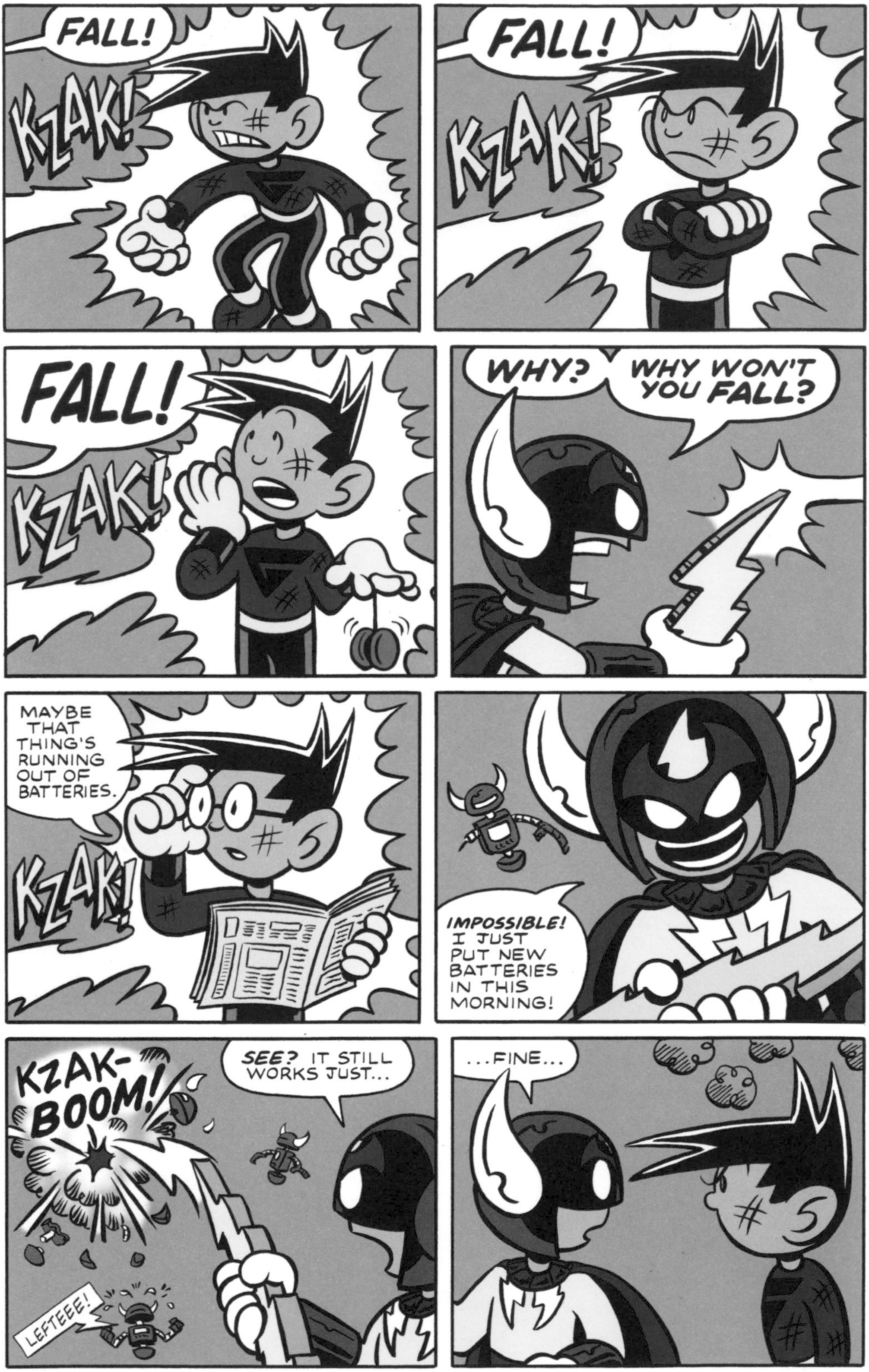
FALL!
KZAK!
FALL!
KZAK!
FALL!
KZAK!
WHY?
WHY WON'T YOU FALL?
MAYBE THAT THING'S RUNNING OUT OF BATTERIES.
KZAK!
IMPOSSIBLE! I JUST PUT NEW BATTERIES IN THIS MORNING!
KZAK-BOOM!
SEE? IT STILL WORKS JUST...
LEFTEEE!
...FINE...

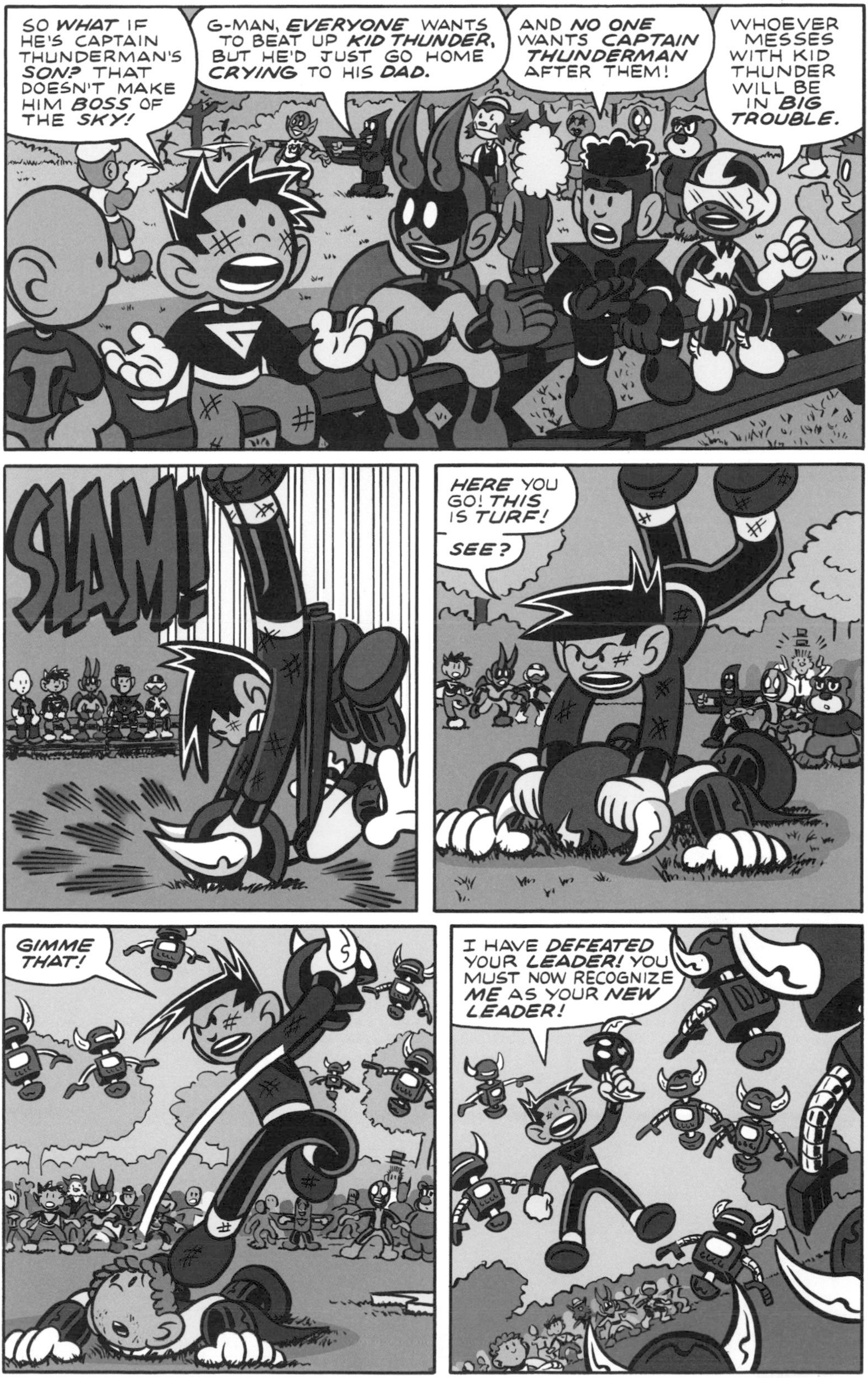
SO WHAT IF HE'S CAPTAIN THUNDERMAN'S SON? THAT DOESN'T MAKE HIM BOSS OF THE SKY!
G-MAN, EVERYONE WANTS TO BEAT UP KID THUNDER, BUT HE'D JUST GO HOME CRYING TO HIS DAD.
AND NO ONE WANTS CAPTAIN THUNDERMAN AFTER THEM!
WHOEVER MESSES WITH KID THUNDER WILL BE IN BIG TROUBLE.
SLAM!
HERE YOU GO! THIS IS TURF!
SEE?
GIMME THAT!
I HAVE DEFEATED YOUR LEADER! YOU MUST NOW RECOGNIZE ME AS YOUR NEW LEADER!

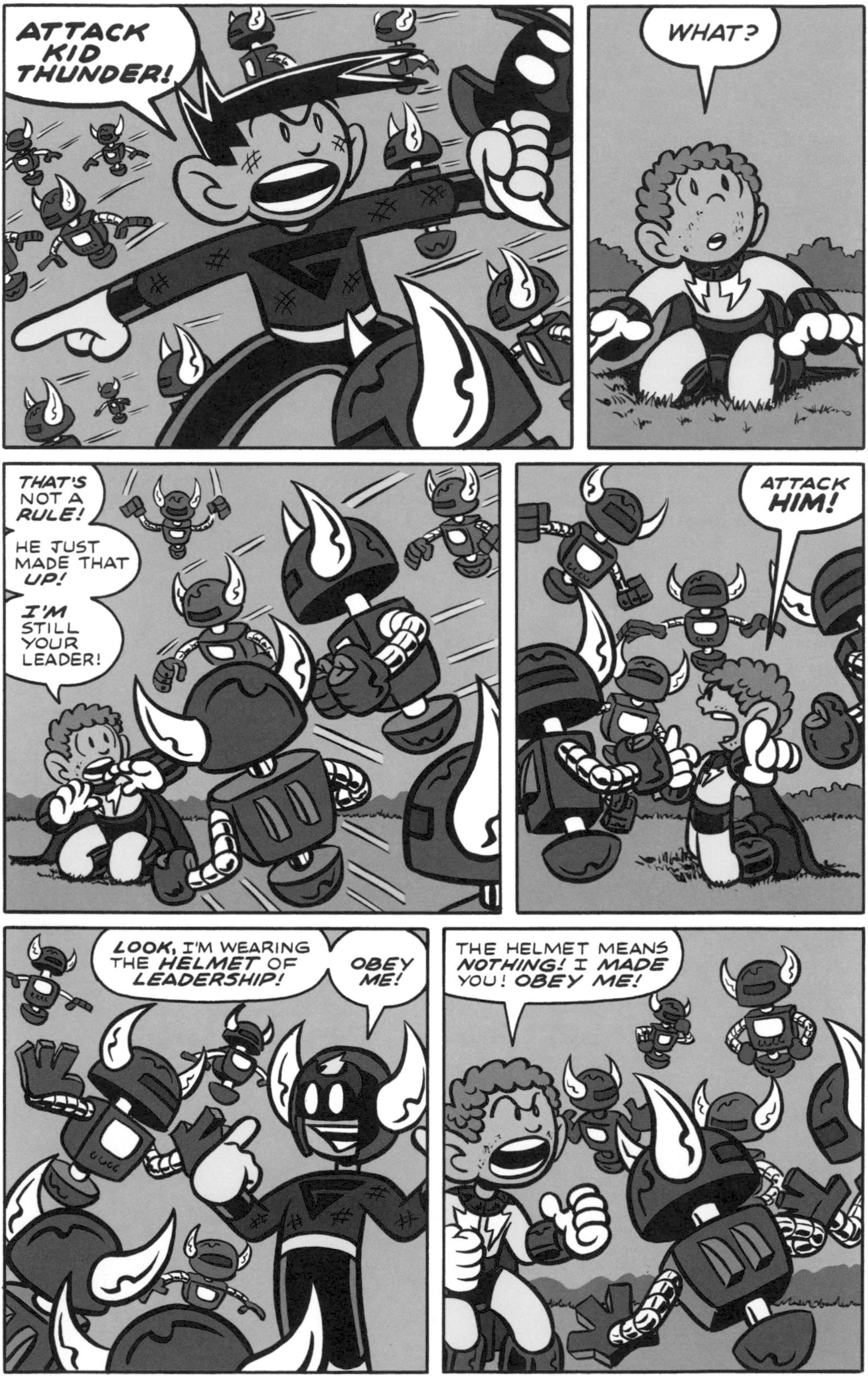
ATTACK KID THUNDER!
WHAT?
THAT'S NOT A RULE!
HE JUST MADE THAT UP!
I'M STILL YOUR LEADER!
ATTACK HIM!
LOOK, I'M WEARING THE HELMET OF LEADERSHIP!
OBEY ME!
THE HELMET MEANS NOTHING! I MADE YOU! OBEY ME!

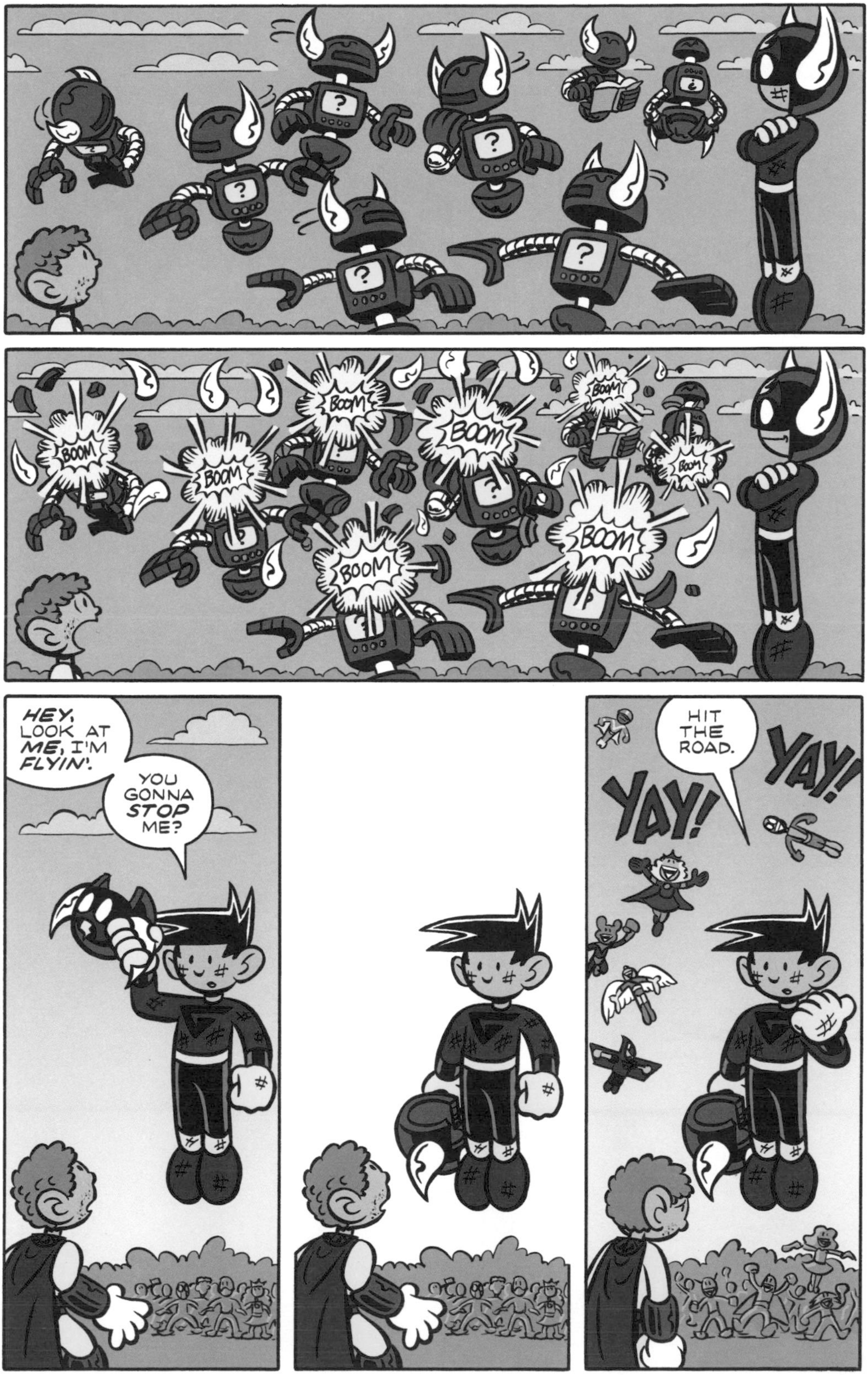
BOOM
BOOM
BOOM
BOOM
BOOM
BOOM
BOOM
BOOM
HEY, LOOK AT ME, I'M FLYIN'.
YOU GONNA STOP ME?
HIT THE ROAD.
YAY!
YAY!

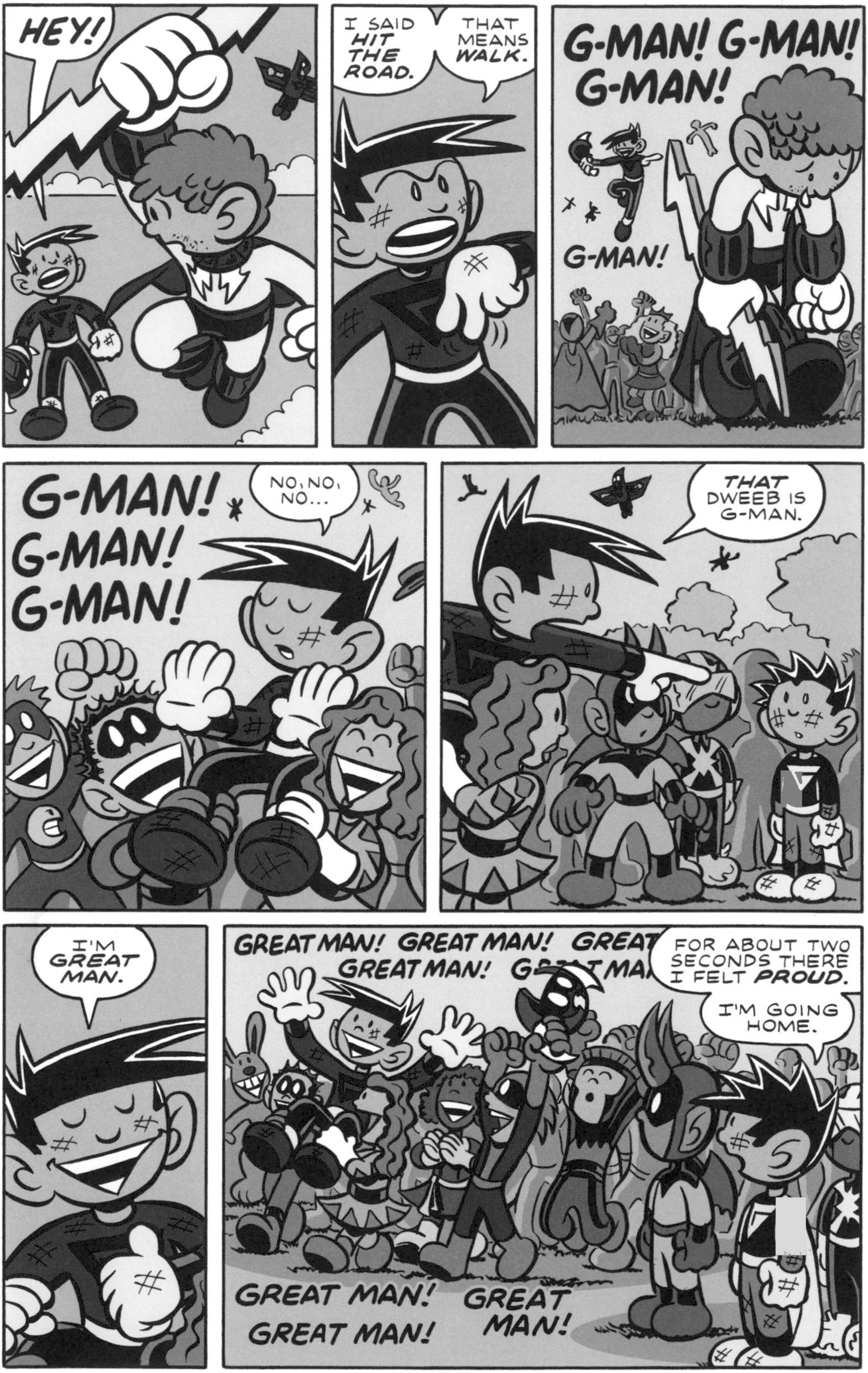
HEY!
I SAID HIT THE ROAD.
THAT MEANS WALK.
G-MAN! G-MAN! G-MAN!
G-MAN!
G-MAN! G-MAN! G-MAN!
NO, NO, NO...
THAT DWEEB IS G-MAN.
I'M GREAT MAN.
GREAT MAN! GREAT MAN! GREAT
GREAT MAN!
FOR ABOUT TWO SECONDS THERE I FELT PROUD.
I'M GOING HOME.
GREAT MAN! GREAT MAN! GREAT MAN!

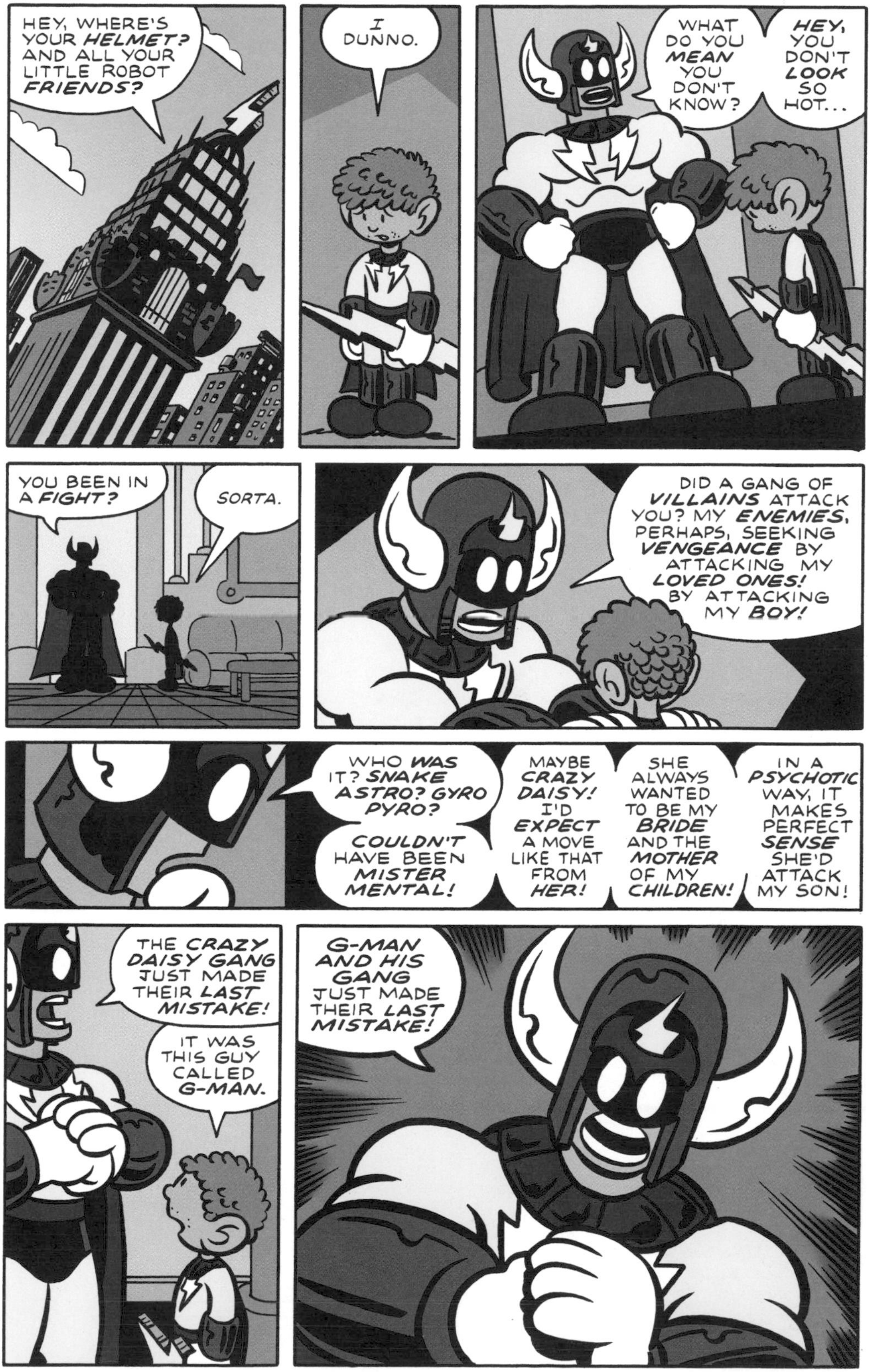
HEY, WHERE'S YOUR HELMET? AND ALL YOUR LITTLE ROBOT FRIENDS?
I DUNNO.
WHAT DO YOU MEAN YOU DON'T KNOW?
HEY, YOU DON'T LOOK SO HOT...
YOU BEEN IN A FIGHT?
SORTA.
DID A GANG OF VILLAINS ATTACK YOU? MY ENEMIES, PERHAPS, SEEKING VENGEANCE BY ATTACKING MY LOVED ONES! BY ATTACKING MY BOY!
WHO WAS IT? SNAKE ASTRO? GYRO PYRO?
COULDN'T HAVE BEEN MISTER MENTAL!
MAYBE CRAZY DAISY! I'D EXPECT A MOVE LIKE THAT FROM HER!
SHE ALWAYS WANTED TO BE MY BRIDE AND THE MOTHER OF MY CHILDREN!
IN A PSYCHOTIC WAY, IT MAKES PERFECT SENSE SHE'D ATTACK MY SON!
THE CRAZY DAISY GANG JUST MADE THEIR LAST MISTAKE!
IT WAS THIS GUY CALLED G-MAN.
G-MAN AND HIS GANG JUST MADE THEIR LAST MISTAKE!

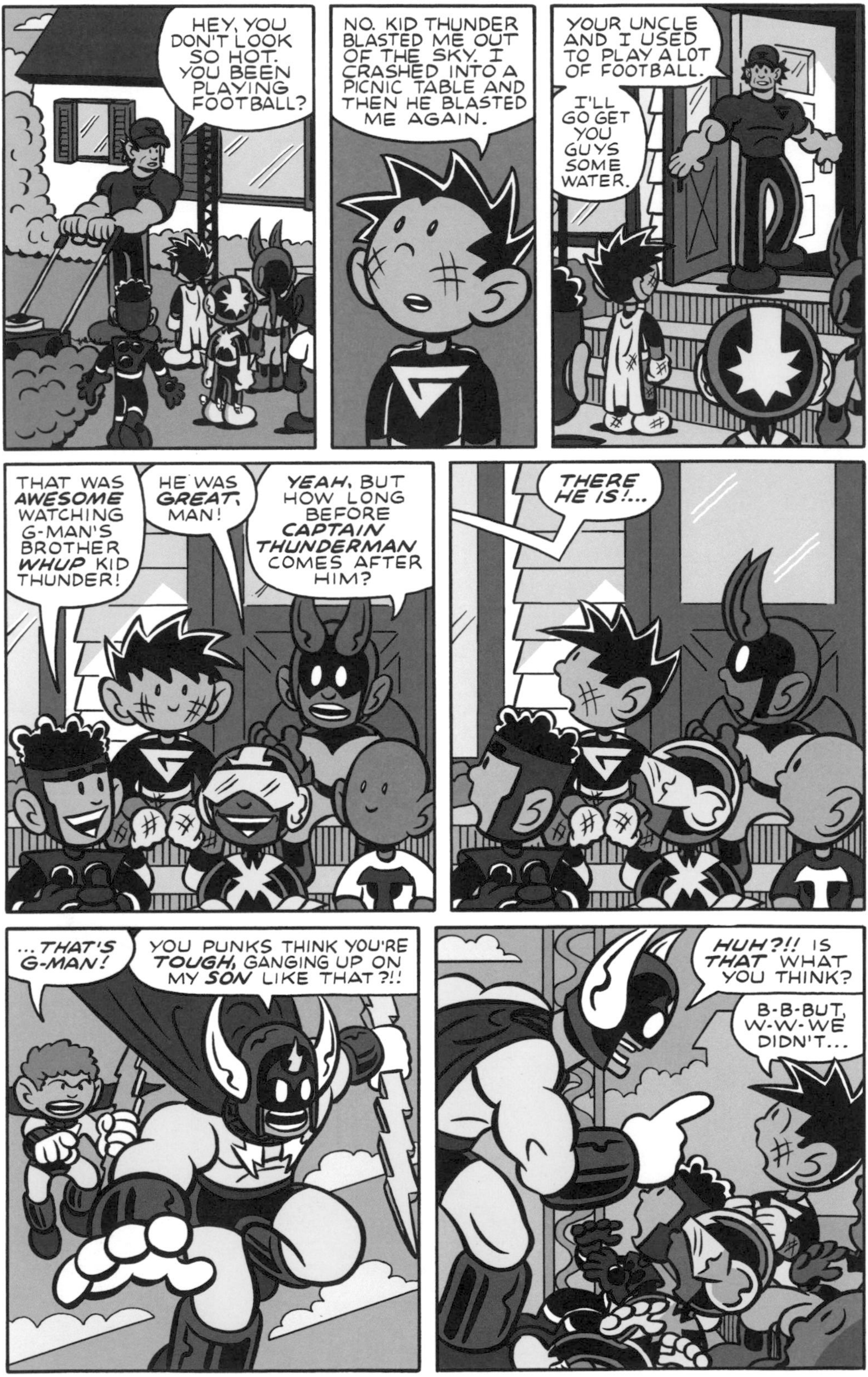
HEY, YOU DON'T LOOK SO HOT. YOU BEEN PLAYING FOOTBALL?
NO. KID THUNDER BLASTED ME OUT OF THE SKY. I CRASHED INTO A PICNIC TABLE AND THEN HE BLASTED ME AGAIN.
YOUR UNCLE AND I USED TO PLAY A LOT OF FOOTBALL.
I'LL GO GET YOU GUYS SOME WATER.
THAT WAS AWESOME WATCHING G-MAN'S BROTHER WHUP KID THUNDER!
HE WAS GREAT, MAN!
YEAH, BUT HOW LONG BEFORE CAPTAIN THUNDERMAN COMES AFTER HIM?
THERE HE IS!...
...THAT'S G-MAN!
YOU PUNKS THINK YOU'RE TOUGH, GANGING UP ON MY SON LIKE THAT?!!
HUH?!! IS THAT WHAT YOU THINK?
B-B-BUT, W-W-WE DIDN'T...

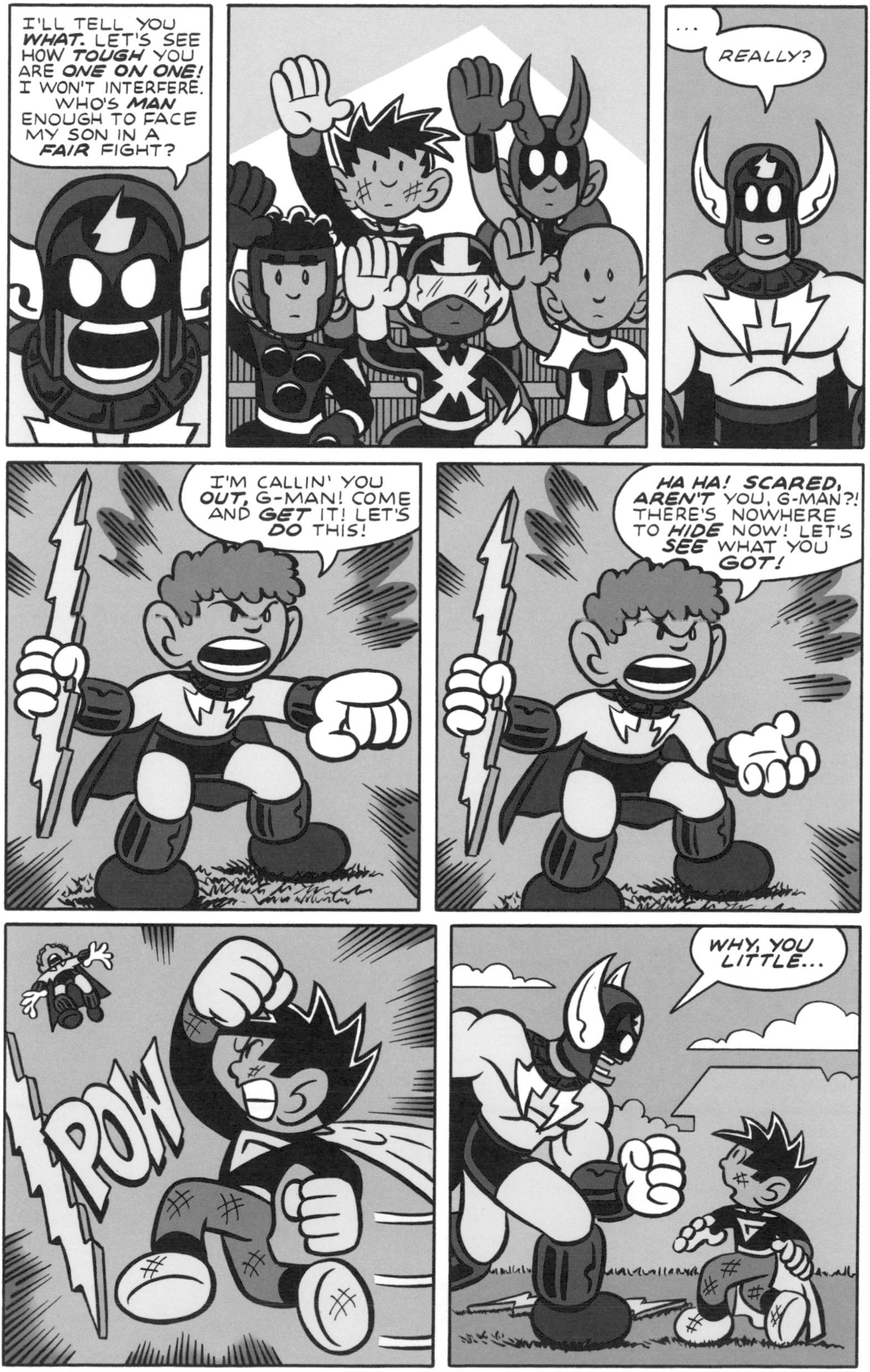

I'LL TELL YOU WHAT. LET'S SEE HOW TOUGH YOU ARE ONE ON ONE! I WON'T INTERFERE. WHO'S MAN ENOUGH TO FACE MY SON IN A FAIR FIGHT?
...
REALLY?
I'M CALLIN' YOU OUT, G-MAN! COME AND GET IT! LET'S DO THIS!
HA HA! SCARED, AREN'T YOU, G-MAN?! THERE'S NOWHERE TO HIDE NOW! LET'S SEE WHAT YOU GOT!
POW
WHY, YOU LITTLE...

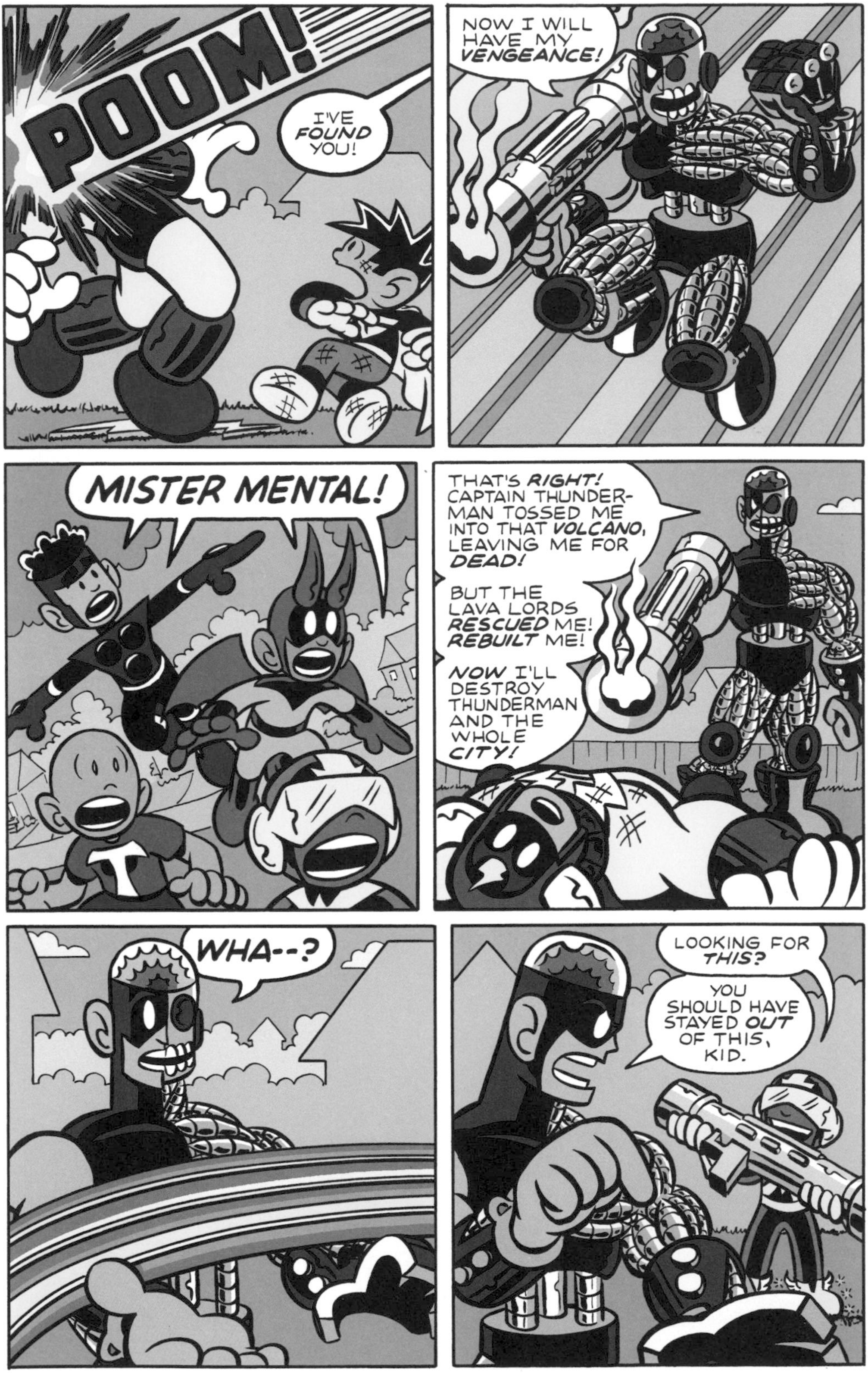
POOM!
I'VE FOUND YOU!
NOW I WILL HAVE MY VENGEANCE!
MISTER MENTAL!
THAT'S RIGHT! CAPTAIN THUNDERMAN TOSSED ME INTO THAT VOLCANO, LEAVING ME FOR DEAD!
BUT THE LAVA LORDS RESCUED ME! REBUILT ME!
NOW I'LL DESTROY THUNDERMAN AND THE WHOLE CITY!
WHA--?
LOOKING FOR THIS?
YOU SHOULD HAVE STAYED OUT OF THIS, KID.

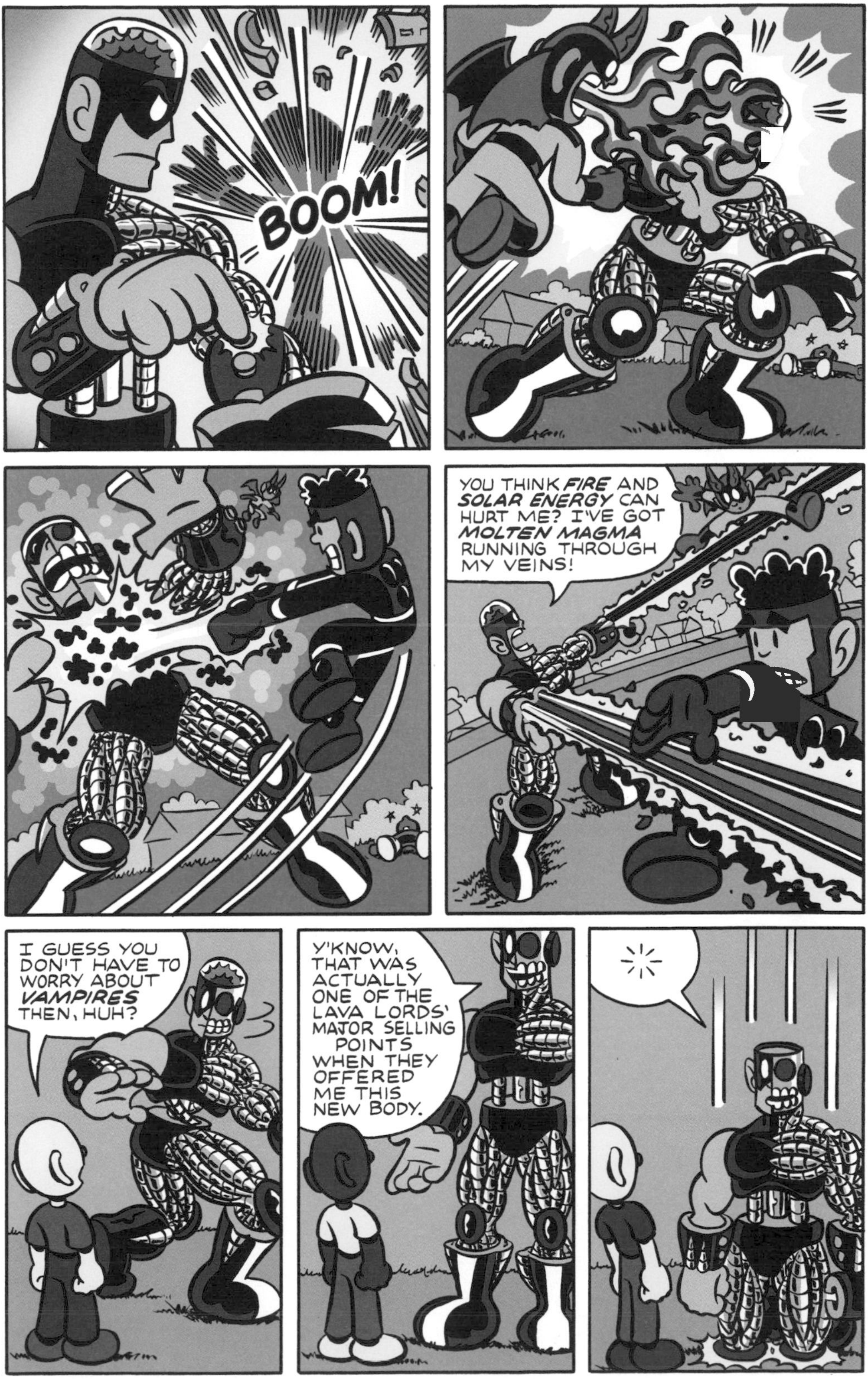
BOOM!
YOU THINK FIRE AND SOLAR ENERGY CAN HURT ME? I'VE GOT MOLTEN MAGMA RUNNING THROUGH MY VEINS!
I GUESS YOU DON'T HAVE TO WORRY ABOUT VAMPIRES THEN, HUH?
Y'KNOW, THAT WAS ACTUALLY ONE OF THE LAVA LORDS' MAJOR SELLING POINTS WHEN THEY OFFERED ME THIS NEW BODY.

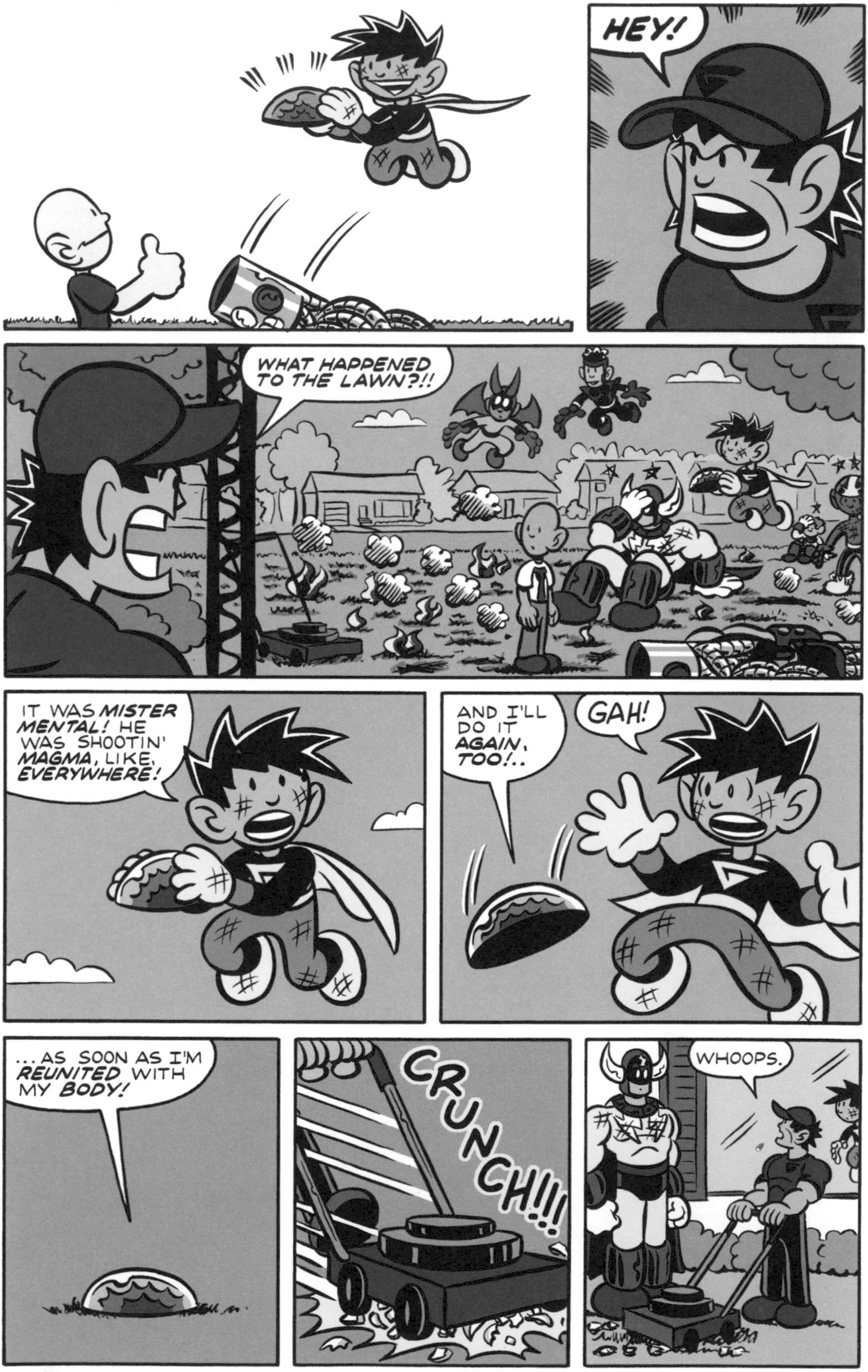
HEY!
WHAT HAPPENED TO THE LAWN?!!
IT WAS MISTER MENTAL! HE WAS SHOOTIN' MAGMA, LIKE, EVERYWHERE!
AND I'LL DO IT AGAIN, TOO!..
GAH!
...AS SOON AS I'M REUNITED WITH MY BODY!
CRUNCH!!!
WHOOPS.

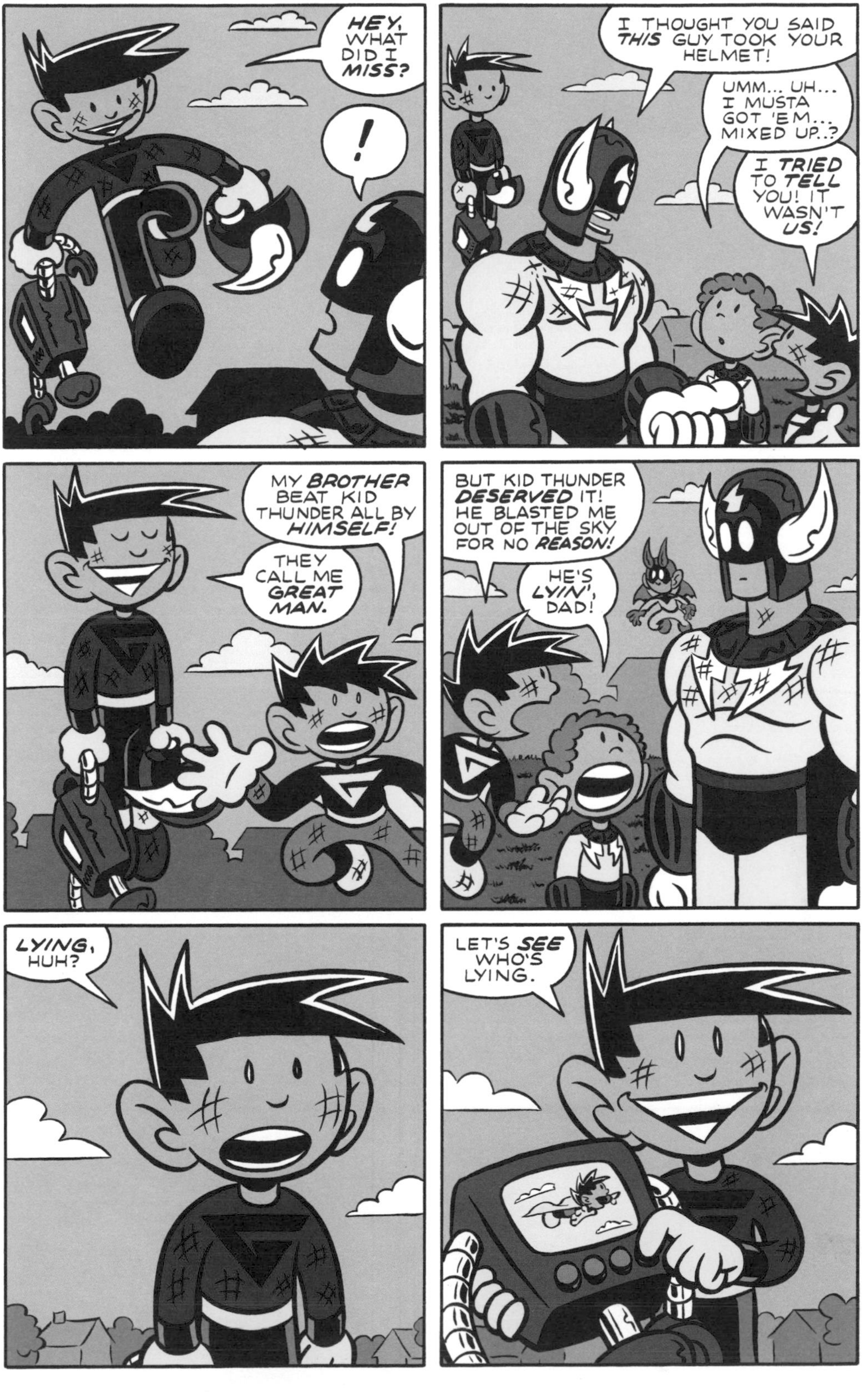
HEY, WHAT DID I MISS?
!
I THOUGHT YOU SAID THIS GUY TOOK YOUR HELMET!
UMM... UH... I MUSTA GOT 'EM... MIXED UP..?
I TRIED TO TELL YOU! IT WASN'T US!
MY BROTHER BEAT KID THUNDER ALL BY HIMSELF!
THEY CALL ME GREAT MAN.
BUT KID THUNDER DESERVED IT! HE BLASTED ME OUT OF THE SKY FOR NO REASON!
HE'S LYIN', DAD!
LYING, HUH?
LET'S SEE WHO'S LYING.

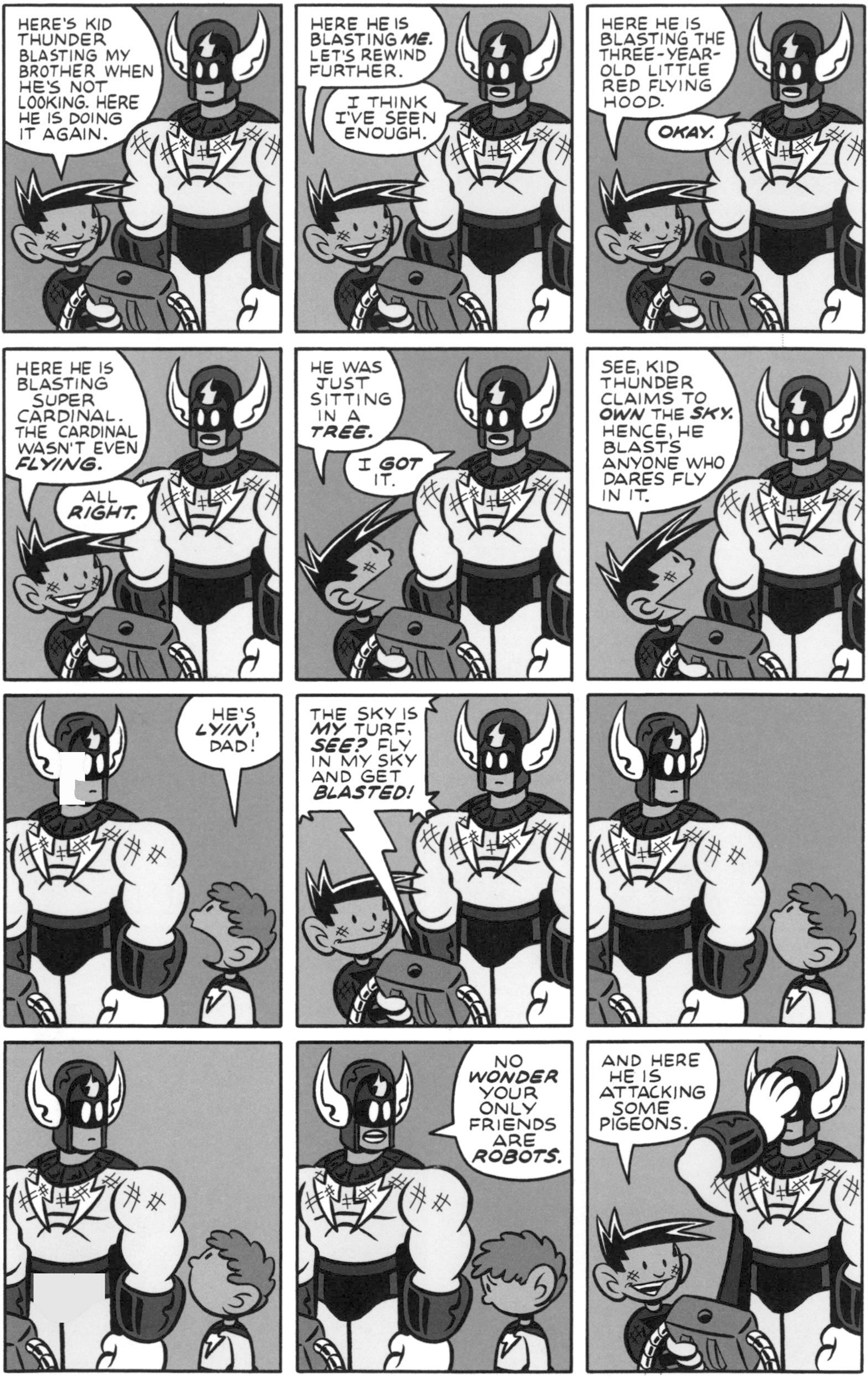
HERE'S KID THUNDER BLASTING MY BROTHER WHEN HE'S NOT LOOKING. HERE HE IS DOING IT AGAIN.
HERE HE IS BLASTING *ME.* LET'S REWIND FURTHER.
I THINK I'VE SEEN ENOUGH.
HERE HE IS BLASTING THE THREE-YEAR-OLD LITTLE RED FLYING HOOD.
OKAY.
HERE HE IS BLASTING SUPER CARDINAL. THE CARDINAL WASN'T EVEN *FLYING.*
ALL *RIGHT.*
HE WAS JUST SITTING IN A *TREE.*
I *GOT* IT.
SEE, KID THUNDER CLAIMS TO *OWN* THE *SKY.* HENCE, HE BLASTS ANYONE WHO DARES FLY IN IT.
HE'S *LYIN'*, DAD!
THE SKY IS *MY* TURF, *SEE?* FLY IN MY SKY AND GET *BLASTED!*
NO *WONDER* YOUR ONLY FRIENDS ARE *ROBOTS.*
AND HERE HE IS ATTACKING SOME PIGEONS.

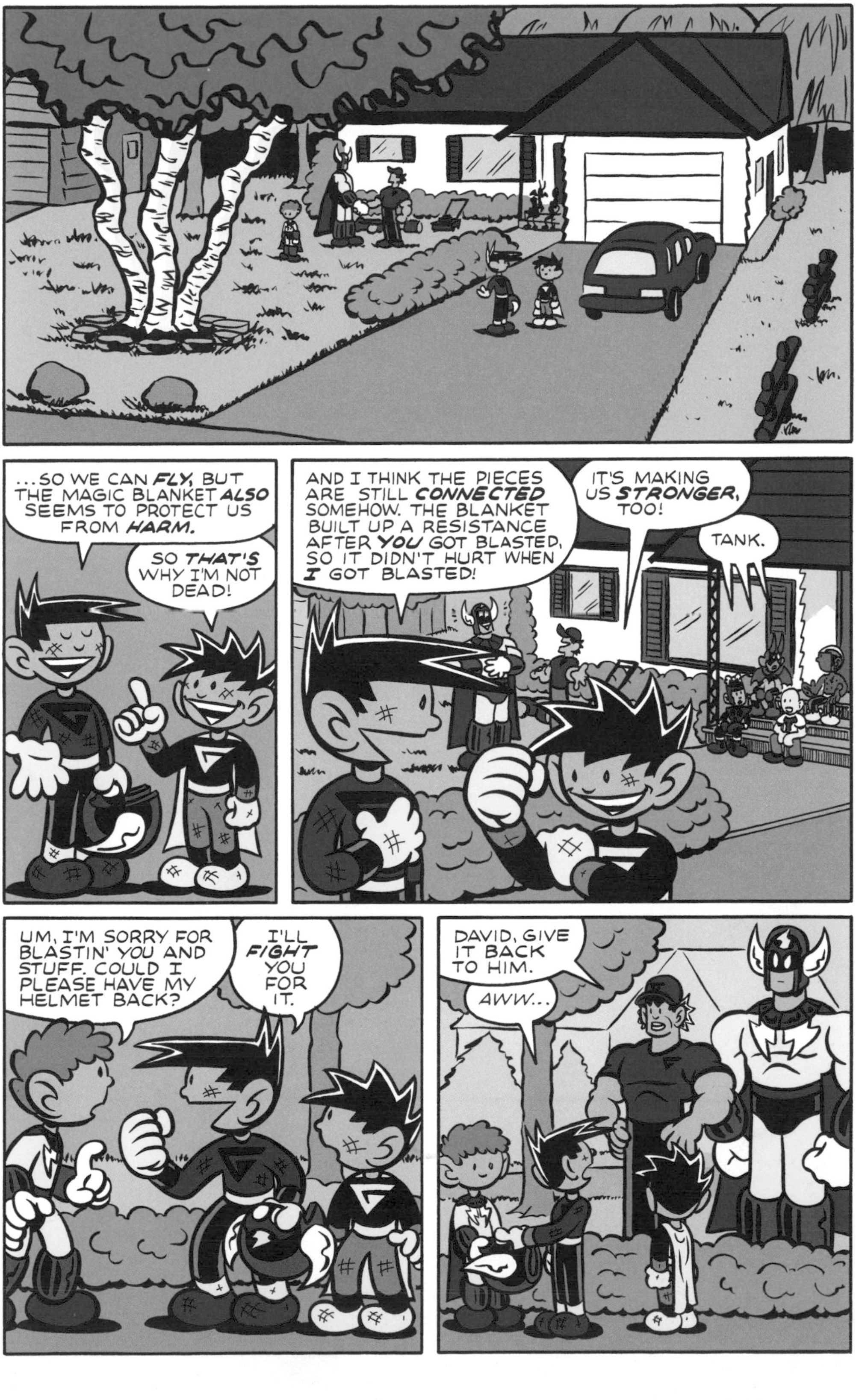
...SO WE CAN FLY, BUT THE MAGIC BLANKET ALSO SEEMS TO PROTECT US FROM HARM.
SO THAT'S WHY I'M NOT DEAD!
AND I THINK THE PIECES ARE STILL CONNECTED SOMEHOW. THE BLANKET BUILT UP A RESISTANCE AFTER YOU GOT BLASTED, SO IT DIDN'T HURT WHEN I GOT BLASTED!
IT'S MAKING US STRONGER, TOO!
TANK.
UM, I'M SORRY FOR BLASTIN' YOU AND STUFF. COULD I PLEASE HAVE MY HELMET BACK?
I'LL FIGHT YOU FOR IT.
DAVID, GIVE IT BACK TO HIM.
AWW...

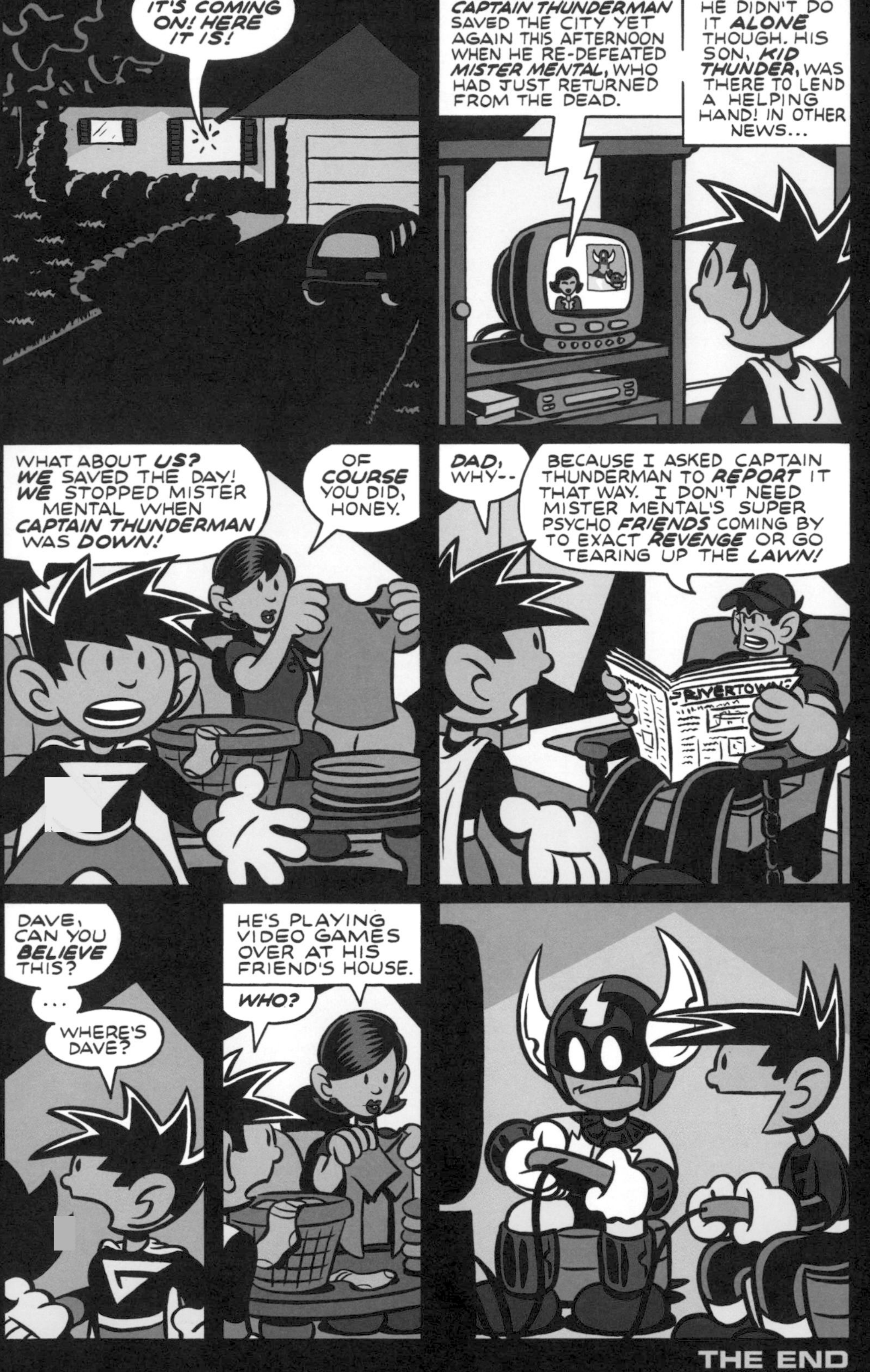

IT'S COMING ON! HERE IT IS!
CAPTAIN THUNDERMAN SAVED THE CITY YET AGAIN THIS AFTERNOON WHEN HE RE-DEFEATED MISTER MENTAL, WHO HAD JUST RETURNED FROM THE DEAD.
HE DIDN'T DO IT ALONE THOUGH. HIS SON, KID THUNDER, WAS THERE TO LEND A HELPING HAND! IN OTHER NEWS...
WHAT ABOUT US? WE SAVED THE DAY! WE STOPPED MISTER MENTAL WHEN CAPTAIN THUNDERMAN WAS DOWN!
OF COURSE YOU DID, HONEY.
DAD, WHY--
BECAUSE I ASKED CAPTAIN THUNDERMAN TO REPORT IT THAT WAY. I DON'T NEED MISTER MENTAL'S SUPER PSYCHO FRIENDS COMING BY TO EXACT REVENGE OR GO TEARING UP THE LAWN!
RIVERTOWN
DAVE, CAN YOU BELIEVE THIS?
...
WHERE'S DAVE?
HE'S PLAYING VIDEO GAMES OVER AT HIS FRIEND'S HOUSE.
WHO?
THE END

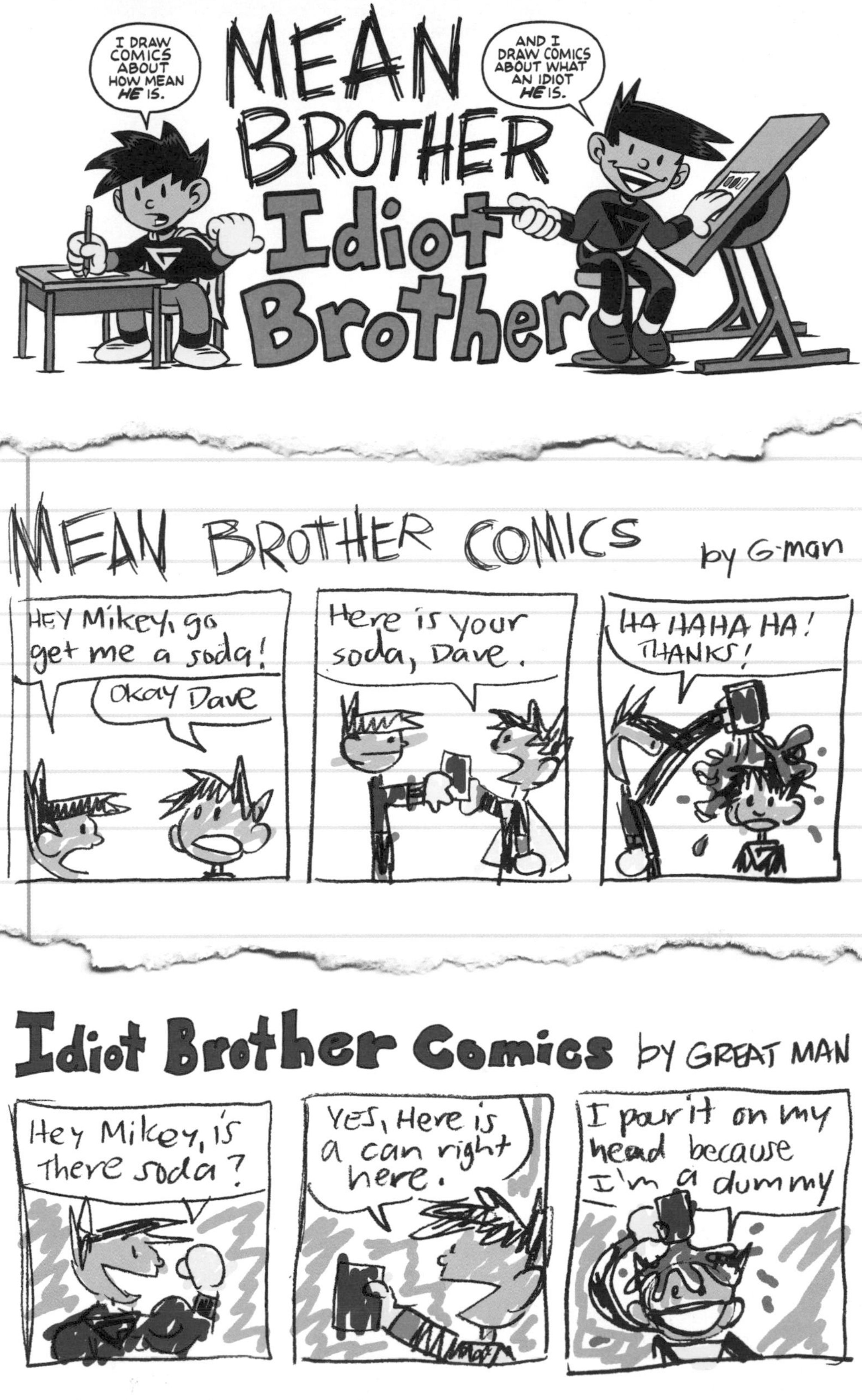

I DRAW COMICS ABOUT HOW MEAN HE IS.
MEAN BROTHER Idiot Brother
AND I DRAW COMICS ABOUT WHAT AN IDIOT HE IS.
MEAN BROTHER COMICS
by G-man
HEY Mikey, go get me a soda!
Okay Dave
Here is your soda, Dave.
HA HAHA HA HA! THANKS!
Idiot Brother Comics
by GREAT MAN
Hey Mikey, is there soda?
YES, Here is a can right here.
I pour it on my head because I'm a dummy

COMIC BITS

BY CHRIS GIARRUSSO

HI. I'M HERE TO CHECK IN.

NAME?

COACH

SUNNYSIDE SUPERHERO SUMMER CAMP

I'M G-MAN.

SO! THE *CHOSEN ONE* HAS ARRIVED! WELCOME TO SUPERHERO CAMP, *CHOSEN ONE!*

CHOSEN ONE?

THAT'S RIGHT, *G-MAN.* YOU ARE THE *CHOSEN ONE* REFERRED TO IN THE *ANCIENT PROPHECIES!*

ANCIENT PROPHECIES OR ARMAGEDDON

"AND LO, WHEN THE FINAL DAYS ARE UPON YOU, LOOK TO HIM WHO BEARS THE *SEVENTH LETTER*..."

"...FOR HE IS THE *CHOSEN ONE,* WHO SHALL LEAD YOU TO *SALVATION.*"

WOW! I'M THE *CHOSEN ONE!*

NAME?

THE *CHOSEN ONE!* BY GOLLY, THAT'S *SOMETHING* ALL RIGHT!

YESSIR, THE *CHOSEN ONE!* YOU DON'T HEAR *THAT* EVERY DAY!

THAT'S RIGHT, *STARGAZE. YOU* ARE THE *CHOSEN ONE!*

"AND LO, LOOK TO HER WHO WEARS A MASK WITH STARS OVER THE EYES PART OF THE *MASK*..."

HEY, MOM, GUESS WHAT! *I'M* THE *CHOSEN ONE!*

SO I SAY TO HER, "DON'T YOU KNOW I'M THE *CHOSEN ONE?*"

YOU PRETENDED YOU WERE ME?

HEY, THERE! I'M THE *CHOSEN ONE!*

GREAT.

CG 02

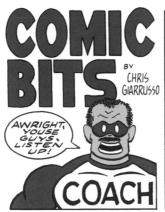

COMIC BITS

BY CHRIS GIARRUSSO

YOUSE CAME HERE TA *SUNNYSIDE SUPERHERO SUMMER CAMP* TA LEARN THE *FUNDAMENTALS* OF *SUPERHEROICS.*

DAT MEANS LOTSA PRACTICE, HARD WORK, AN' *DRILLS, DRILLS, DRILLS!*

AWRIGHT, YOUSE GUYS, LISTEN UP!

COACH

FIRST UP IS THE *BULLET DODGIN'* DRILL. BULLET DODGIN' IS AN IMPORTANT SKILL TA MASTER. I WANNA SEE EVERYONE TAKE A TURN IN THE *BULLET CAGE.*

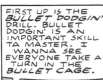

BULLE CAGE

RATATATAT

GREAT REFLEXES, *BILLY DEMON!*

RATATAT

HA HA! *SPARKY,* YER A SHOW-OFF!

BANG

AH!

CONCENTRATE, *G-MAN!*

AH!

STAY FOCUSED!

AH!

KEEP YER *EYE* ON THE *BULLETS!*

AH!

COAC

G-MAN, YER STAYIN' IN DAT CAGE UNTIL YA GET IT *RIGHT!*

AH!

G-MAN'S GETTING *TORN UP* IN THAT CAGE!

I CAN'T BELIEVE COACH IS MAKING HIM STAY *IN* THERE!

WAIT! IT LOOKS LIKE HE'S GETTING THE *HANG* OF IT!

THERE'S NOT A SINGLE BULLET *TOUCHING* HIM!

WAY TO GO, G-MAN!

YEAH, *G!*

RATATAT

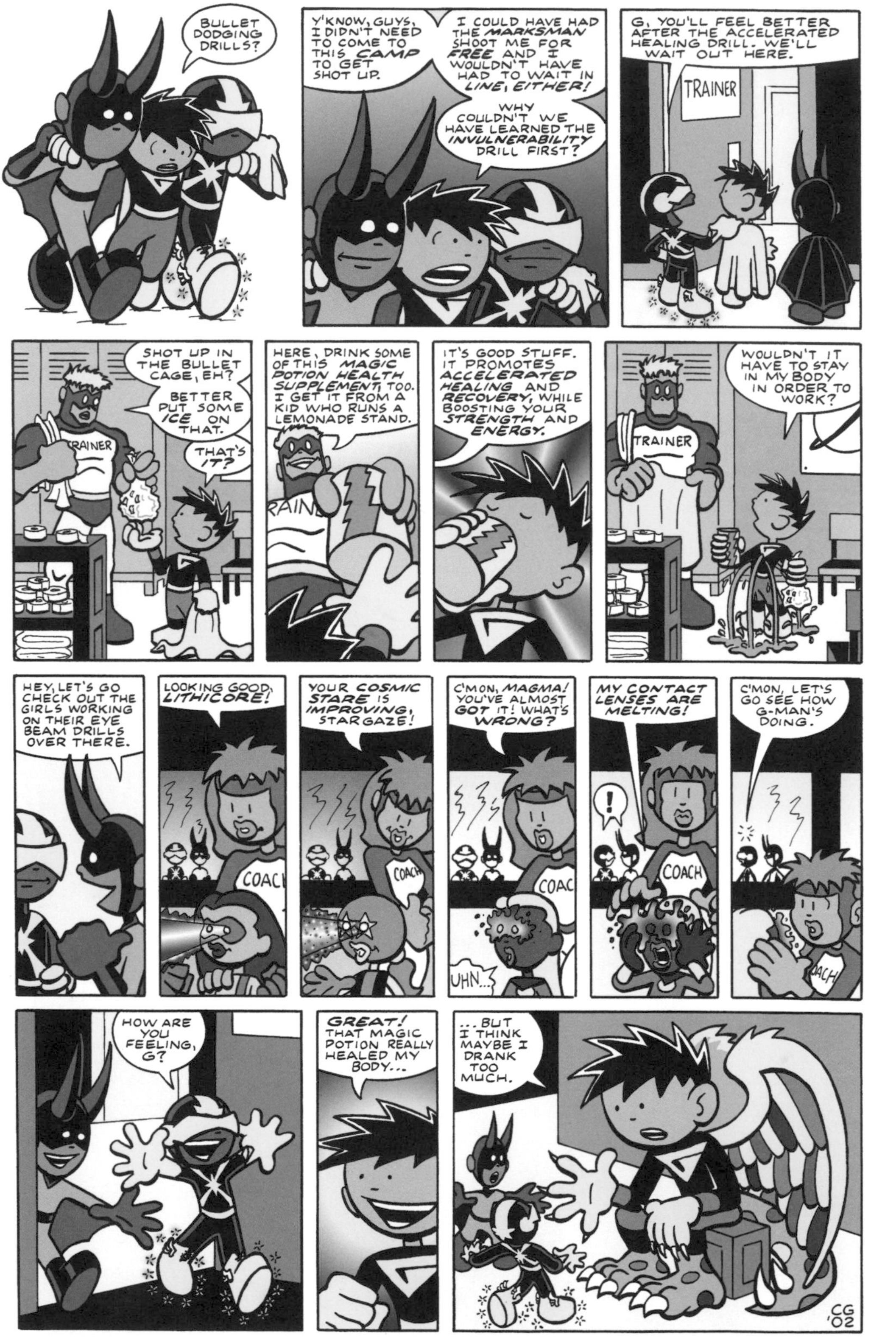
BULLET DODGING DRILLS?
Y'KNOW, GUYS, I DIDN'T NEED TO COME TO THIS CAMP TO GET SHOT UP.
I COULD HAVE HAD THE MARKSMAN SHOOT ME FOR FREE AND I WOULDN'T HAVE HAD TO WAIT IN LINE, EITHER!
WHY COULDN'T WE HAVE LEARNED THE INVULNERABILITY DRILL FIRST?
G, YOU'LL FEEL BETTER AFTER THE ACCELERATED HEALING DRILL. WE'LL WAIT OUT HERE.
TRAINER
SHOT UP IN THE BULLET CAGE, EH?
BETTER PUT SOME ICE ON THAT.
THAT'S IT?
TRAINER
HERE, DRINK SOME OF THIS MAGIC POTION HEALTH SUPPLEMENT, TOO. I GET IT FROM A KID WHO RUNS A LEMONADE STAND.
IT'S GOOD STUFF. IT PROMOTES ACCELERATED HEALING AND RECOVERY, WHILE BOOSTING YOUR STRENGTH AND ENERGY.
WOULDN'T IT HAVE TO STAY IN MY BODY IN ORDER TO WORK?
TRAINER
HEY, LET'S GO CHECK OUT THE GIRLS WORKING ON THEIR EYE BEAM DRILLS OVER THERE.
LOOKING GOOD, LITHICORE!
COACH
YOUR COSMIC STARE IS IMPROVING, STARGAZE!
COACH
C'MON, MAGMA! YOU'VE ALMOST GOT IT! WHAT'S WRONG?
UHN...
MY CONTACT LENSES ARE MELTING!
!
COACH
C'MON, LET'S GO SEE HOW G-MAN'S DOING.
HOW ARE YOU FEELING, G?
GREAT! THAT MAGIC POTION REALLY HEALED MY BODY...
...BUT I THINK MAYBE I DRANK TOO MUCH.
CG '02

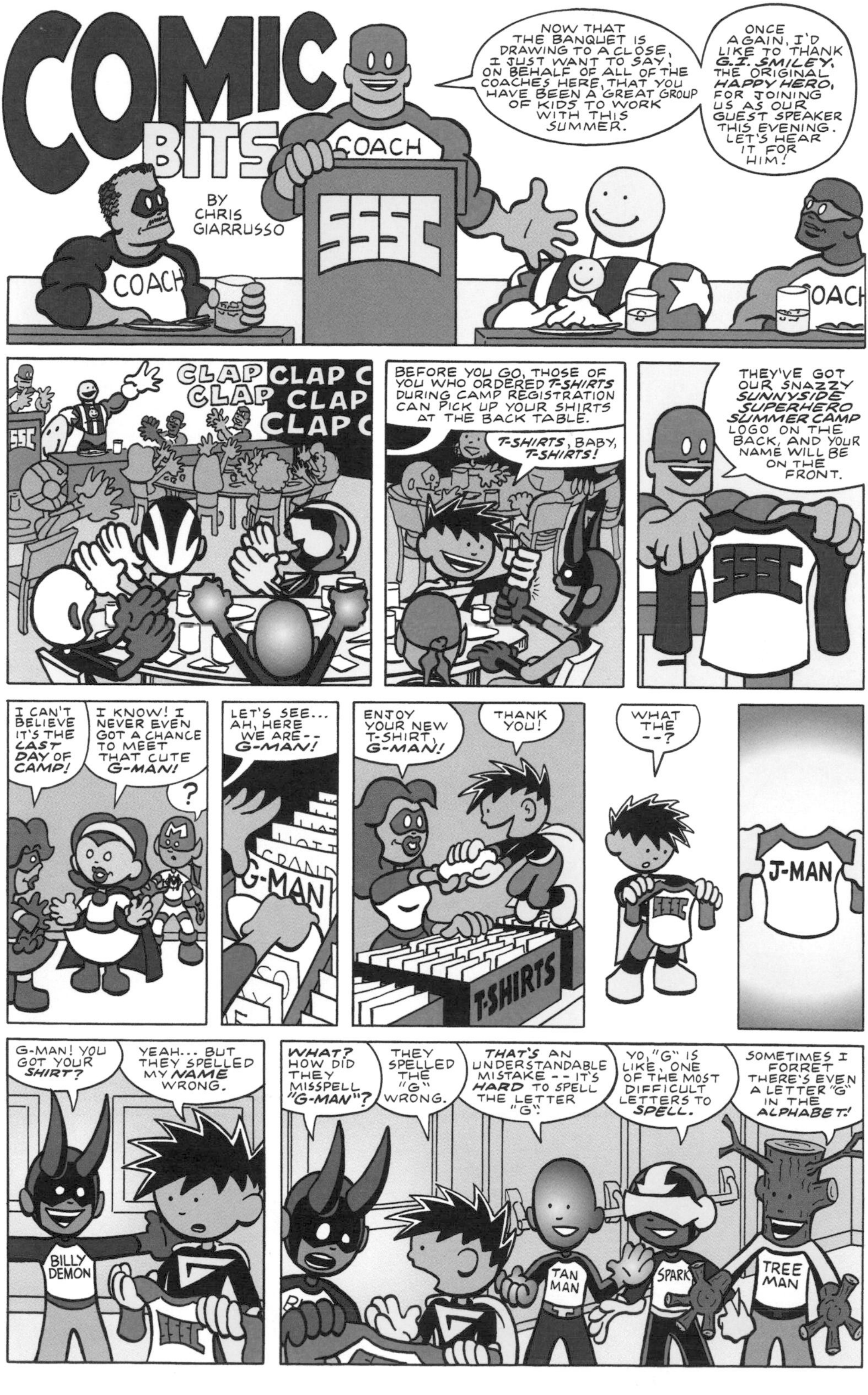
COMIC BITS
BY CHRIS GIARRUSSO
NOW THAT THE BANQUET IS DRAWING TO A CLOSE, I JUST WANT TO SAY, ON BEHALF OF ALL OF THE COACHES HERE, THAT YOU HAVE BEEN A GREAT GROUP OF KIDS TO WORK WITH THIS SUMMER.
ONCE AGAIN, I'D LIKE TO THANK G.I. SMILEY, THE ORIGINAL HAPPY HERO, FOR JOINING US AS OUR GUEST SPEAKER THIS EVENING. LET'S HEAR IT FOR HIM!
COACH
SSSC
COACH
COACH
CLAP CLAP CLAP C CLAP CLAP C
BEFORE YOU GO, THOSE OF YOU WHO ORDERED T-SHIRTS DURING CAMP REGISTRATION CAN PICK UP YOUR SHIRTS AT THE BACK TABLE.
T-SHIRTS, BABY, T-SHIRTS!
THEY'VE GOT OUR SNAZZY SUNNYSIDE SUPERHERO SUMMER CAMP LOGO ON THE BACK, AND YOUR NAME WILL BE ON THE FRONT.
SSSC
I CAN'T BELIEVE IT'S THE LAST DAY OF CAMP!
I KNOW! I NEVER EVEN GOT A CHANCE TO MEET THAT CUTE G-MAN!
?
LET'S SEE... AH, HERE WE ARE -- G-MAN!
G-MAN
GRAND
ENJOY YOUR NEW T-SHIRT, G-MAN!
THANK YOU!
T-SHIRTS
WHAT THE --?
J-MAN
G-MAN! YOU GOT YOUR SHIRT?
YEAH... BUT THEY SPELLED MY NAME WRONG.
BILLY DEMON
WHAT? HOW DID THEY MISSPELL "G-MAN"?
THEY SPELLED THE "G" WRONG.
THAT'S AN UNDERSTANDABLE MISTAKE -- IT'S HARD TO SPELL THE LETTER "G".
YO, "G" IS LIKE, ONE OF THE MOST DIFFICULT LETTERS TO SPELL.
SOMETIMES I FORRET THERE'S EVEN A LETTER "G" IN THE ALPHABET!
TAN MAN
SPARK
TREE MAN

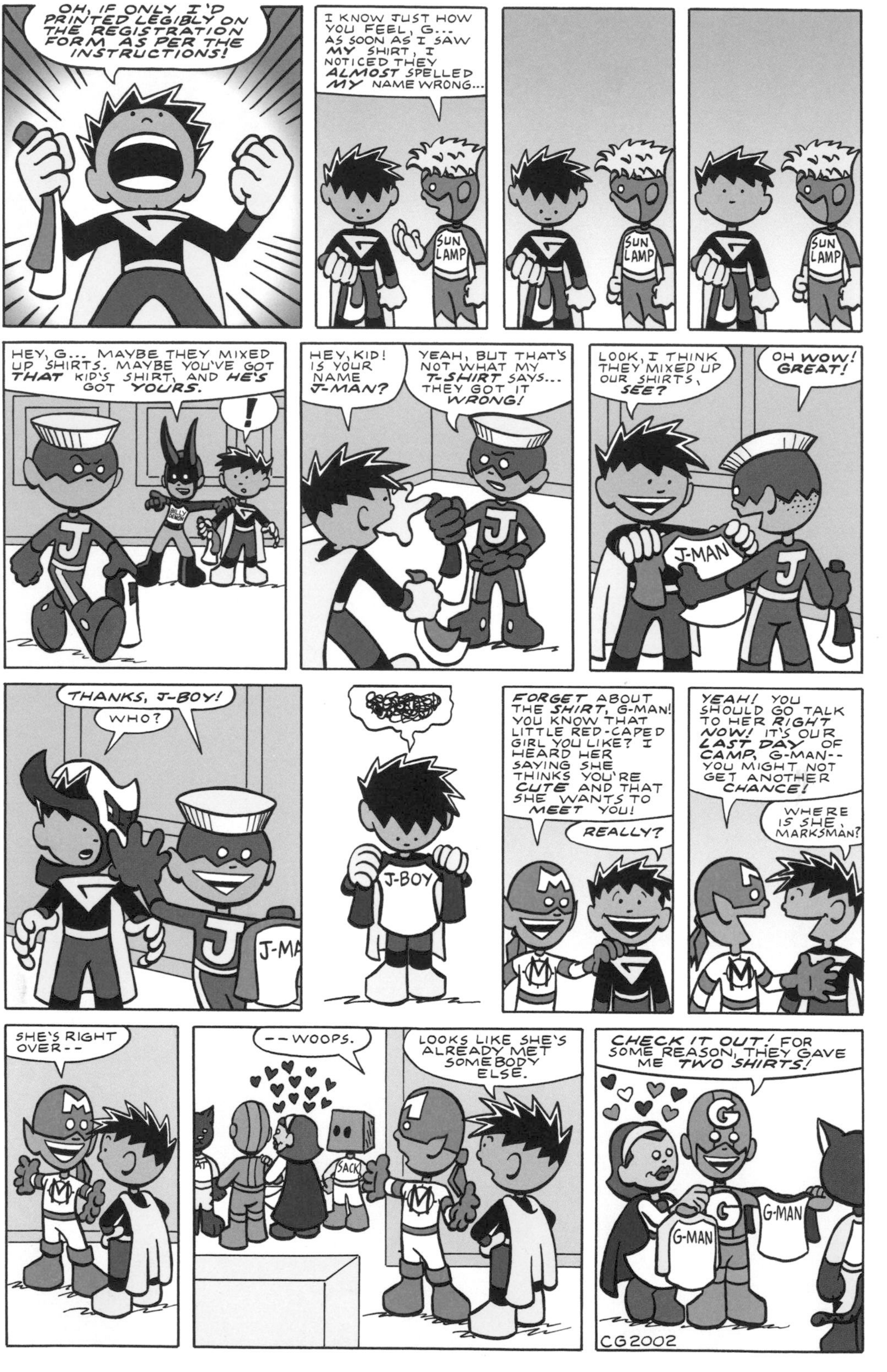
OH, IF ONLY I'D PRINTED LEGIBLY ON THE REGISTRATION FORM AS PER THE INSTRUCTIONS!
I KNOW JUST HOW YOU FEEL, G... AS SOON AS I SAW MY SHIRT, I NOTICED THEY ALMOST SPELLED MY NAME WRONG...
SUN LAMP
SUN LAMP
SUN LAMP
HEY, G... MAYBE THEY MIXED UP SHIRTS. MAYBE YOU'VE GOT THAT KID'S SHIRT, AND HE'S GOT YOURS.
!
BILLY DEMON
HEY, KID! IS YOUR NAME J-MAN?
YEAH, BUT THAT'S NOT WHAT MY T-SHIRT SAYS... THEY GOT IT WRONG!
LOOK, I THINK THEY MIXED UP OUR SHIRTS, SEE?
OH WOW! GREAT!
J-MAN
THANKS, J-BOY!
WHO?
J-MA
J-BOY
FORGET ABOUT THE SHIRT, G-MAN! YOU KNOW THAT LITTLE RED-CAPED GIRL YOU LIKE? I HEARD HER SAYING SHE THINKS YOU'RE CUTE AND THAT SHE WANTS TO MEET YOU!
REALLY?
YEAH! YOU SHOULD GO TALK TO HER RIGHT NOW! IT'S OUR LAST DAY OF CAMP, G-MAN-- YOU MIGHT NOT GET ANOTHER CHANCE!
WHERE IS SHE, MARKSMAN?
SHE'S RIGHT OVER--
--WOOPS.
SACK
LOOKS LIKE SHE'S ALREADY MET SOMEBODY ELSE.
CHECK IT OUT! FOR SOME REASON, THEY GAVE ME TWO SHIRTS!
G-MAN
G-MAN
CG2002

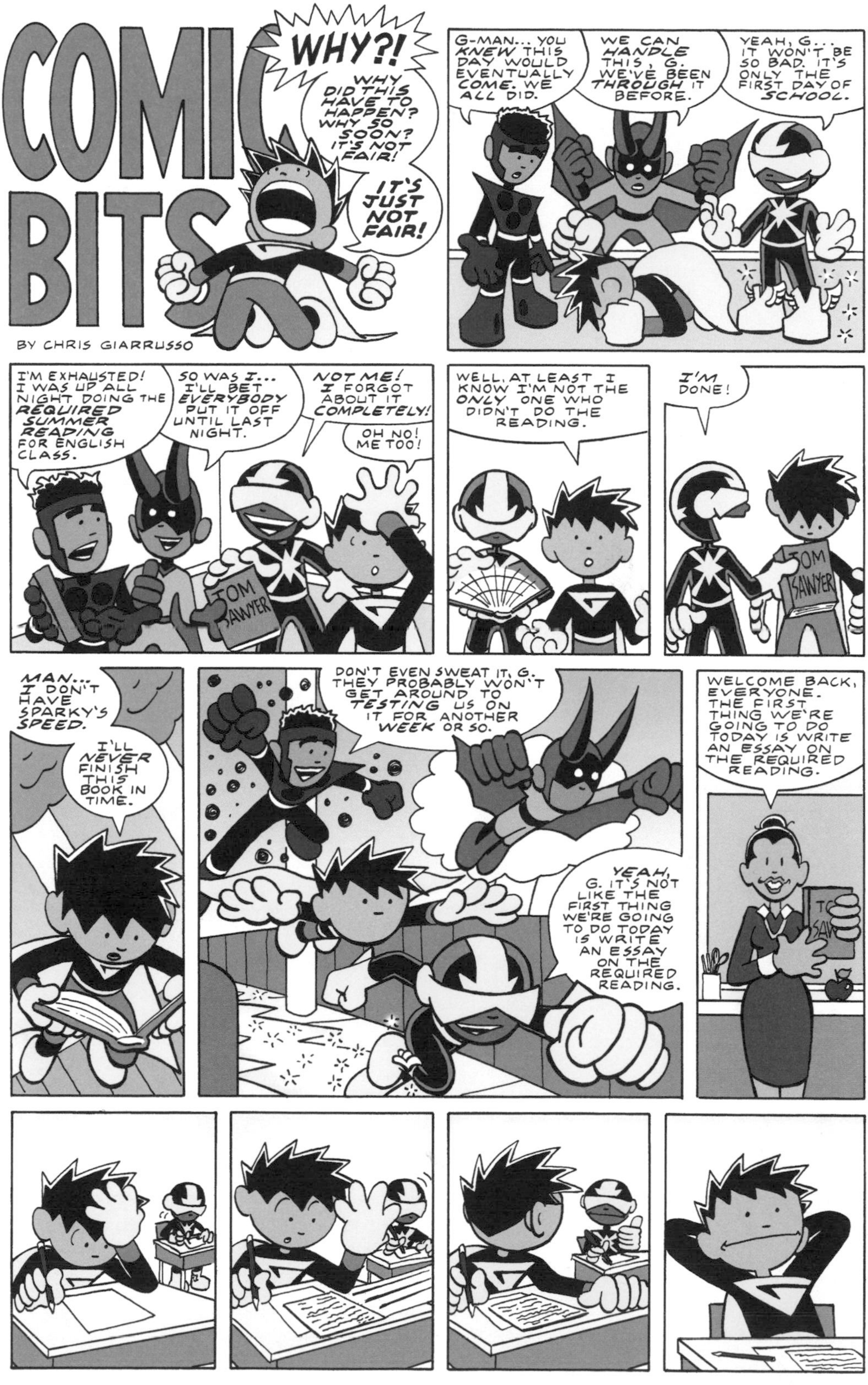
COMIC BITS
BY CHRIS GIARRUSSO
WHY?!
WHY DID THIS HAVE TO HAPPEN? WHY SO SOON? IT'S NOT FAIR!
IT'S JUST NOT FAIR!
G-MAN... YOU KNEW THIS DAY WOULD EVENTUALLY COME. WE ALL DID.
WE CAN HANDLE THIS, G. WE'VE BEEN THROUGH IT BEFORE.
YEAH, G... IT WON'T BE SO BAD. IT'S ONLY THE FIRST DAY OF SCHOOL.
I'M EXHAUSTED! I WAS UP ALL NIGHT DOING THE REQUIRED SUMMER READING FOR ENGLISH CLASS.
SO WAS I... I'LL BET EVERYBODY PUT IT OFF UNTIL LAST NIGHT.
NOT ME! I FORGOT ABOUT IT COMPLETELY!
OH NO! ME TOO!
TOM SAWYER
WELL, AT LEAST I KNOW I'M NOT THE ONLY ONE WHO DIDN'T DO THE READING.
I'M DONE!
TOM SAWYER
MAN... I DON'T HAVE SPARKY'S SPEED.
I'LL NEVER FINISH THIS BOOK IN TIME.
DON'T EVEN SWEAT IT, G. THEY PROBABLY WON'T GET AROUND TO TESTING US ON IT FOR ANOTHER WEEK OR SO.
YEAH, G. IT'S NOT LIKE THE FIRST THING WE'RE GOING TO DO TODAY IS WRITE AN ESSAY ON THE REQUIRED READING.
WELCOME BACK, EVERYONE. THE FIRST THING WE'RE GOING TO DO TODAY IS WRITE AN ESSAY ON THE REQUIRED READING.

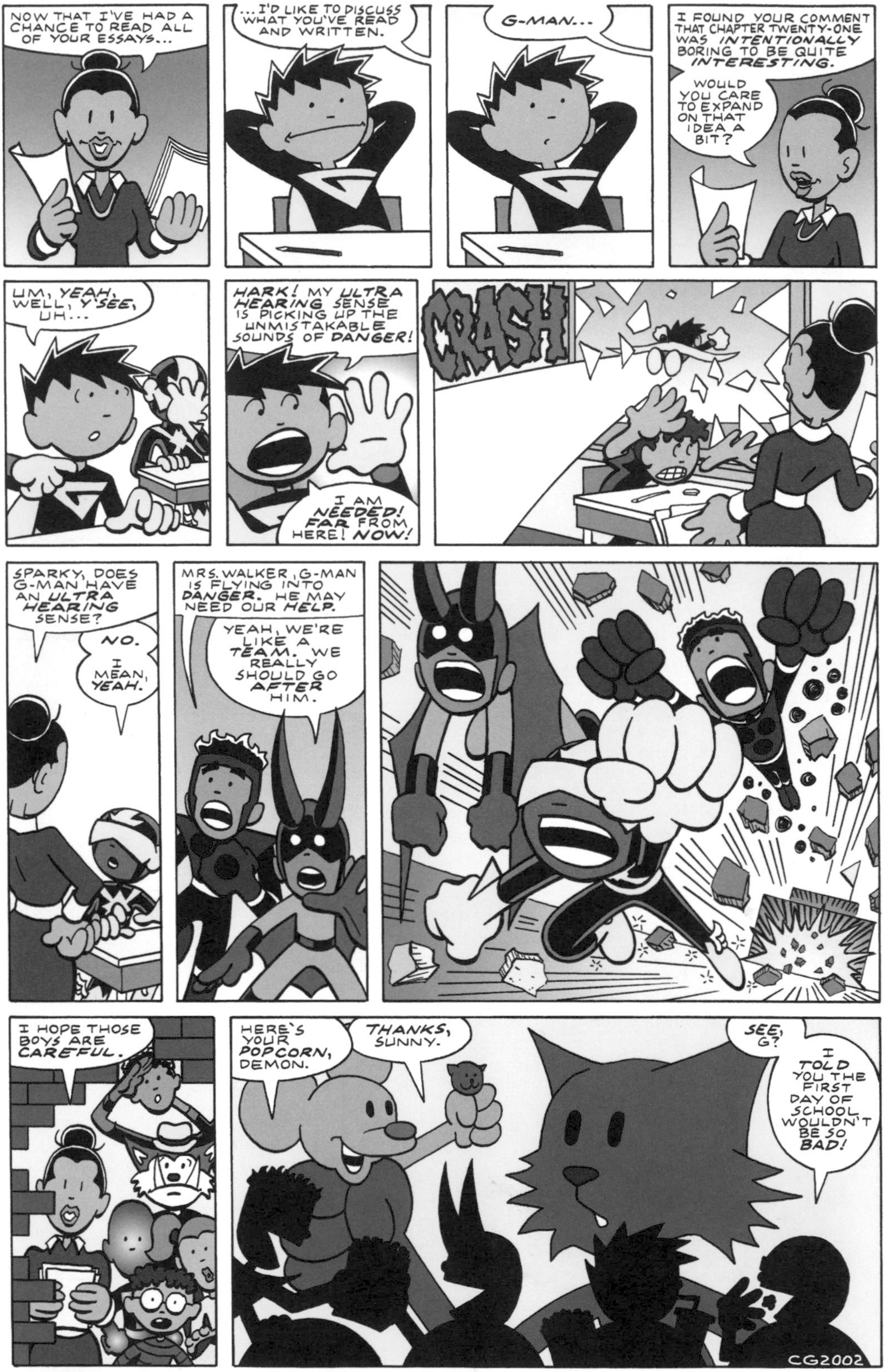
NOW THAT I'VE HAD A CHANCE TO READ ALL OF YOUR ESSAYS...
...I'D LIKE TO DISCUSS WHAT YOU'VE READ AND WRITTEN.
G-MAN...
I FOUND YOUR COMMENT THAT CHAPTER TWENTY-ONE WAS INTENTIONALLY BORING TO BE QUITE INTERESTING.
WOULD YOU CARE TO EXPAND ON THAT IDEA A BIT?
UM, YEAH, WELL, Y'SEE, UH...
HARK! MY ULTRA HEARING SENSE IS PICKING UP THE UNMISTAKABLE SOUNDS OF DANGER!
I AM NEEDED! FAR FROM HERE! NOW!
CRASH
SPARKY, DOES G-MAN HAVE AN ULTRA HEARING SENSE?
NO.
I MEAN, YEAH.
MRS. WALKER, G-MAN IS FLYING INTO DANGER. HE MAY NEED OUR HELP.
YEAH, WE'RE LIKE A TEAM. WE REALLY SHOULD GO AFTER HIM.
I HOPE THOSE BOYS ARE CAREFUL.
HERE'S YOUR POPCORN, DEMON.
THANKS, SUNNY.
SEE, G?
I TOLD YOU THE FIRST DAY OF SCHOOL WOULDN'T BE SO BAD!
CG2002

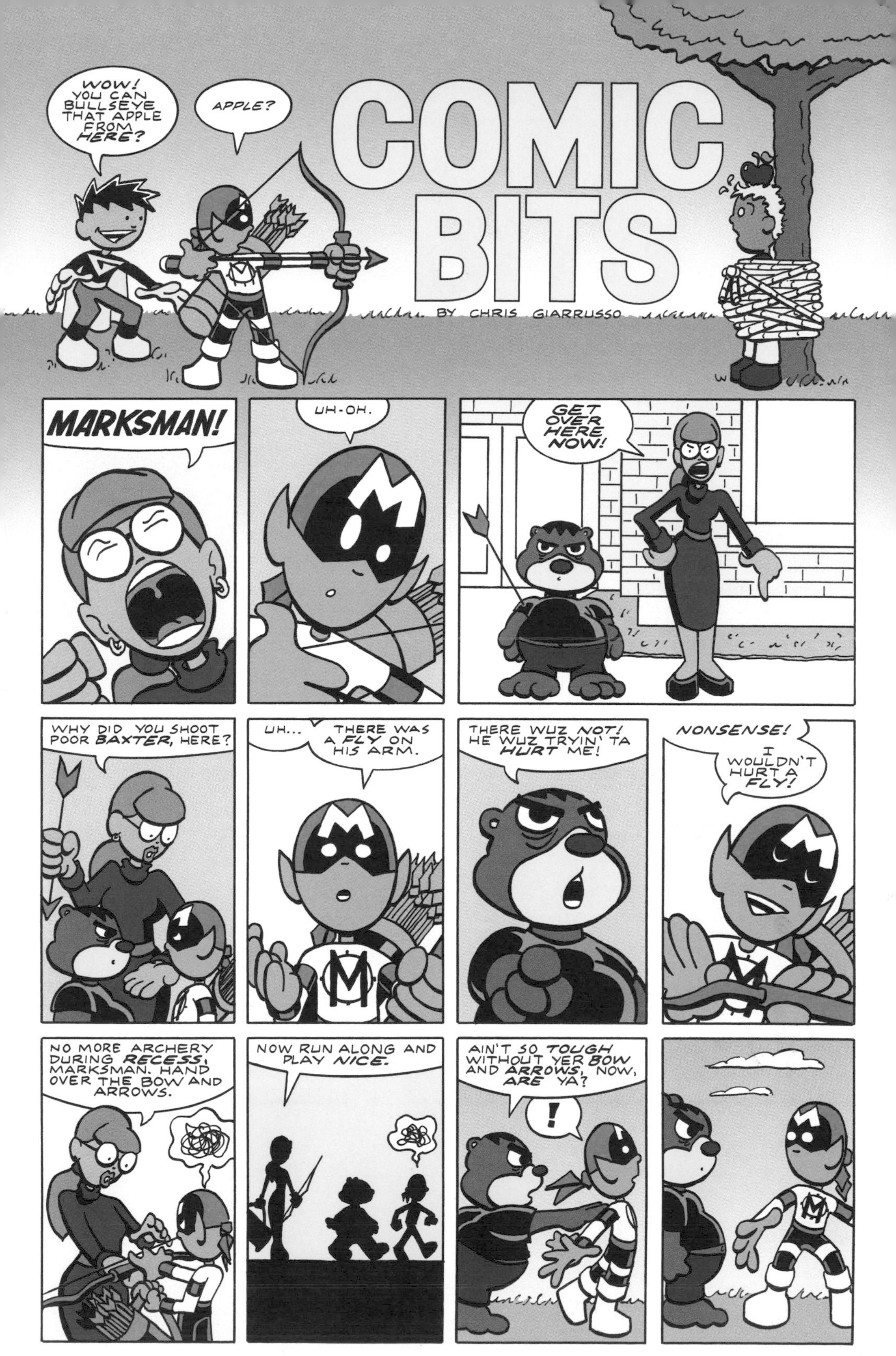
WOW! YOU CAN BULLSEYE THAT APPLE FROM HERE?
APPLE?
COMIC BITS
BY CHRIS GIARRUSSO
MARKSMAN!
UH-OH.
GET OVER HERE NOW!
WHY DID YOU SHOOT POOR BAXTER, HERE?
UH...
THERE WAS A FLY ON HIS ARM.
THERE WUZ NOT! HE WUZ TRYIN' TA HURT ME!
NONSENSE!
I WOULDN'T HURT A FLY!
NO MORE ARCHERY DURING RECESS, MARKSMAN. HAND OVER THE BOW AND ARROWS.
NOW RUN ALONG AND PLAY NICE.
AIN'T SO TOUGH WITHOUT YER BOW AND ARROWS, NOW, ARE YA?
!

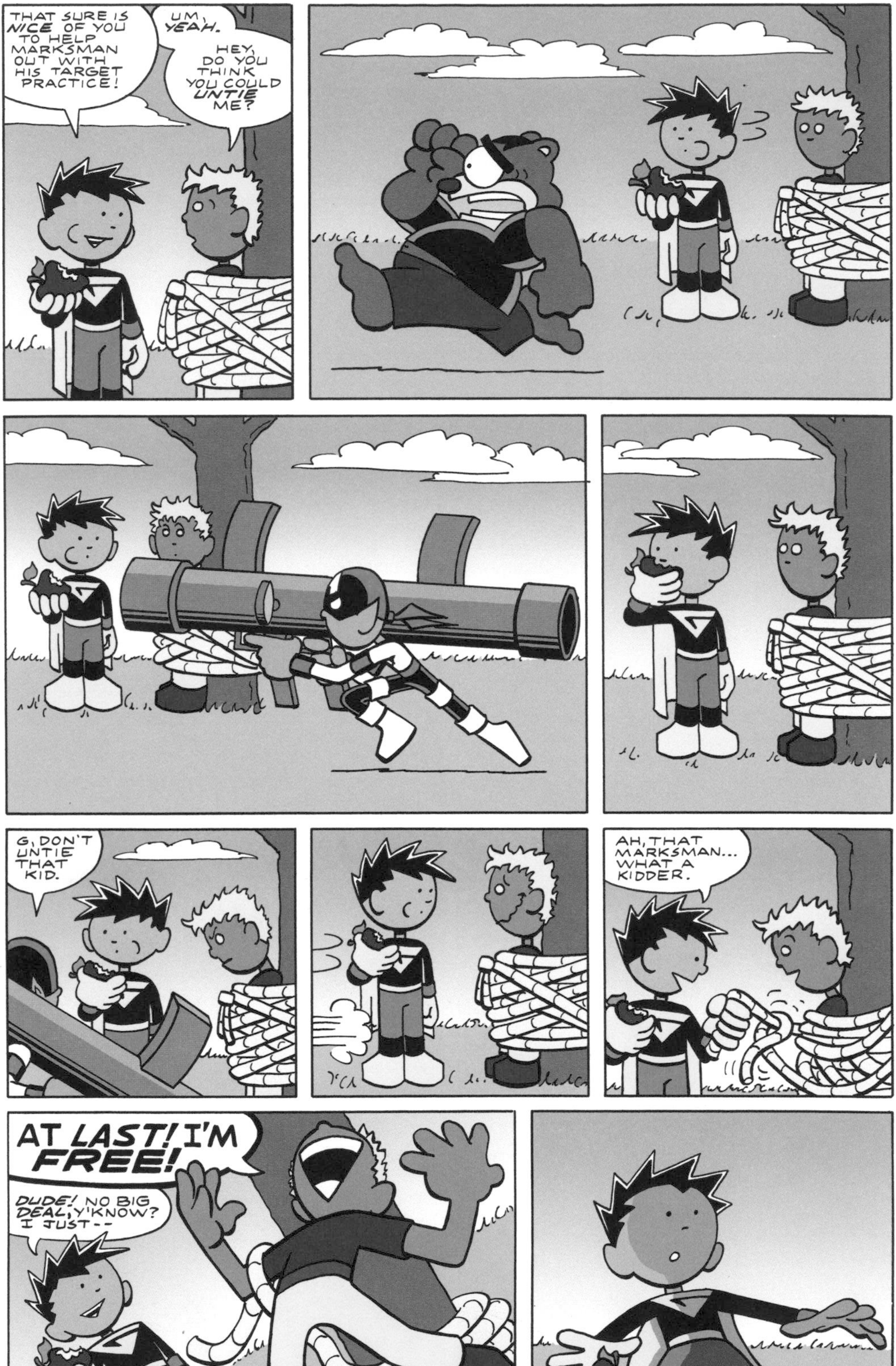
THAT SURE IS NICE OF YOU TO HELP MARKSMAN OUT WITH HIS TARGET PRACTICE!
UM, YEAH.
HEY, DO YOU THINK YOU COULD UNTIE ME?
G, DON'T UNTIE THAT KID.
AH, THAT MARKSMAN... WHAT A KIDDER.
AT LAST! I'M FREE!
DUDE! NO BIG DEAL, Y'KNOW? I JUST--

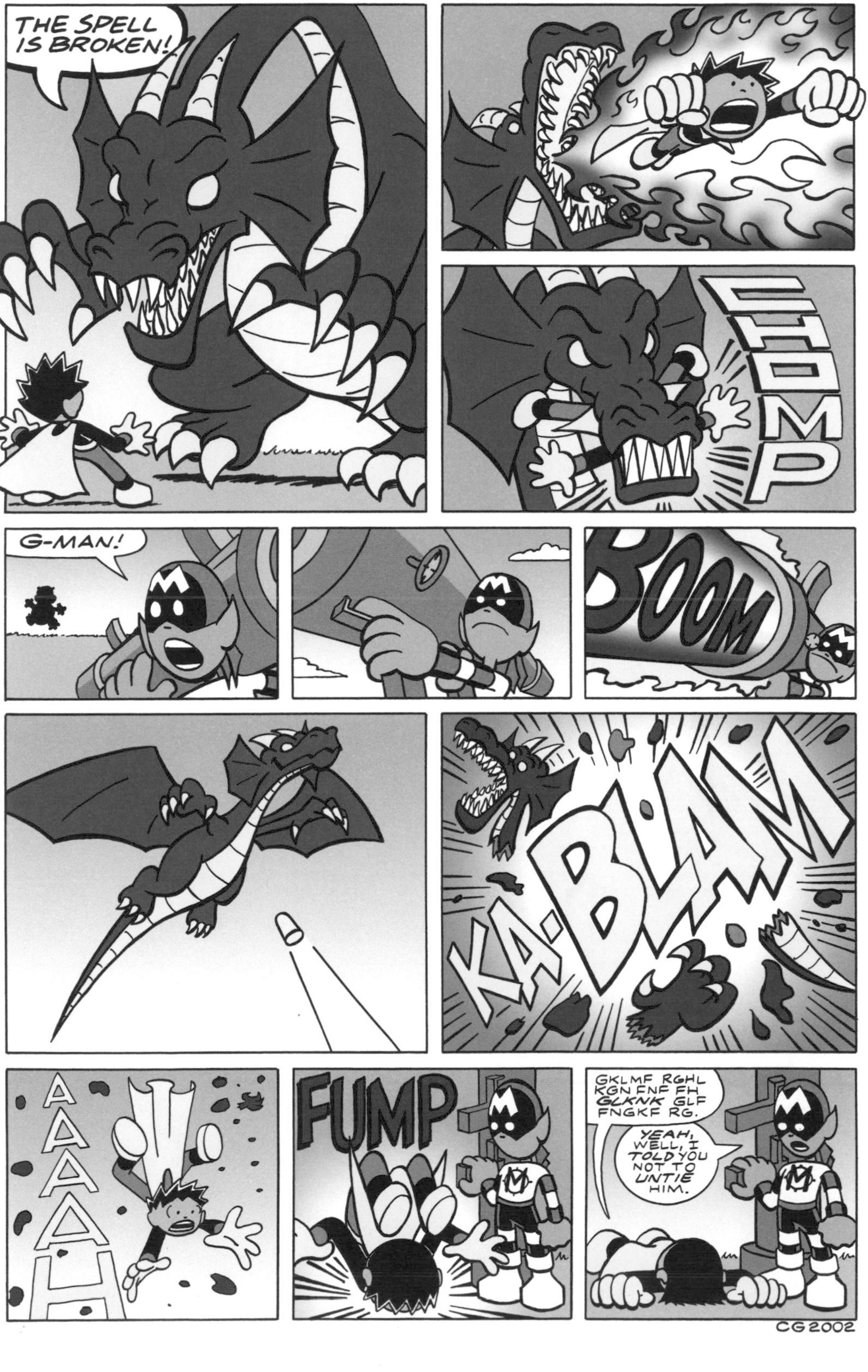
THE SPELL IS BROKEN!
CHOMP
G-MAN!
BOOM
KA-BLAM
AAAAAH
FUMP
GKLMF RGHL KGN FNF FH GLKNK GLF FNGKF RG.
YEAH, WELL, I TOLD YOU NOT TO UNTIE HIM.
CG 2002

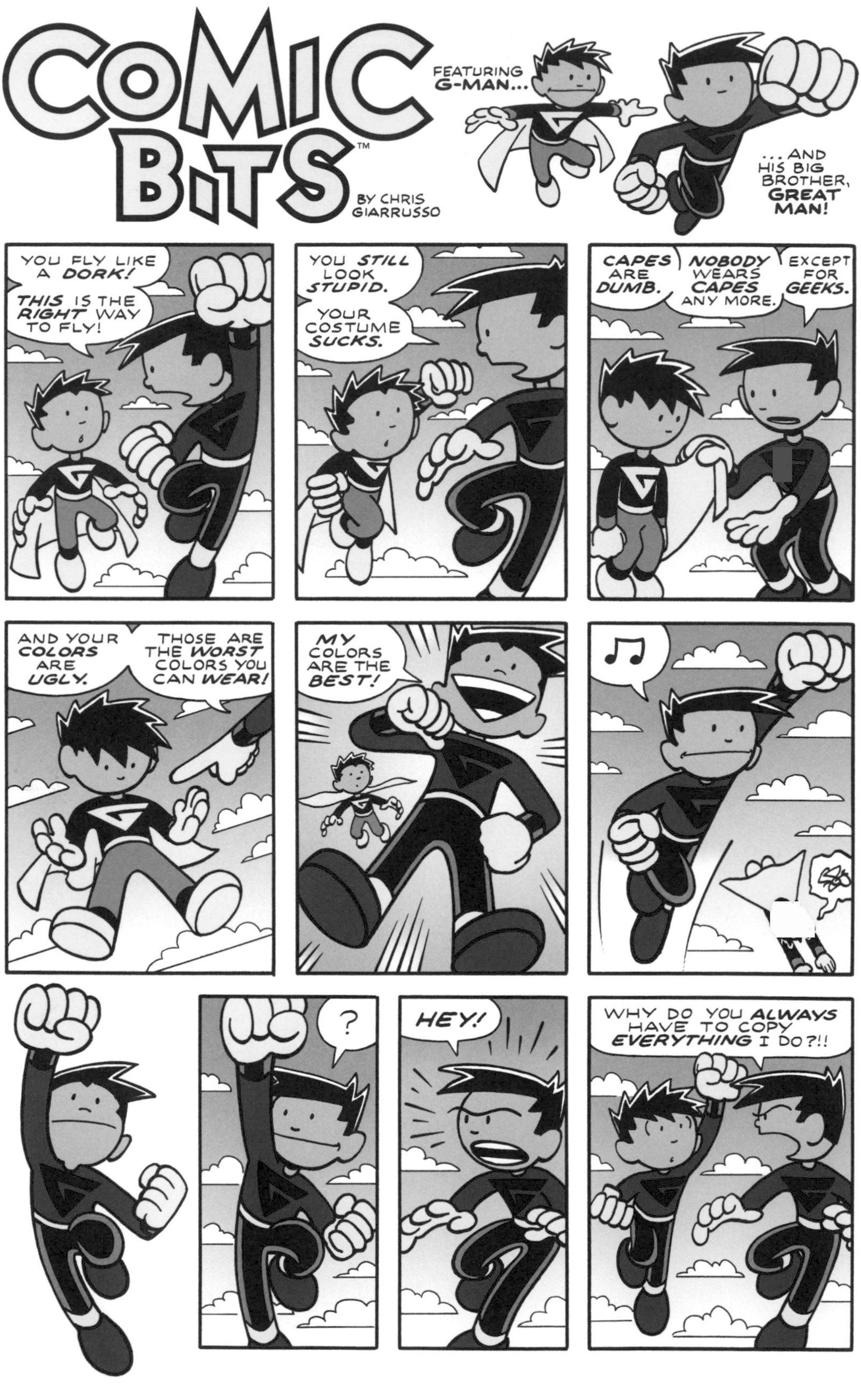
COMIC BITS™
BY CHRIS GIARRUSSO
FEATURING G-MAN...
...AND HIS BIG BROTHER, GREAT MAN!
YOU FLY LIKE A DORK!
THIS IS THE RIGHT WAY TO FLY!
YOU STILL LOOK STUPID.
YOUR COSTUME SUCKS.
CAPES ARE DUMB.
NOBODY WEARS CAPES ANY MORE.
EXCEPT FOR GEEKS.
AND YOUR COLORS ARE UGLY.
THOSE ARE THE WORST COLORS YOU CAN WEAR!
MY COLORS ARE THE BEST!
♫
?
HEY!
WHY DO YOU ALWAYS HAVE TO COPY EVERYTHING I DO?!!

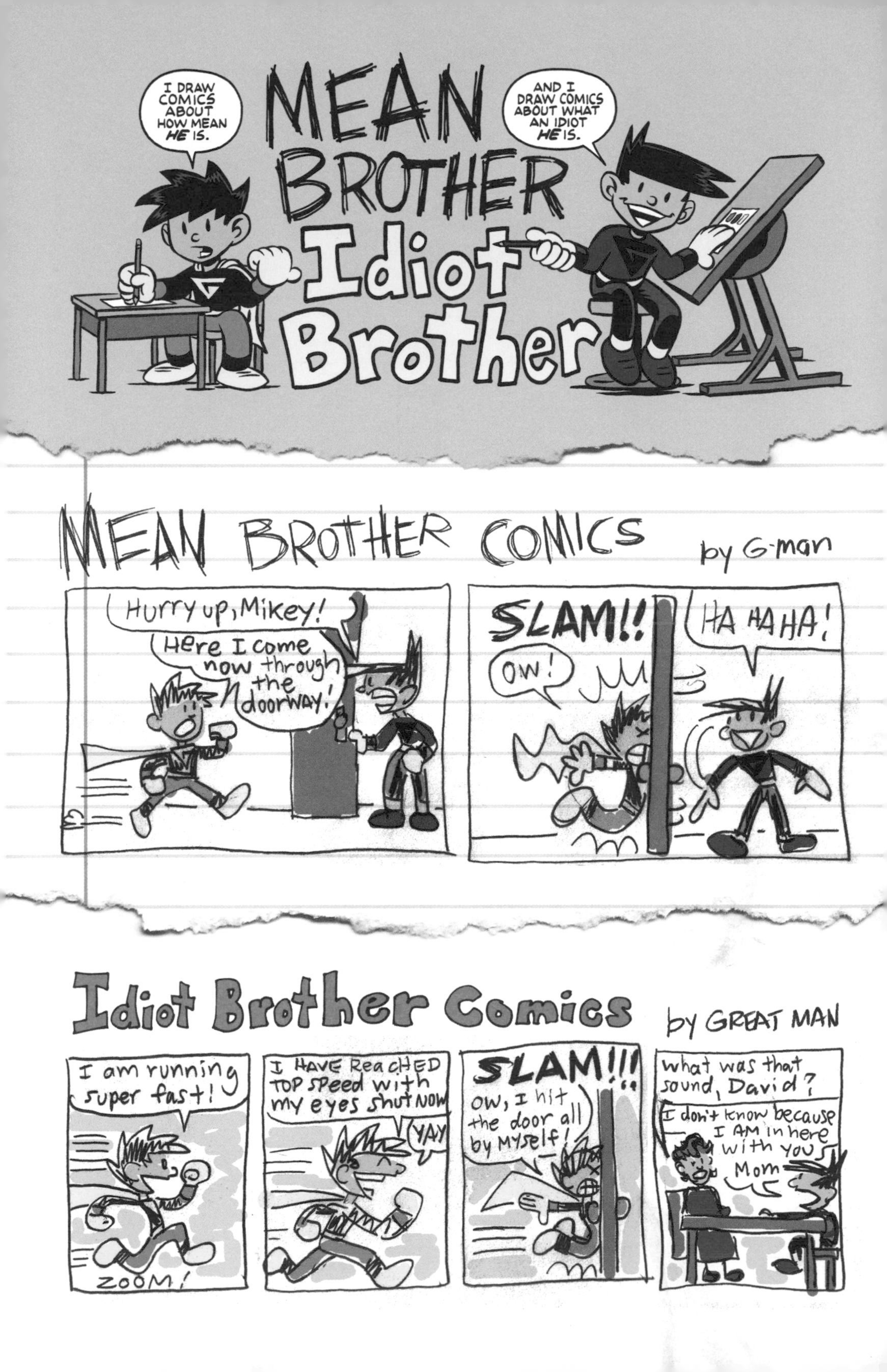

I DRAW COMICS ABOUT HOW MEAN HE IS.
MEAN BROTHER Idiot Brother
AND I DRAW COMICS ABOUT WHAT AN IDIOT HE IS.
MEAN BROTHER COMICS
by G-man
Hurry up, Mikey!
Here I come now through the doorway!
SLAM!!
OW!
HA HA HA!
Idiot Brother Comics
by GREAT MAN
I am running super fast!
ZOOM!
I HAVE REACHED TOP SPEED with my eyes shut NOW
YAY
SLAM!!!
OW, I hit the door all by MYself!
What was that sound, David?
I don't know because I AM in here with you Mom

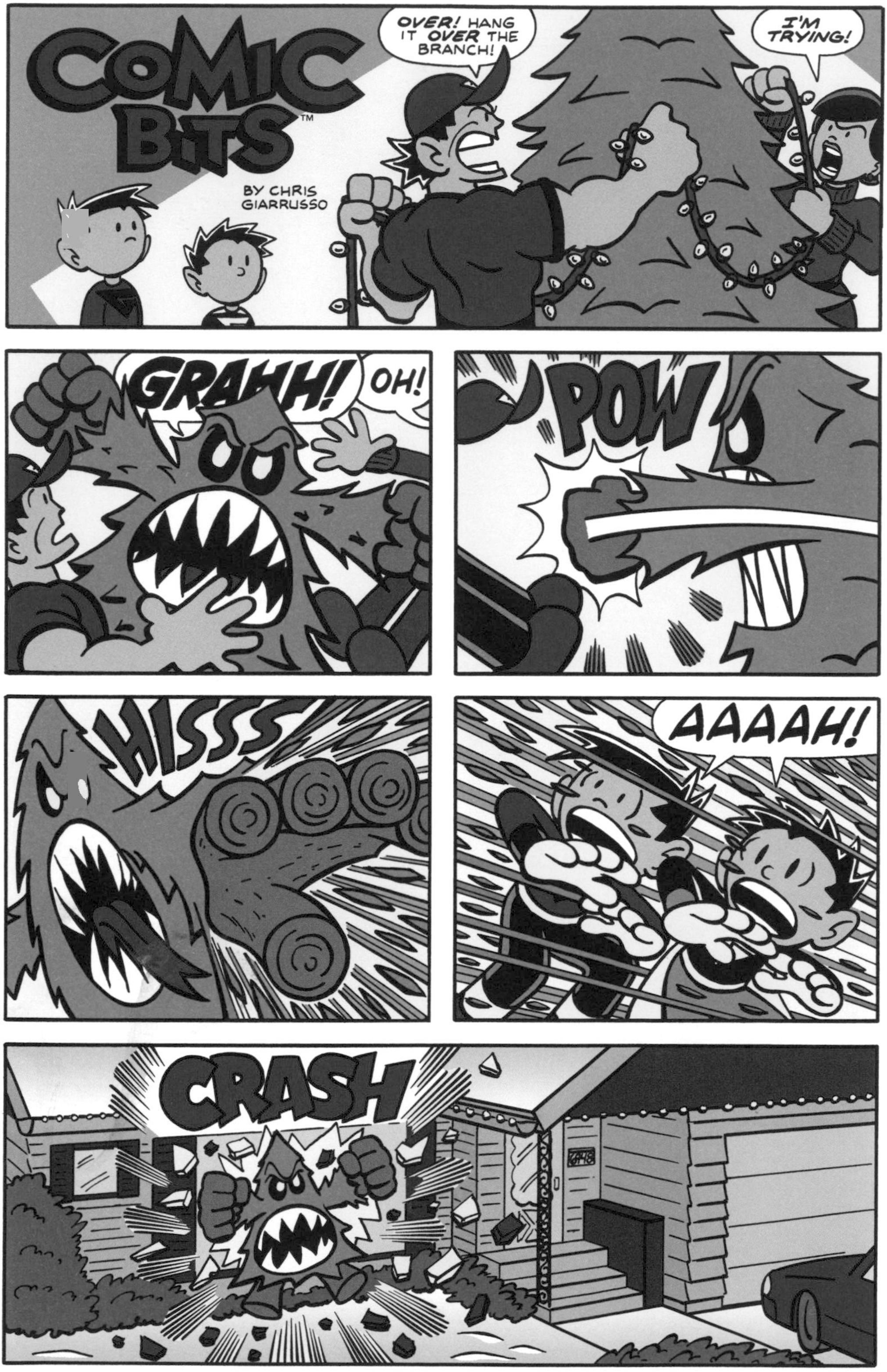

COMIC BITS™
BY CHRIS GIARRUSSO
OVER! HANG IT OVER THE BRANCH!
I'M TRYING!
GRAHH!
OH!
POW
HISSS
AAAAH!
CRASH

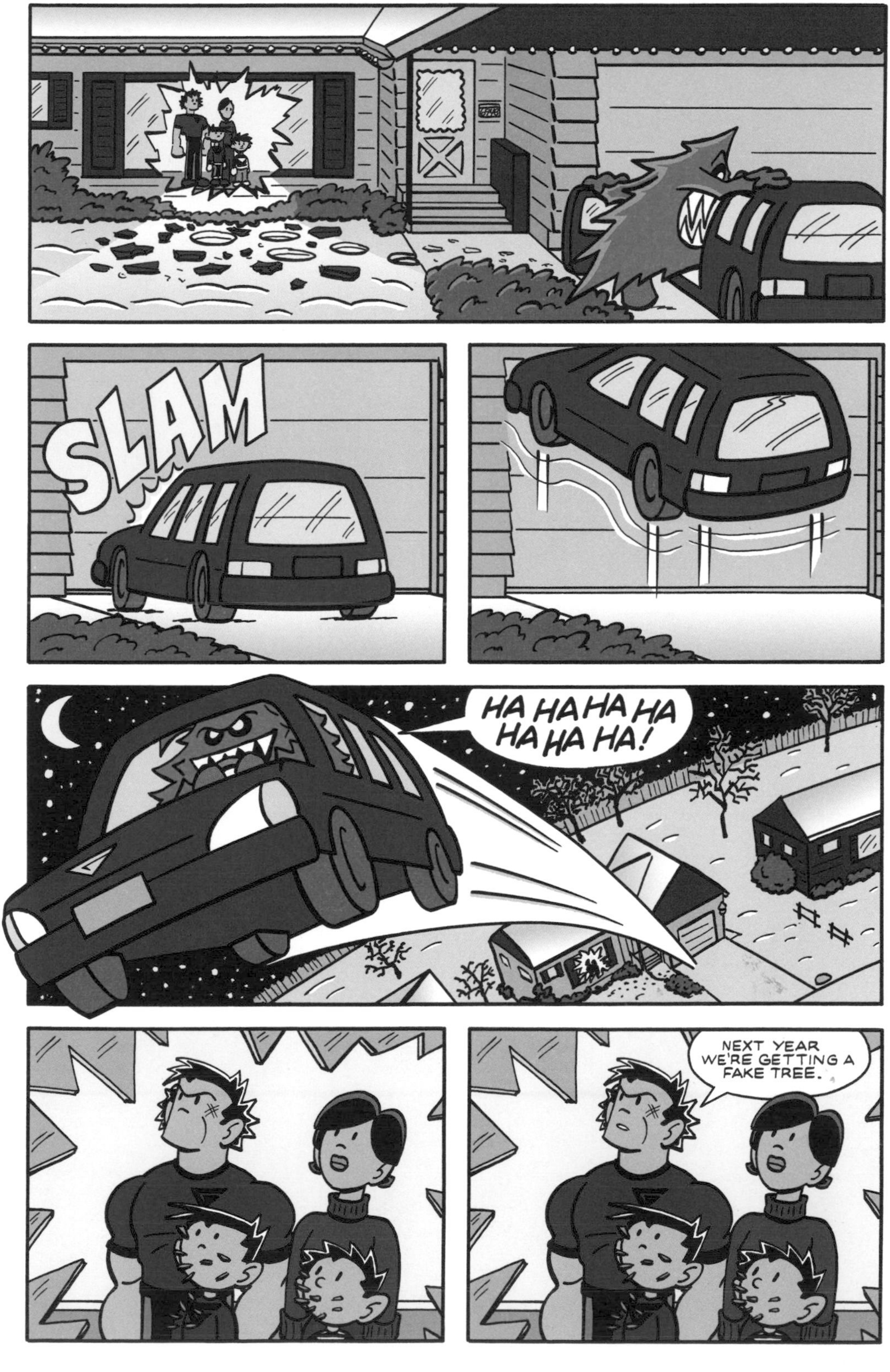
SLAM
HA HAHA HA HA HA HA!
NEXT YEAR WE'RE GETTING A FAKE TREE.

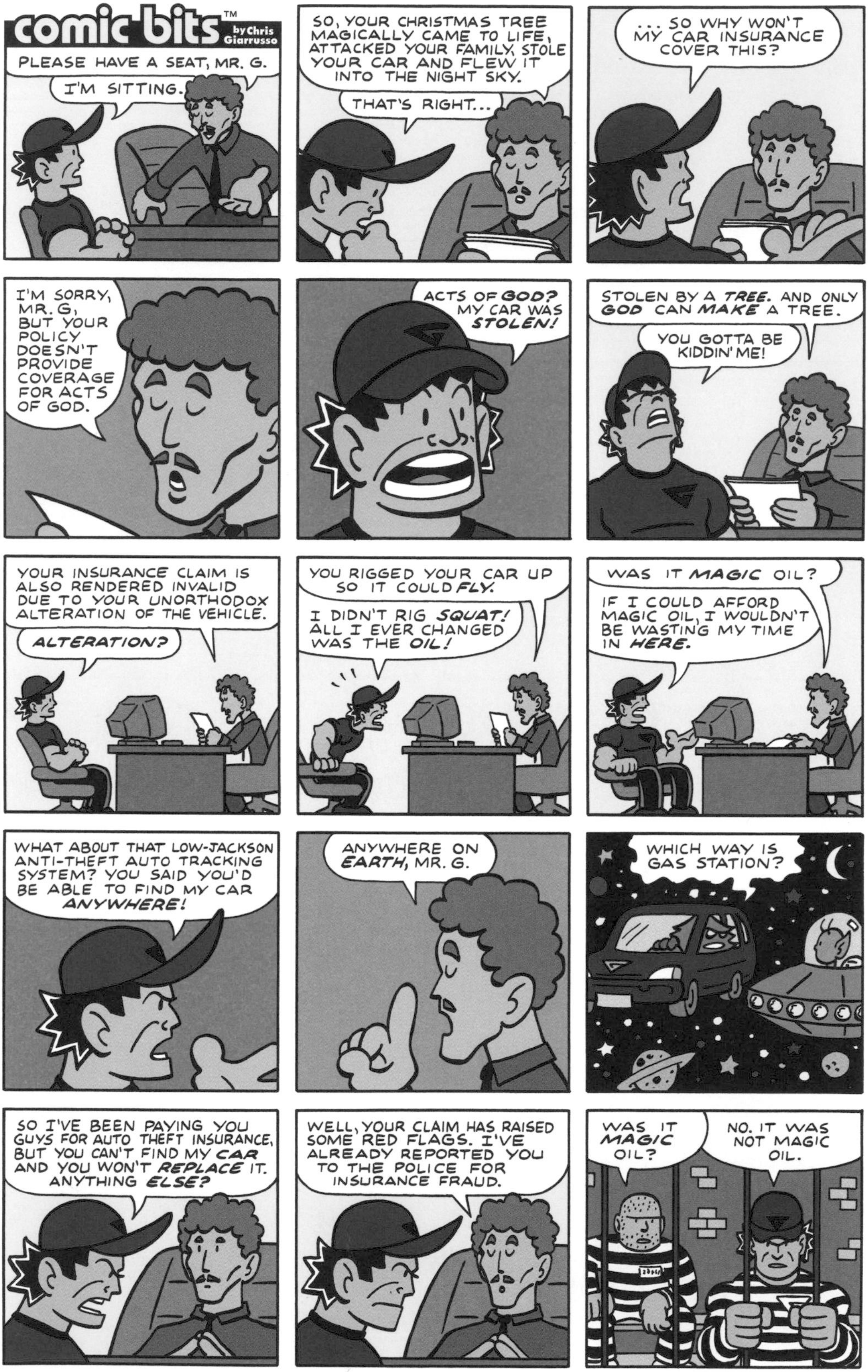
comic bits™ by Chris Giarrusso
PLEASE HAVE A SEAT, MR. G.
I'M SITTING.
SO, YOUR CHRISTMAS TREE MAGICALLY CAME TO LIFE, ATTACKED YOUR FAMILY, STOLE YOUR CAR AND FLEW IT INTO THE NIGHT SKY.
THAT'S RIGHT...
... SO WHY WON'T MY CAR INSURANCE COVER THIS?
I'M SORRY, MR. G, BUT YOUR POLICY DOESN'T PROVIDE COVERAGE FOR ACTS OF GOD.
ACTS OF GOD? MY CAR WAS STOLEN!
STOLEN BY A TREE. AND ONLY GOD CAN MAKE A TREE.
YOU GOTTA BE KIDDIN' ME!
YOUR INSURANCE CLAIM IS ALSO RENDERED INVALID DUE TO YOUR UNORTHODOX ALTERATION OF THE VEHICLE.
ALTERATION?
YOU RIGGED YOUR CAR UP SO IT COULD FLY.
I DIDN'T RIG SQUAT! ALL I EVER CHANGED WAS THE OIL!
WAS IT MAGIC OIL?
IF I COULD AFFORD MAGIC OIL, I WOULDN'T BE WASTING MY TIME IN HERE.
WHAT ABOUT THAT LOW-JACKSON ANTI-THEFT AUTO TRACKING SYSTEM? YOU SAID YOU'D BE ABLE TO FIND MY CAR ANYWHERE!
ANYWHERE ON EARTH, MR. G.
WHICH WAY IS GAS STATION?
SO I'VE BEEN PAYING YOU GUYS FOR AUTO THEFT INSURANCE, BUT YOU CAN'T FIND MY CAR AND YOU WON'T REPLACE IT. ANYTHING ELSE?
WELL, YOUR CLAIM HAS RAISED SOME RED FLAGS. I'VE ALREADY REPORTED YOU TO THE POLICE FOR INSURANCE FRAUD.
WAS IT MAGIC OIL?
NO. IT WAS NOT MAGIC OIL.

G-MAN™ and the Christmas Tree of Doom

by Chris Giarrusso

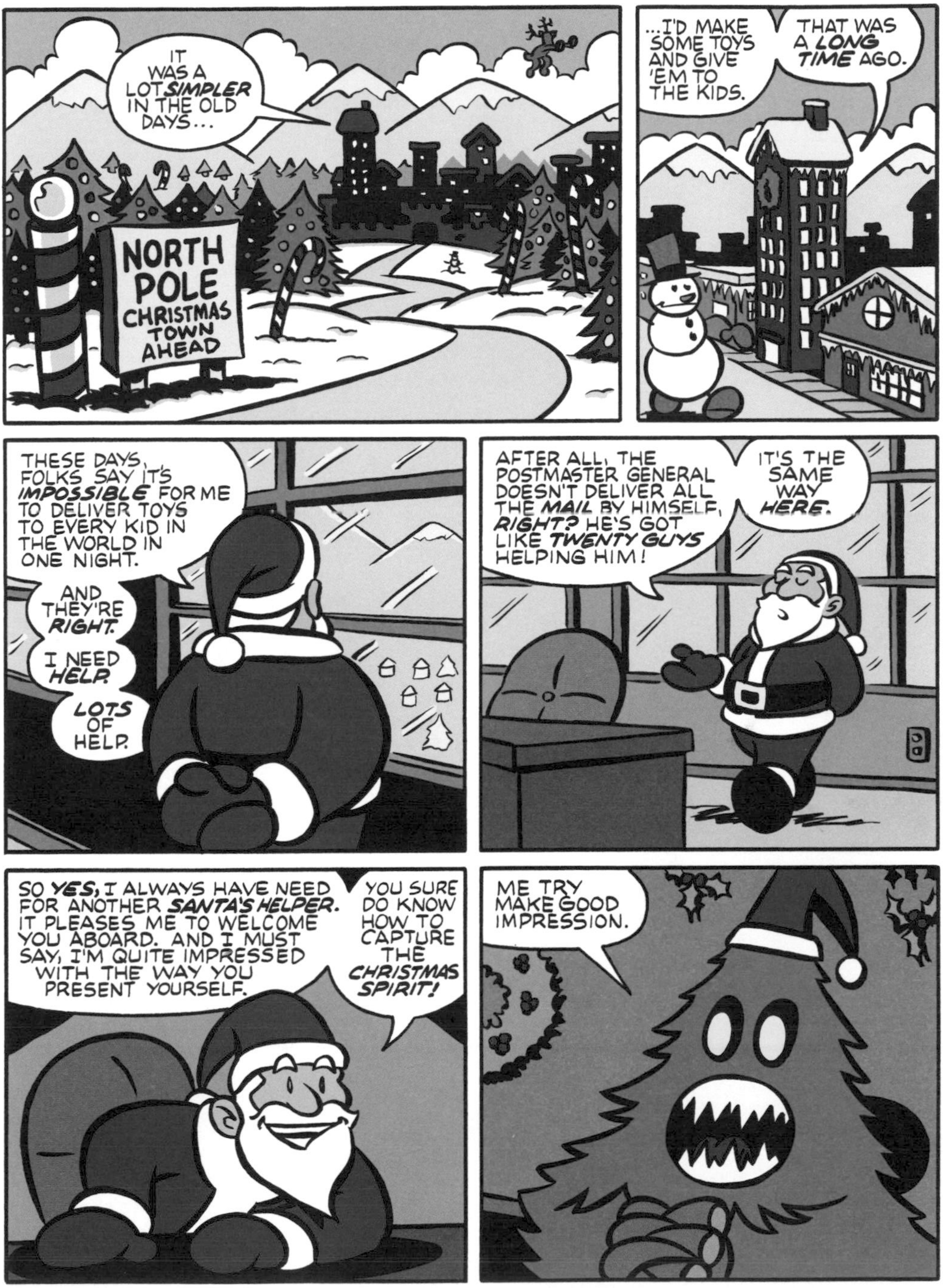

IT WAS A LOT SIMPLER IN THE OLD DAYS...
NORTH POLE CHRISTMAS TOWN AHEAD
...I'D MAKE SOME TOYS AND GIVE 'EM TO THE KIDS.
THAT WAS A LONG TIME AGO.
THESE DAYS, FOLKS SAY IT'S IMPOSSIBLE FOR ME TO DELIVER TOYS TO EVERY KID IN THE WORLD IN ONE NIGHT.
AND THEY'RE RIGHT.
I NEED HELP.
LOTS OF HELP.
AFTER ALL, THE POSTMASTER GENERAL DOESN'T DELIVER ALL THE MAIL BY HIMSELF, RIGHT? HE'S GOT LIKE TWENTY GUYS HELPING HIM!
IT'S THE SAME WAY HERE.
SO YES, I ALWAYS HAVE NEED FOR ANOTHER SANTA'S HELPER. IT PLEASES ME TO WELCOME YOU ABOARD. AND I MUST SAY, I'M QUITE IMPRESSED WITH THE WAY YOU PRESENT YOURSELF.
YOU SURE DO KNOW HOW TO CAPTURE THE CHRISTMAS SPIRIT!
ME TRY MAKE GOOD IMPRESSION.

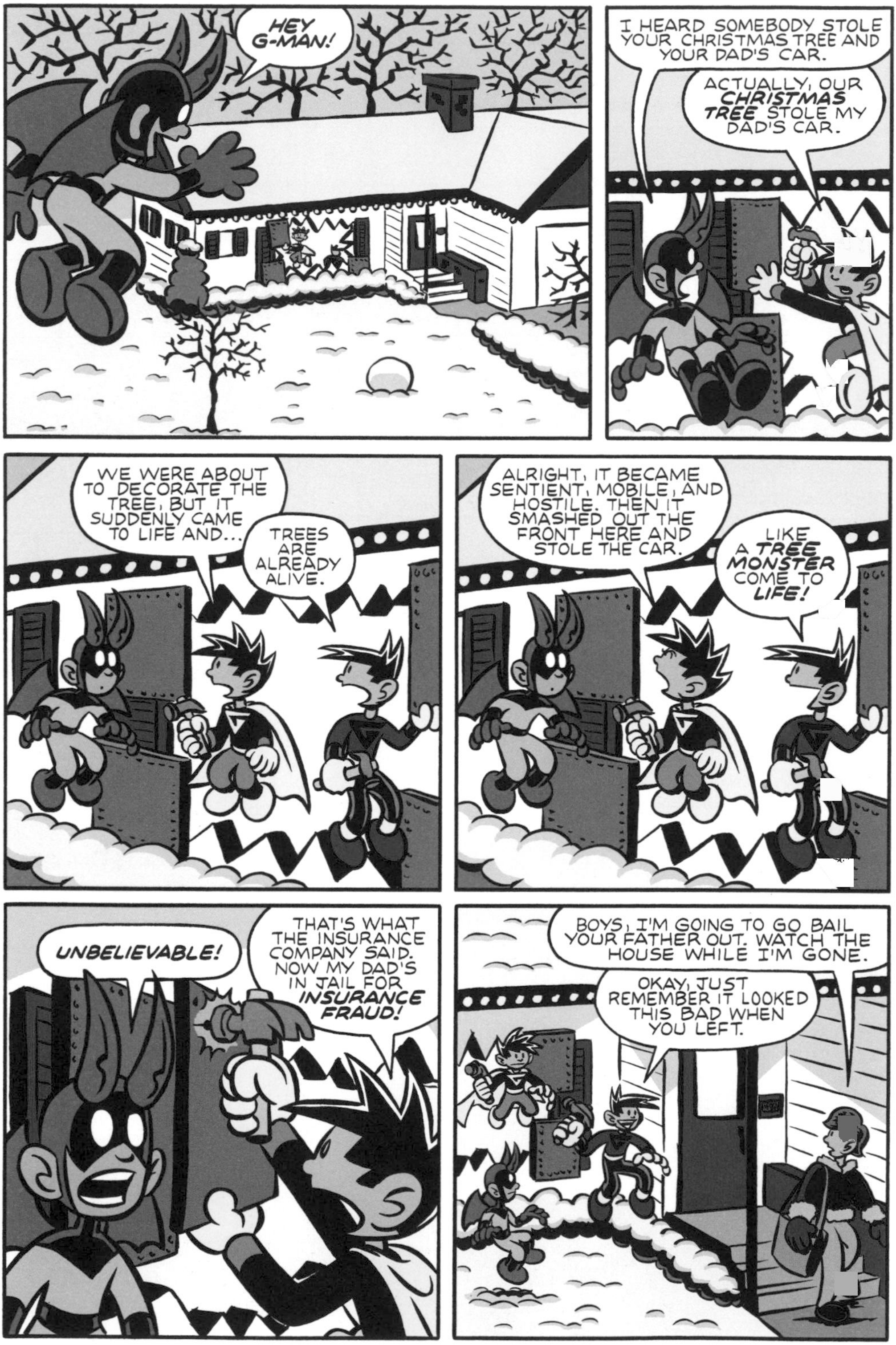
HEY G-MAN!
I HEARD SOMEBODY STOLE YOUR CHRISTMAS TREE AND YOUR DAD'S CAR.
ACTUALLY, OUR CHRISTMAS TREE STOLE MY DAD'S CAR.
WE WERE ABOUT TO DECORATE THE TREE, BUT IT SUDDENLY CAME TO LIFE AND...
TREES ARE ALREADY ALIVE.
ALRIGHT, IT BECAME SENTIENT, MOBILE, AND HOSTILE. THEN IT SMASHED OUT THE FRONT HERE AND STOLE THE CAR.
LIKE A TREE MONSTER COME TO LIFE!
UNBELIEVABLE!
THAT'S WHAT THE INSURANCE COMPANY SAID. NOW MY DAD'S IN JAIL FOR INSURANCE FRAUD!
BOYS, I'M GOING TO GO BAIL YOUR FATHER OUT. WATCH THE HOUSE WHILE I'M GONE.
OKAY, JUST REMEMBER IT LOOKED THIS BAD WHEN YOU LEFT.

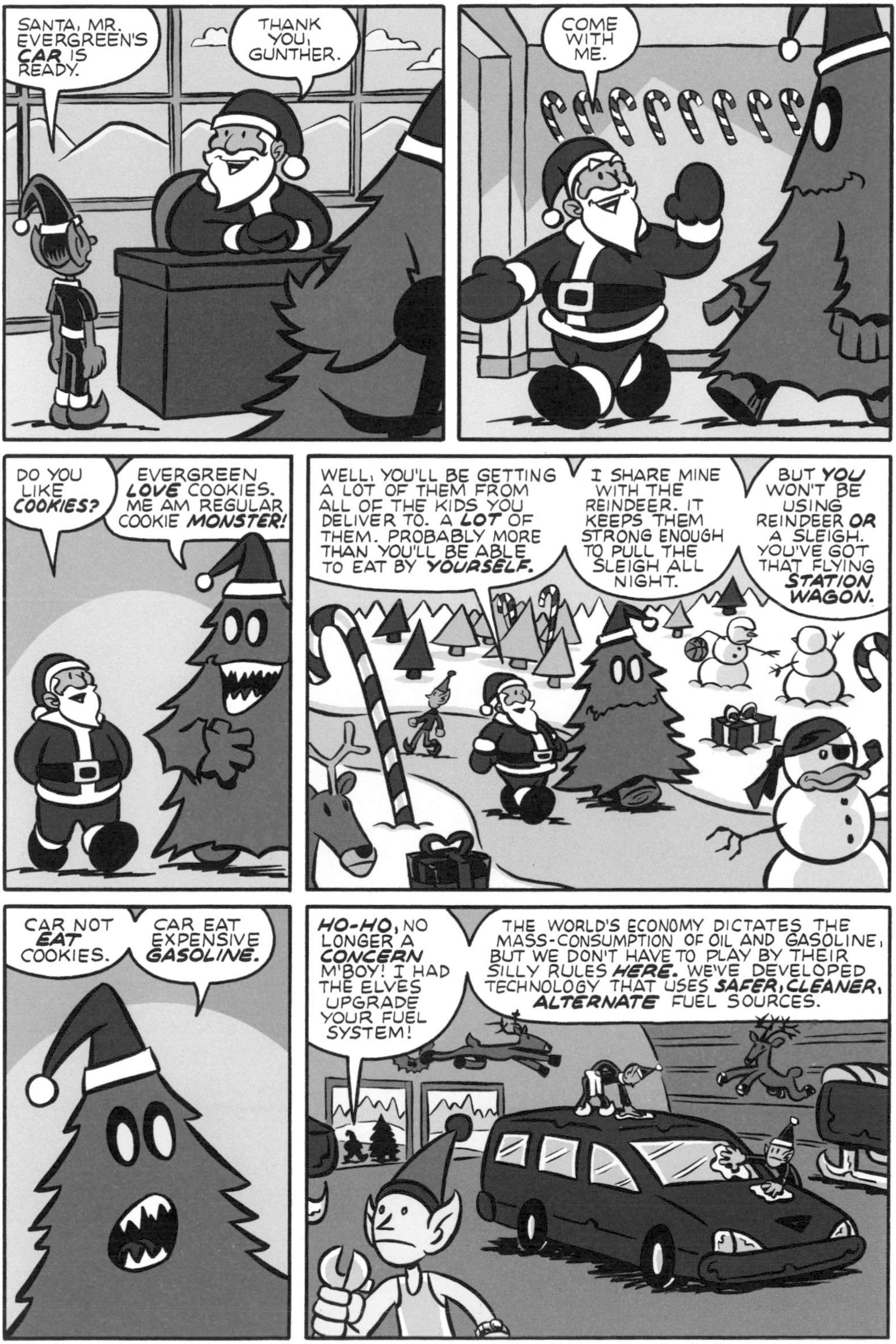
SANTA, MR. EVERGREEN'S **CAR** IS READY.
THANK YOU, GUNTHER.
COME WITH ME.
DO YOU LIKE **COOKIES?**
EVERGREEN **LOVE** COOKIES. ME AM REGULAR COOKIE **MONSTER!**
WELL, YOU'LL BE GETTING A LOT OF THEM FROM ALL OF THE KIDS YOU DELIVER TO. A **LOT** OF THEM. PROBABLY MORE THAN YOU'LL BE ABLE TO EAT BY **YOURSELF.**
I SHARE MINE WITH THE REINDEER. IT KEEPS THEM STRONG ENOUGH TO PULL THE SLEIGH ALL NIGHT.
BUT **YOU** WON'T BE USING REINDEER **OR** A SLEIGH. YOU'VE GOT THAT FLYING **STATION WAGON.**
CAR NOT **EAT** COOKIES.
CAR EAT EXPENSIVE **GASOLINE.**
HO-HO, NO LONGER A **CONCERN** M'BOY! I HAD THE ELVES UPGRADE YOUR FUEL SYSTEM!
THE WORLD'S ECONOMY DICTATES THE MASS-CONSUMPTION OF OIL AND GASOLINE, BUT WE DON'T HAVE TO PLAY BY THEIR SILLY RULES **HERE.** WE'VE DEVELOPED TECHNOLOGY THAT USES **SAFER, CLEANER, ALTERNATE** FUEL SOURCES.

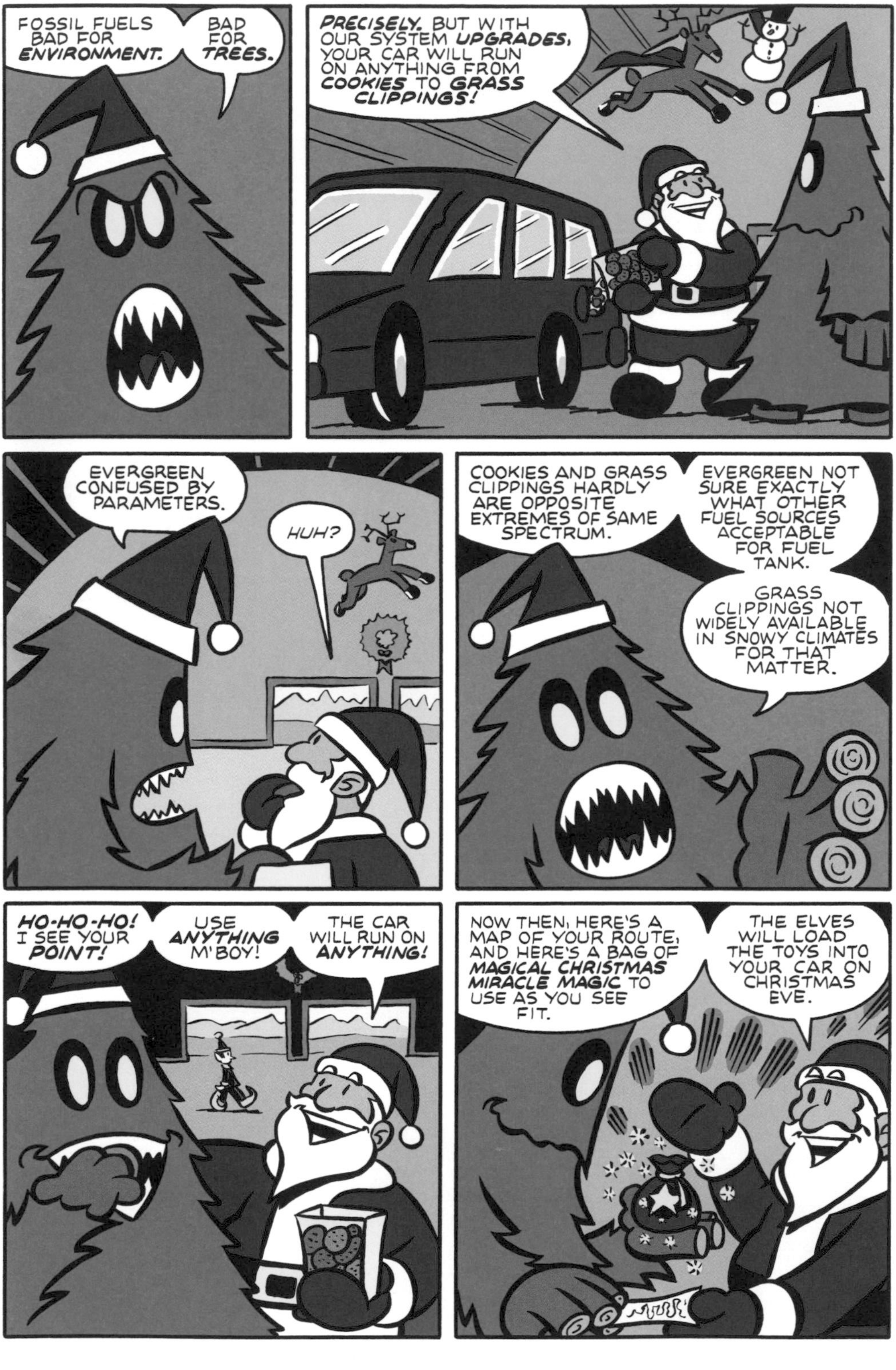
FOSSIL FUELS BAD FOR ENVIRONMENT.
BAD FOR TREES.
PRECISELY. BUT WITH OUR SYSTEM UPGRADES, YOUR CAR WILL RUN ON ANYTHING FROM COOKIES TO GRASS CLIPPINGS!
EVERGREEN CONFUSED BY PARAMETERS.
HUH?
COOKIES AND GRASS CLIPPINGS HARDLY ARE OPPOSITE EXTREMES OF SAME SPECTRUM.
EVERGREEN NOT SURE EXACTLY WHAT OTHER FUEL SOURCES ACCEPTABLE FOR FUEL TANK.
GRASS CLIPPINGS NOT WIDELY AVAILABLE IN SNOWY CLIMATES FOR THAT MATTER.
HO-HO-HO! I SEE YOUR POINT!
USE ANYTHING M'BOY!
THE CAR WILL RUN ON ANYTHING!
NOW THEN, HERE'S A MAP OF YOUR ROUTE, AND HERE'S A BAG OF MAGICAL CHRISTMAS MIRACLE MAGIC TO USE AS YOU SEE FIT.
THE ELVES WILL LOAD THE TOYS INTO YOUR CAR ON CHRISTMAS EVE.

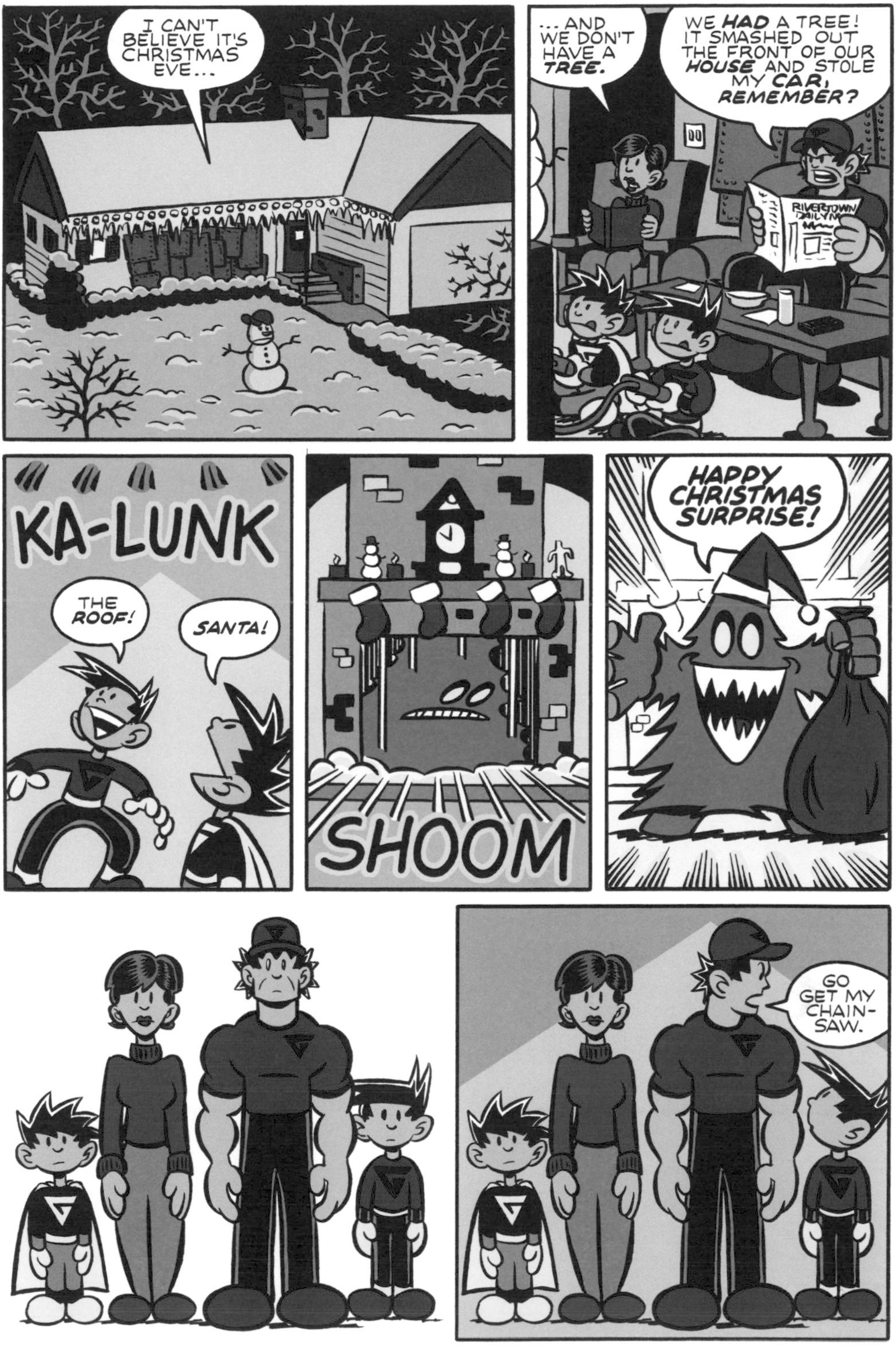
I CAN'T BELIEVE IT'S CHRISTMAS EVE...
...AND WE DON'T HAVE A TREE.
WE HAD A TREE! IT SMASHED OUT THE FRONT OF OUR HOUSE AND STOLE MY CAR, REMEMBER?
RIVERTOWN DAILY
KA-LUNK
THE ROOF!
SANTA!
SHOOM
HAPPY CHRISTMAS SURPRISE!
GO GET MY CHAIN-SAW.

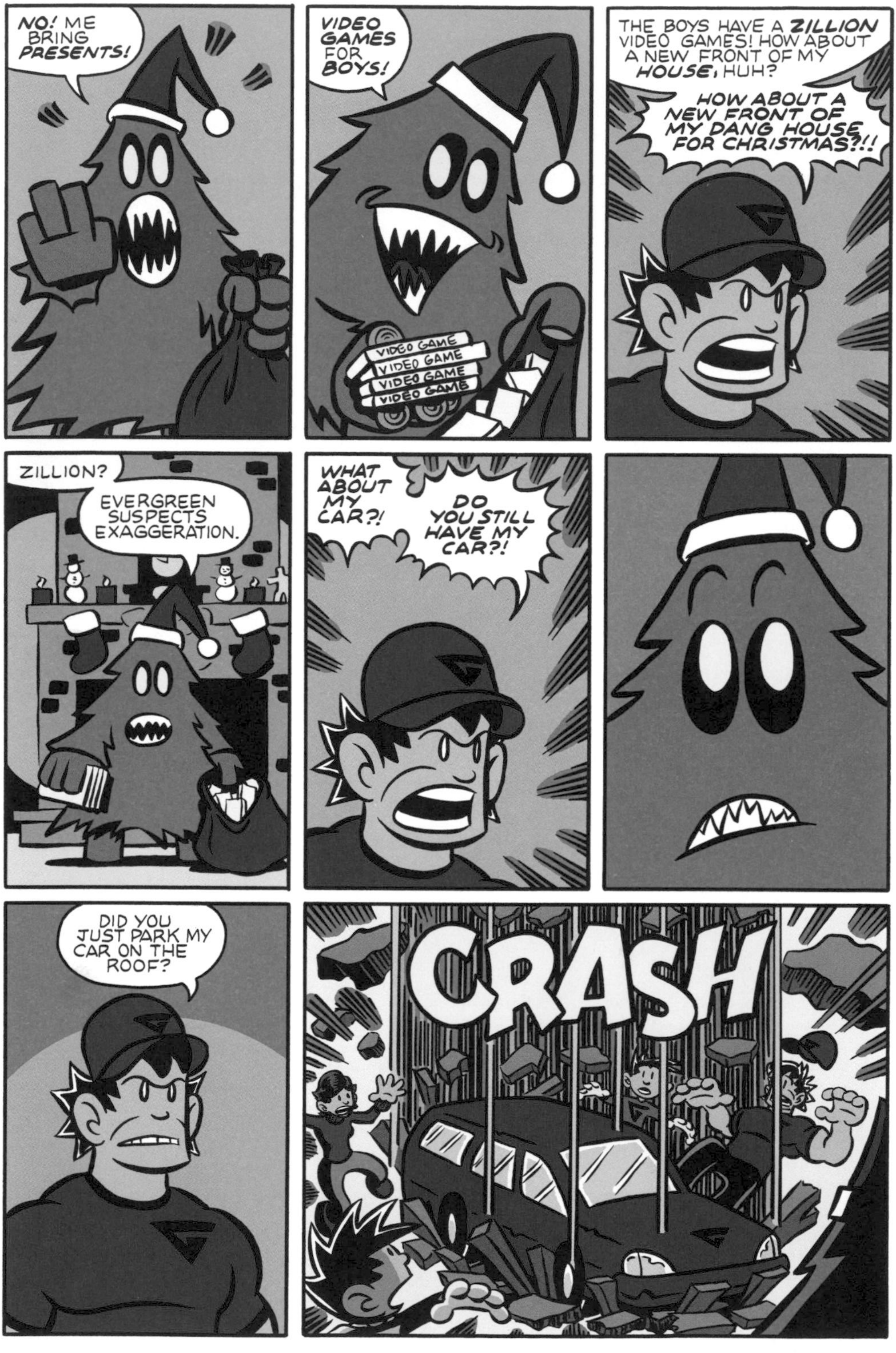
NO! ME BRING PRESENTS!
VIDEO GAMES FOR BOYS!
VIDEO GAME
VIDEO GAME
VIDEO GAME
VIDEO GAME
THE BOYS HAVE A ZILLION VIDEO GAMES! HOW ABOUT A NEW FRONT OF MY HOUSE, HUH?
HOW ABOUT A NEW FRONT OF MY DANG HOUSE FOR CHRISTMAS?!!
ZILLION?
EVERGREEN SUSPECTS EXAGGERATION.
WHAT ABOUT MY CAR?!
DO YOU STILL HAVE MY CAR?!
DID YOU JUST PARK MY CAR ON THE ROOF?
CRASH

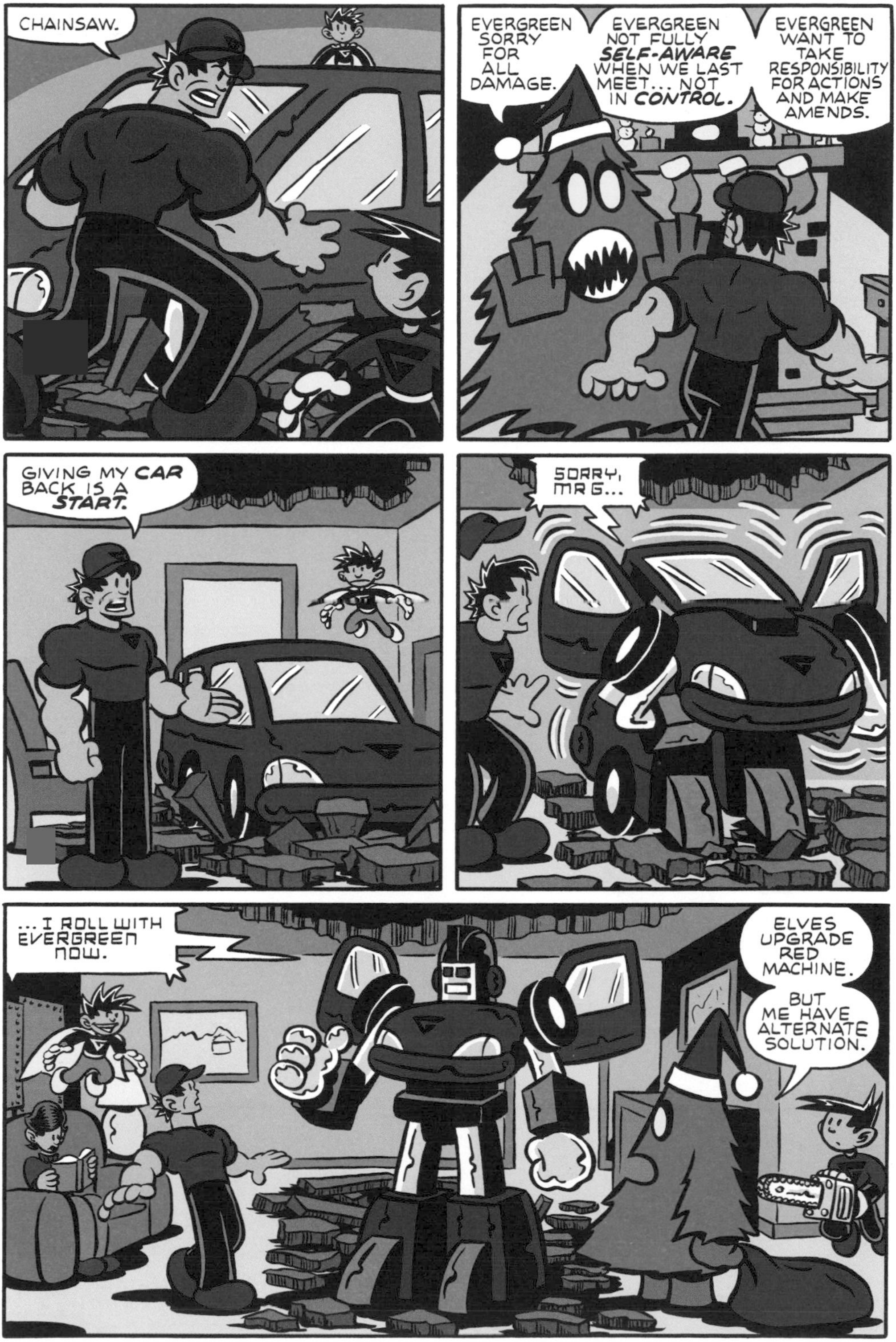
CHAINSAW.
EVERGREEN SORRY FOR ALL DAMAGE.
EVERGREEN NOT FULLY SELF-AWARE WHEN WE LAST MEET... NOT IN CONTROL.
EVERGREEN WANT TO TAKE RESPONSIBILITY FOR ACTIONS AND MAKE AMENDS.
GIVING MY CAR BACK IS A START.
SORRY, MR G...
...I ROLL WITH EVERGREEN NOW.
ELVES UPGRADE RED MACHINE.
BUT ME HAVE ALTERNATE SOLUTION.

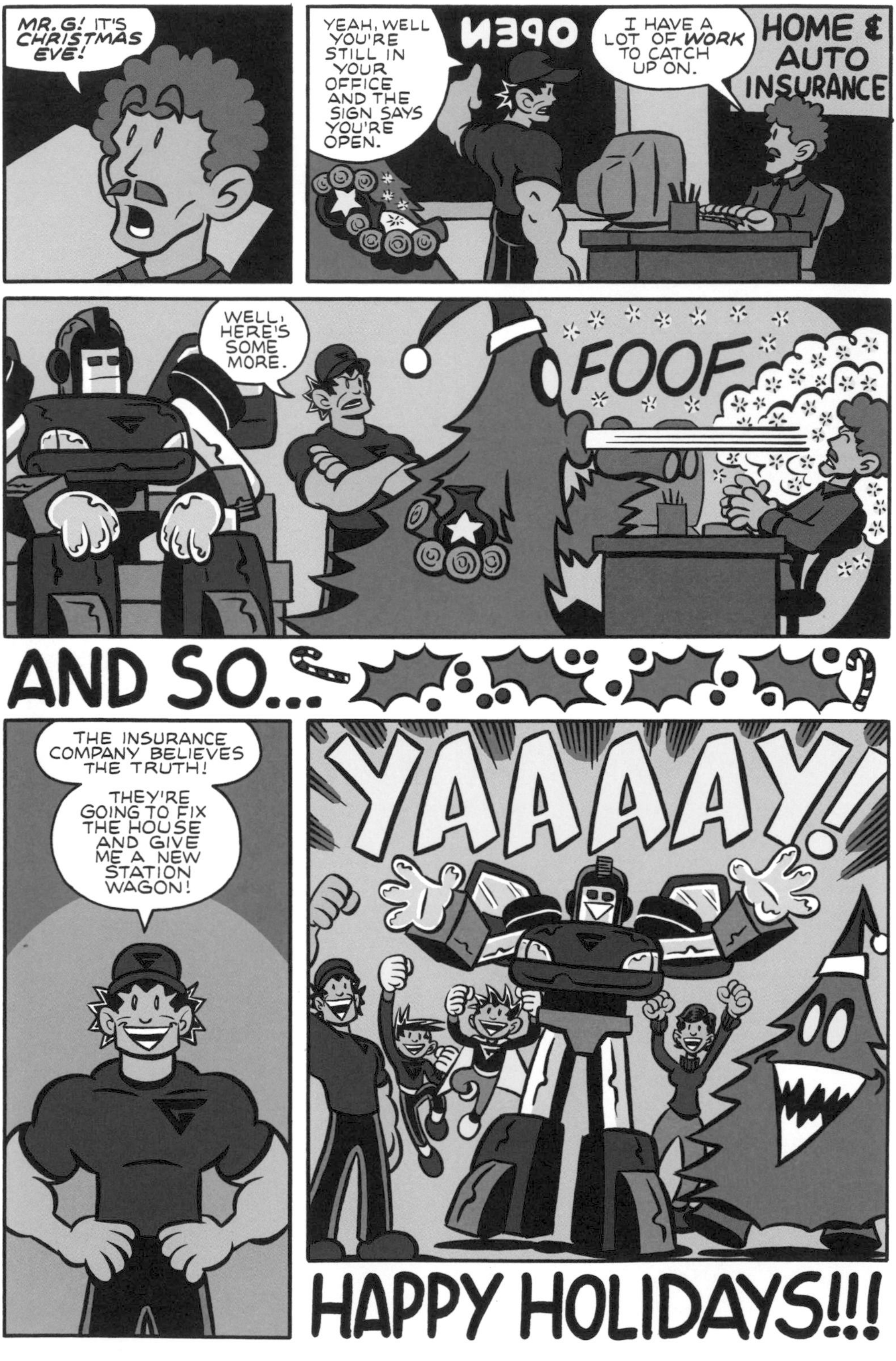
MR. G! IT'S CHRISTMAS EVE!
YEAH, WELL YOU'RE STILL IN YOUR OFFICE AND THE SIGN SAYS YOU'RE OPEN.
OPEN
I HAVE A LOT OF WORK TO CATCH UP ON.
HOME & AUTO INSURANCE
WELL, HERE'S SOME MORE.
FOOF
AND SO...
THE INSURANCE COMPANY BELIEVES THE TRUTH!
THEY'RE GOING TO FIX THE HOUSE AND GIVE ME A NEW STATION WAGON!
YAAAAY!
HAPPY HOLIDAYS!!!

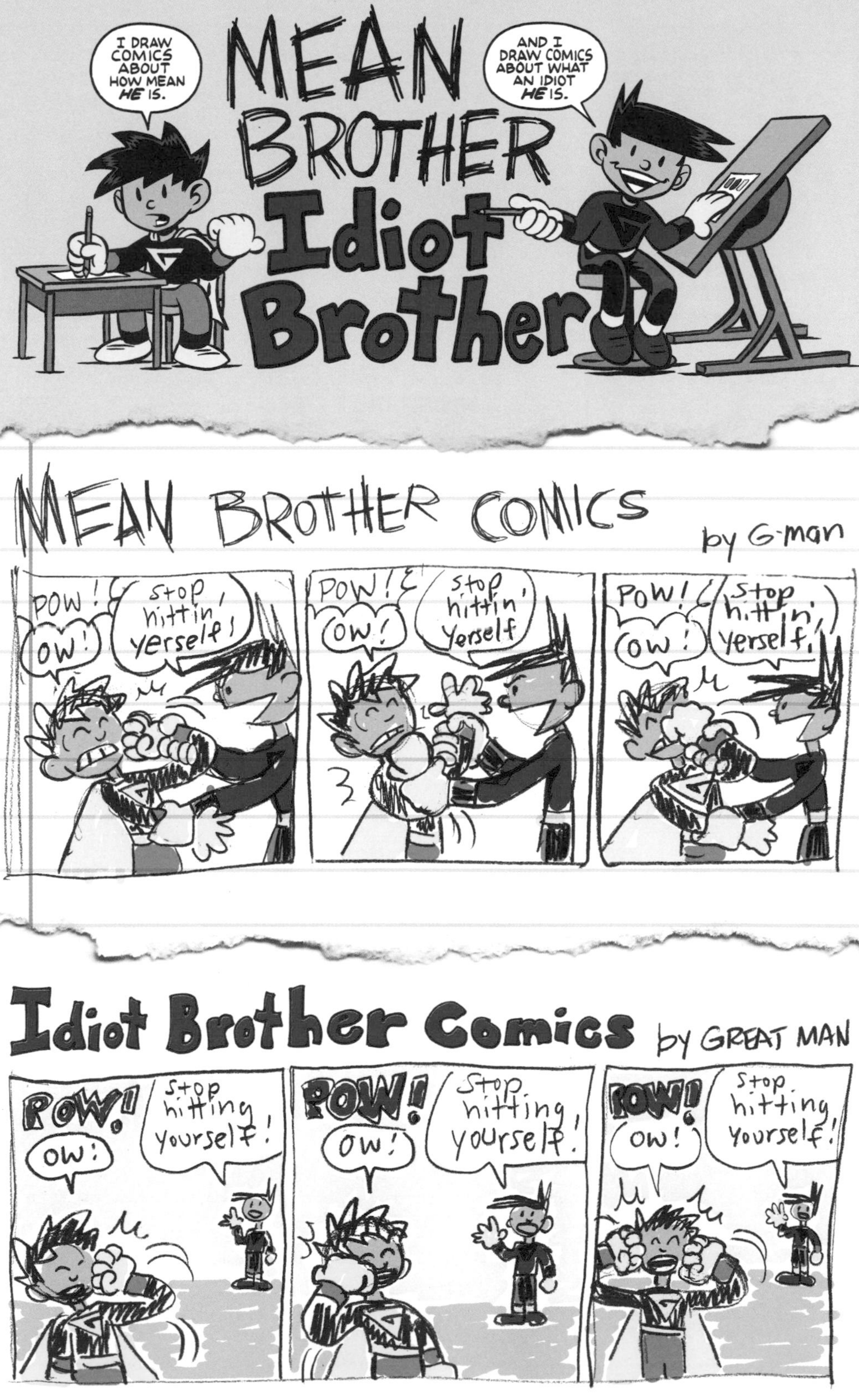
I DRAW COMICS ABOUT HOW MEAN HE IS.
MEAN BROTHER Idiot Brother
AND I DRAW COMICS ABOUT WHAT AN IDIOT HE IS.
MEAN BROTHER COMICS
by G-man
POW!
OW!
Stop hittin' yerself!
POW!
OW!
Stop hittin' yerself
POW!
OW!
Stop hittin' yerself!
Idiot Brother Comics
by GREAT MAN
POW!
OW!
Stop hitting yourself!
POW!
OW!
Stop hitting yourself!
POW!
OW!
Stop hitting yourself!

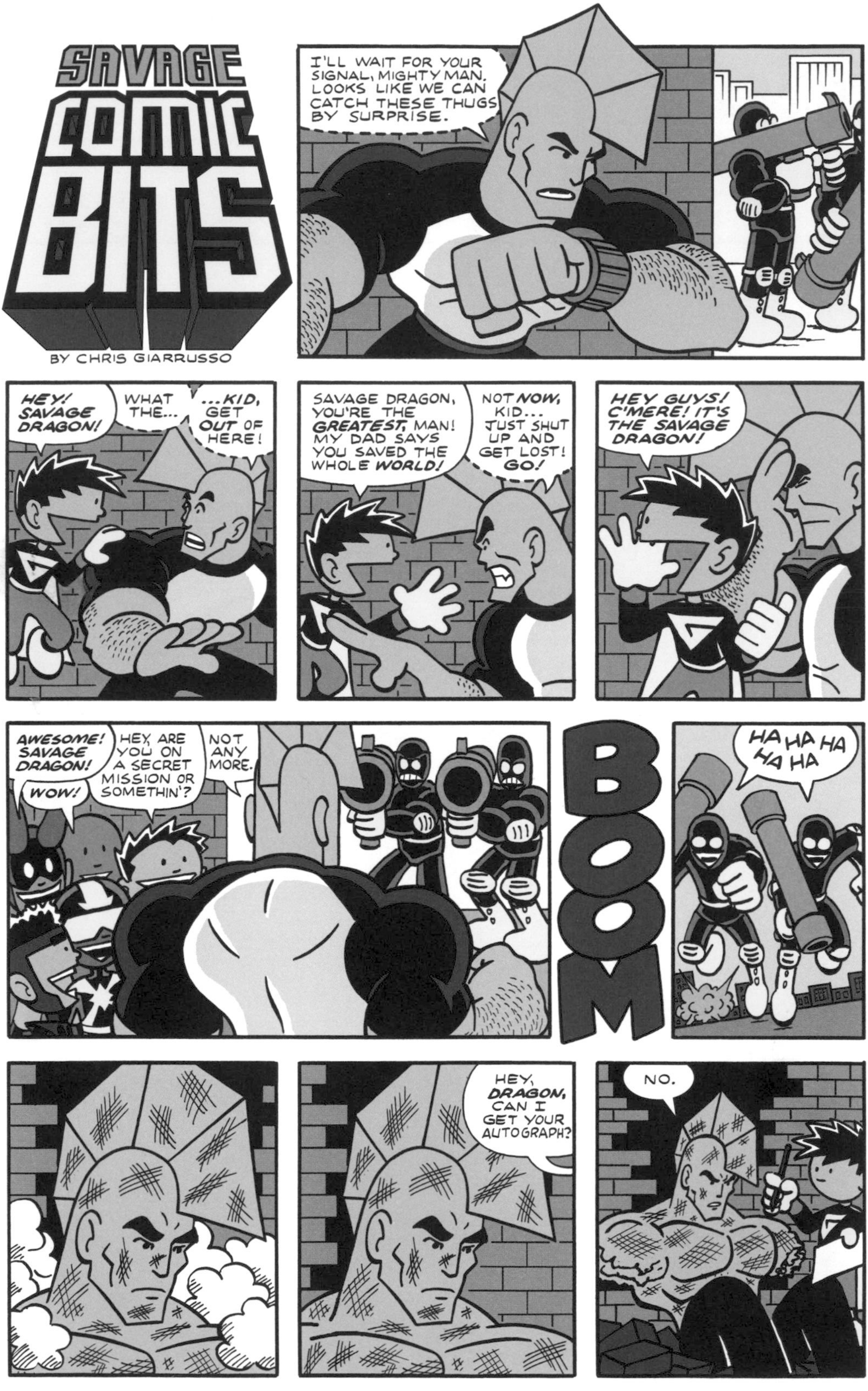
SAVAGE COMIC BITS
BY CHRIS GIARRUSSO
I'LL WAIT FOR YOUR SIGNAL, MIGHTY MAN. LOOKS LIKE WE CAN CATCH THESE THUGS BY SURPRISE.
HEY! SAVAGE DRAGON!
WHAT THE...
...KID, GET OUT OF HERE!
SAVAGE DRAGON, YOU'RE THE GREATEST, MAN! MY DAD SAYS YOU SAVED THE WHOLE WORLD!
NOT NOW, KID... JUST SHUT UP AND GET LOST! GO!
HEY GUYS! C'MERE! IT'S THE SAVAGE DRAGON!
AWESOME! SAVAGE DRAGON!
WOW!
HEY, ARE YOU ON A SECRET MISSION OR SOMETHIN'?
NOT ANY MORE.
BOOOM
HA HA HA HA HA
HEY, DRAGON, CAN I GET YOUR AUTOGRAPH?
NO.

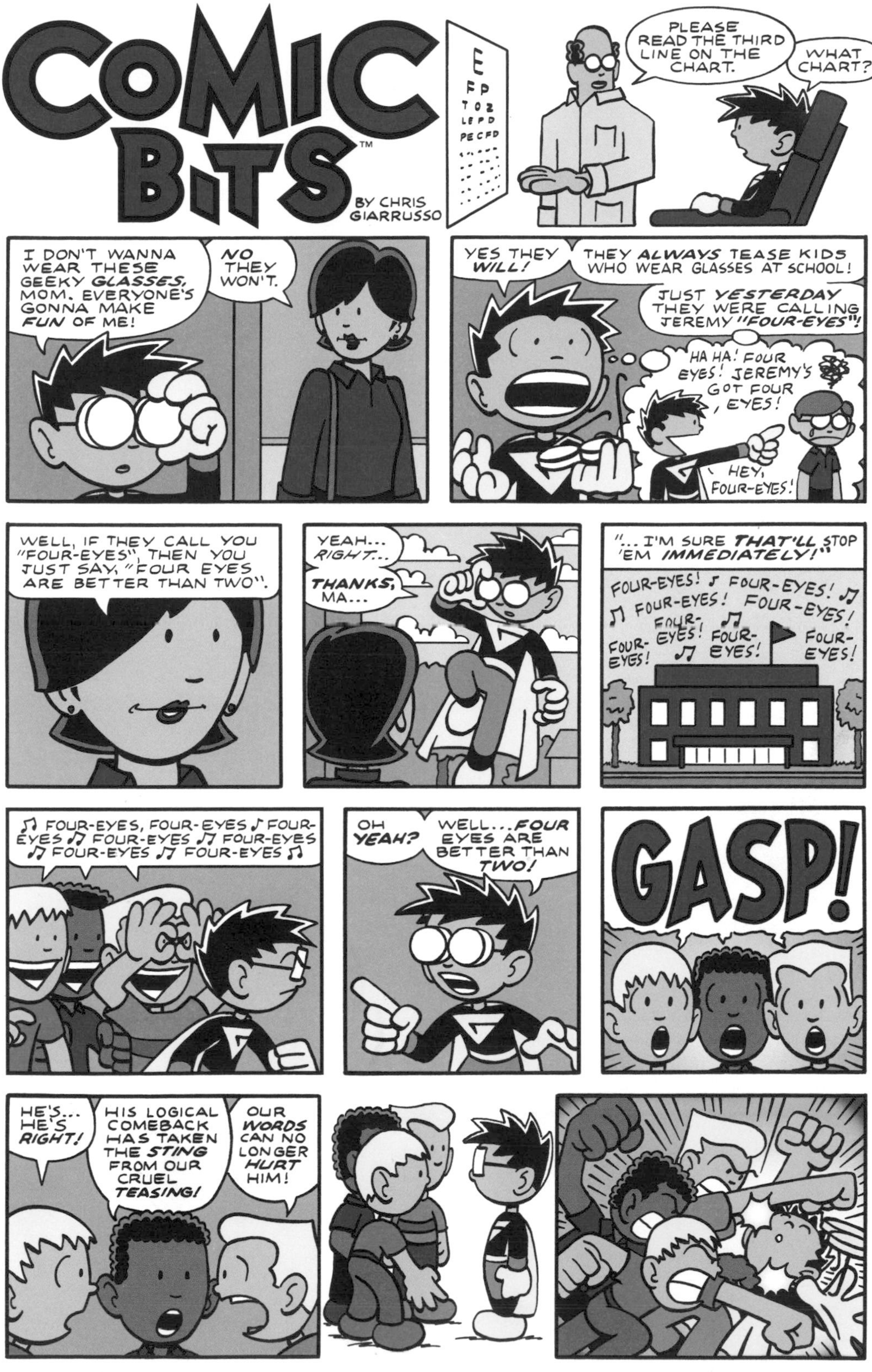

COMIC BITS™
BY CHRIS GIARRUSSO
E
F P
T O Z
L E P D
P E C F D
PLEASE READ THE THIRD LINE ON THE CHART.
WHAT CHART?
I DON'T WANNA WEAR THESE GEEKY GLASSES, MOM. EVERYONE'S GONNA MAKE FUN OF ME!
NO THEY WON'T.
YES THEY WILL!
THEY ALWAYS TEASE KIDS WHO WEAR GLASSES AT SCHOOL!
JUST YESTERDAY THEY WERE CALLING JEREMY "FOUR-EYES"!
HA HA! FOUR EYES! JEREMY'S GOT FOUR EYES!
HEY, FOUR-EYES!
WELL, IF THEY CALL YOU "FOUR-EYES", THEN YOU JUST SAY, "FOUR EYES ARE BETTER THAN TWO".
YEAH... RIGHT...
THANKS, MA...
"... I'M SURE THAT'LL STOP 'EM IMMEDIATELY!"
FOUR-EYES! FOUR-EYES! FOUR-EYES! FOUR-EYES! FOUR-EYES! FOUR-EYES! FOUR-EYES! FOUR-EYES!
FOUR-EYES, FOUR-EYES FOUR-EYES FOUR-EYES FOUR-EYES FOUR-EYES FOUR-EYES
OH YEAH?
WELL... FOUR EYES ARE BETTER THAN TWO!
GASP!
HE'S... HE'S RIGHT!
HIS LOGICAL COMEBACK HAS TAKEN THE STING FROM OUR CRUEL TEASING!
OUR WORDS CAN NO LONGER HURT HIM!

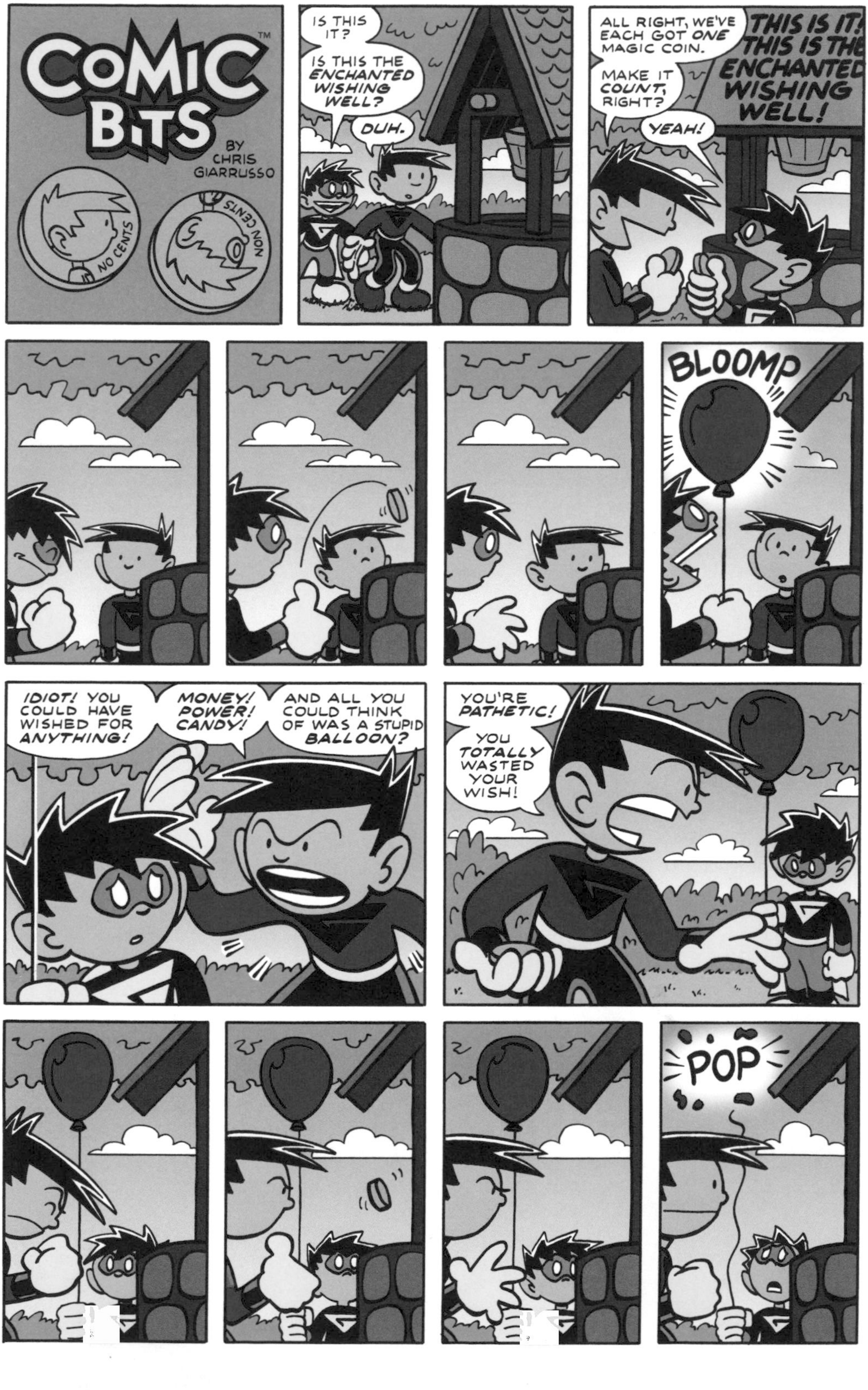
COMIC BITS™
BY CHRIS GIARRUSSO
NO CENTS
NON CENTS
IS THIS IT?
IS THIS THE ENCHANTED WISHING WELL?
DUH.
ALL RIGHT, WE'VE EACH GOT ONE MAGIC COIN.
MAKE IT COUNT, RIGHT?
YEAH!
THIS IS IT! THIS IS THE ENCHANTED WISHING WELL!
BLOOMP
IDIOT! YOU COULD HAVE WISHED FOR ANYTHING!
MONEY! POWER! CANDY!
AND ALL YOU COULD THINK OF WAS A STUPID BALLOON?
YOU'RE PATHETIC!
YOU TOTALLY WASTED YOUR WISH!
POP

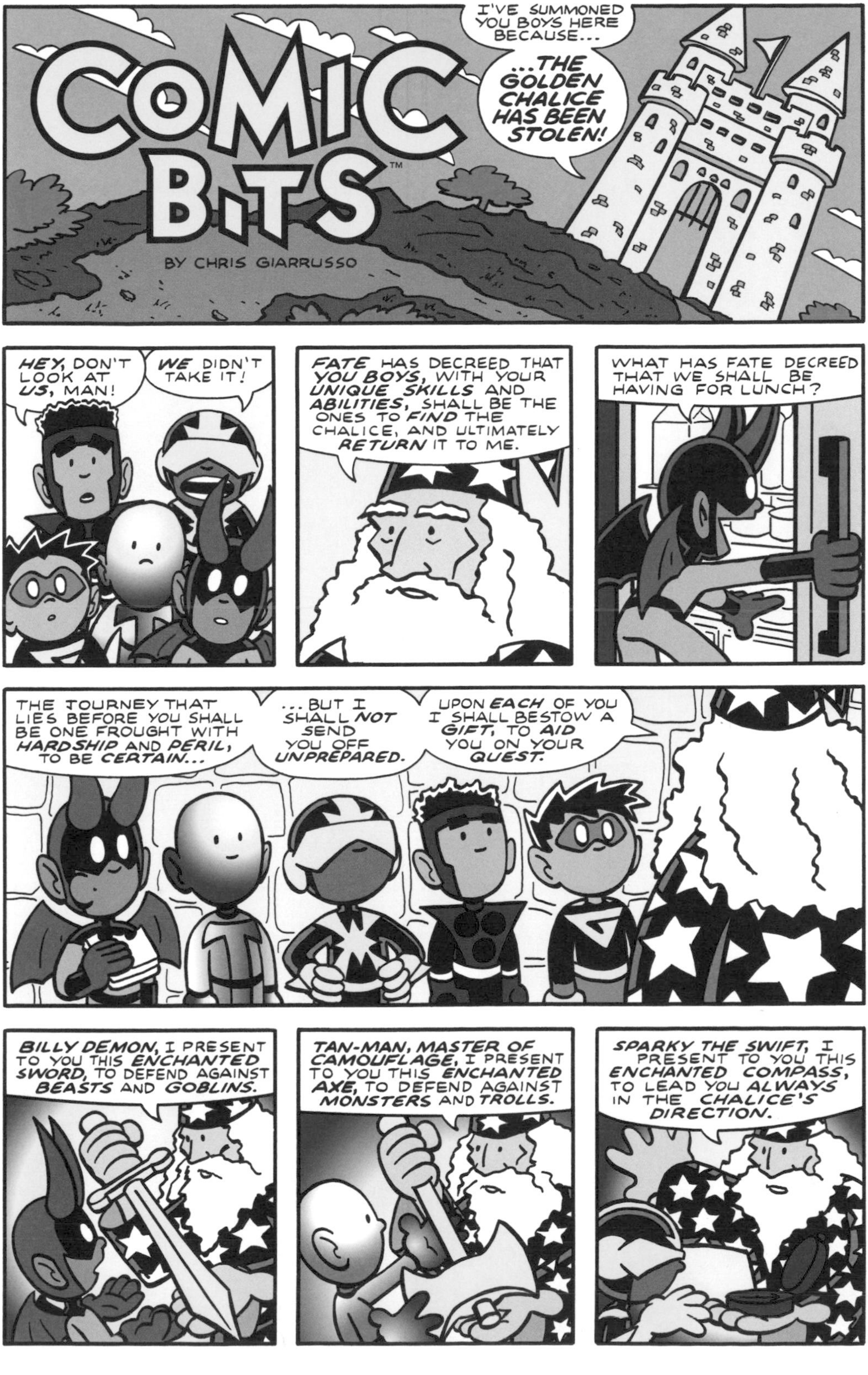
COMIC BITS™
BY CHRIS GIARRUSSO
I'VE SUMMONED YOU BOYS HERE BECAUSE...
...THE GOLDEN CHALICE HAS BEEN STOLEN!
HEY, DON'T LOOK AT US, MAN!
WE DIDN'T TAKE IT!
FATE HAS DECREED THAT YOU BOYS, WITH YOUR UNIQUE SKILLS AND ABILITIES, SHALL BE THE ONES TO FIND THE CHALICE, AND ULTIMATELY RETURN IT TO ME.
WHAT HAS FATE DECREED THAT WE SHALL BE HAVING FOR LUNCH?
THE JOURNEY THAT LIES BEFORE YOU SHALL BE ONE FROUGHT WITH HARDSHIP AND PERIL, TO BE CERTAIN...
...BUT I SHALL NOT SEND YOU OFF UNPREPARED.
UPON EACH OF YOU I SHALL BESTOW A GIFT, TO AID YOU ON YOUR QUEST.
BILLY DEMON, I PRESENT TO YOU THIS ENCHANTED SWORD, TO DEFEND AGAINST BEASTS AND GOBLINS.
TAN-MAN, MASTER OF CAMOUFLAGE, I PRESENT TO YOU THIS ENCHANTED AXE, TO DEFEND AGAINST MONSTERS AND TROLLS.
SPARKY THE SWIFT, I PRESENT TO YOU THIS ENCHANTED COMPASS, TO LEAD YOU ALWAYS IN THE CHALICE'S DIRECTION.

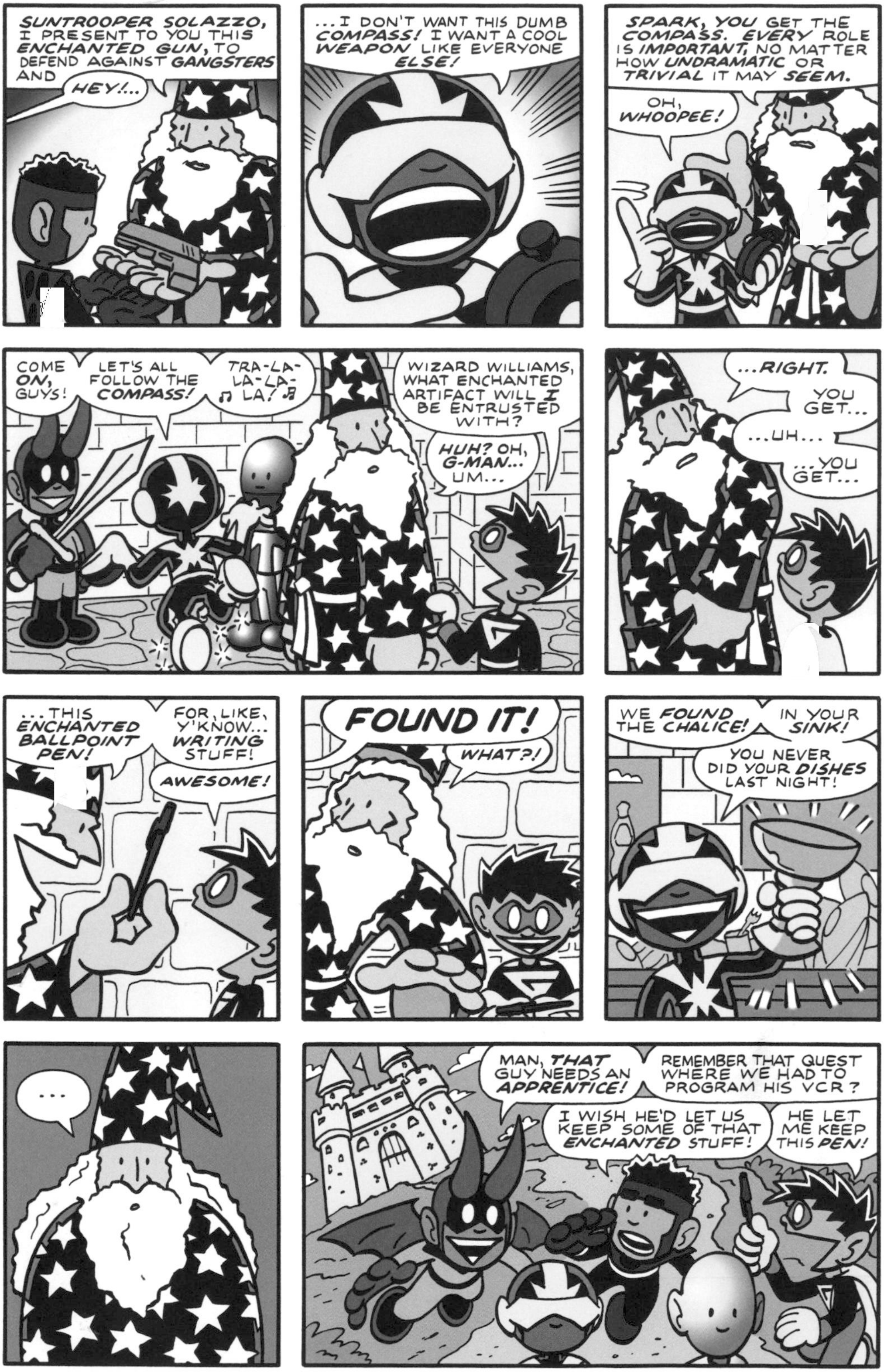

SUNTROOPER SOLAZZO, I PRESENT TO YOU THIS ENCHANTED GUN, TO DEFEND AGAINST GANGSTERS AND
HEY!...
...I DON'T WANT THIS DUMB COMPASS! I WANT A COOL WEAPON LIKE EVERYONE ELSE!
SPARK, YOU GET THE COMPASS. EVERY ROLE IS IMPORTANT, NO MATTER HOW UNDRAMATIC OR TRIVIAL IT MAY SEEM.
OH, WHOOPEE!
COME ON, GUYS!
LET'S ALL FOLLOW THE COMPASS!
TRA-LA-LA-LA-LA!
WIZARD WILLIAMS, WHAT ENCHANTED ARTIFACT WILL I BE ENTRUSTED WITH?
HUH? OH, G-MAN... UM...
...RIGHT.
YOU GET...
...UH...
...YOU GET...
...THIS ENCHANTED BALLPOINT PEN!
FOR, LIKE, Y'KNOW... WRITING STUFF!
AWESOME!
FOUND IT!
WHAT?!
WE FOUND THE CHALICE!
IN YOUR SINK!
YOU NEVER DID YOUR DISHES LAST NIGHT!
...
MAN, THAT GUY NEEDS AN APPRENTICE!
REMEMBER THAT QUEST WHERE WE HAD TO PROGRAM HIS VCR?
I WISH HE'D LET US KEEP SOME OF THAT ENCHANTED STUFF!
HE LET ME KEEP THIS PEN!

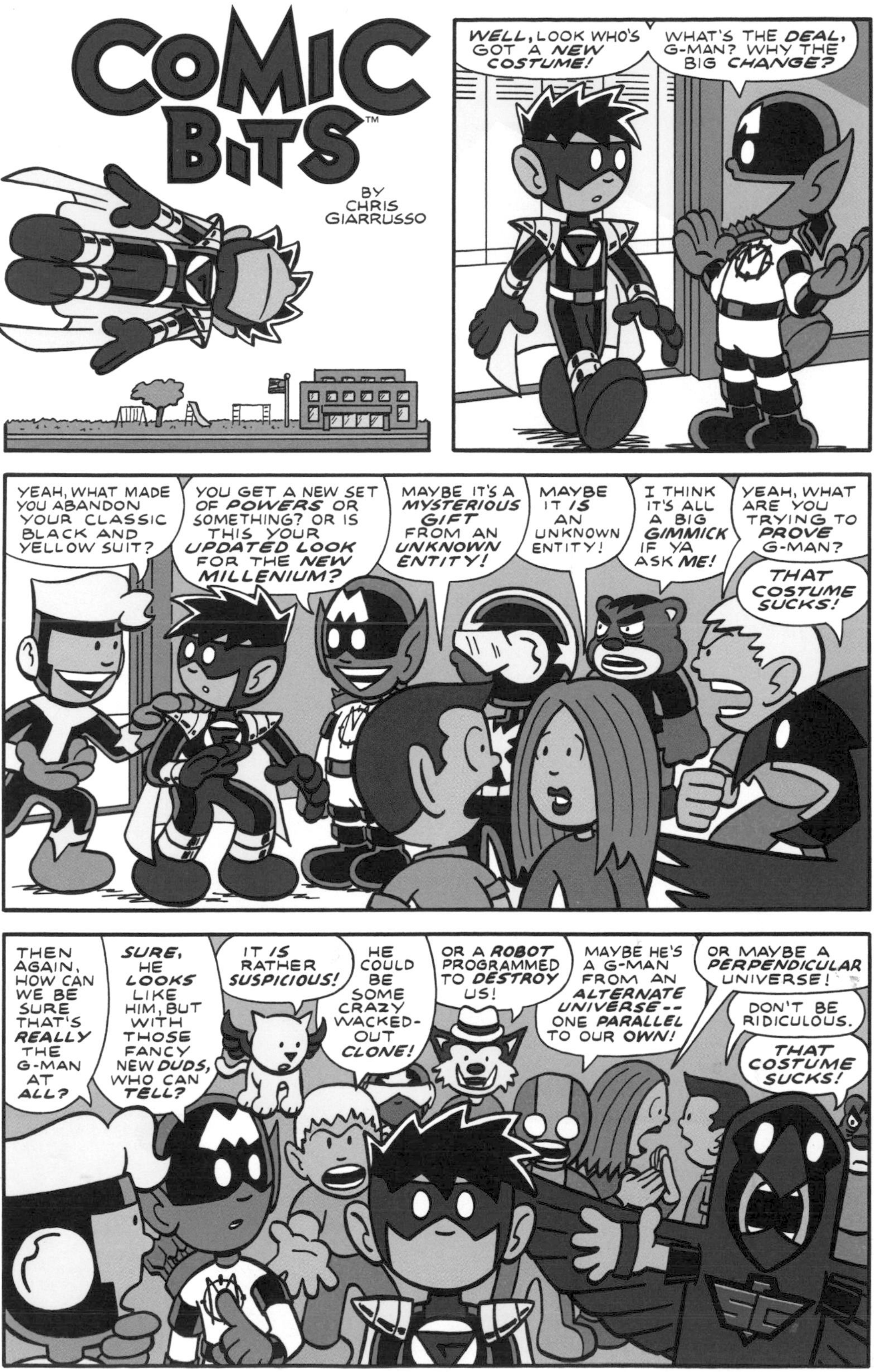
COMIC BITS™
BY CHRIS GIARRUSSO
WELL, LOOK WHO'S GOT A NEW COSTUME!
WHAT'S THE DEAL, G-MAN? WHY THE BIG CHANGE?
YEAH, WHAT MADE YOU ABANDON YOUR CLASSIC BLACK AND YELLOW SUIT?
YOU GET A NEW SET OF POWERS OR SOMETHING? OR IS THIS YOUR UPDATED LOOK FOR THE NEW MILLENIUM?
MAYBE IT'S A MYSTERIOUS GIFT FROM AN UNKNOWN ENTITY!
MAYBE IT IS AN UNKNOWN ENTITY!
I THINK IT'S ALL A BIG GIMMICK IF YA ASK ME!
YEAH, WHAT ARE YOU TRYING TO PROVE G-MAN?
THAT COSTUME SUCKS!
THEN AGAIN, HOW CAN WE BE SURE THAT'S REALLY THE G-MAN AT ALL?
SURE, HE LOOKS LIKE HIM, BUT WITH THOSE FANCY NEW DUDS, WHO CAN TELL?
IT IS RATHER SUSPICIOUS!
HE COULD BE SOME CRAZY WACKED-OUT CLONE!
OR A ROBOT PROGRAMMED TO DESTROY US!
MAYBE HE'S A G-MAN FROM AN ALTERNATE UNIVERSE -- ONE PARALLEL TO OUR OWN!
OR MAYBE A PERPENDICULAR UNIVERSE!
DON'T BE RIDICULOUS.
THAT COSTUME SUCKS!

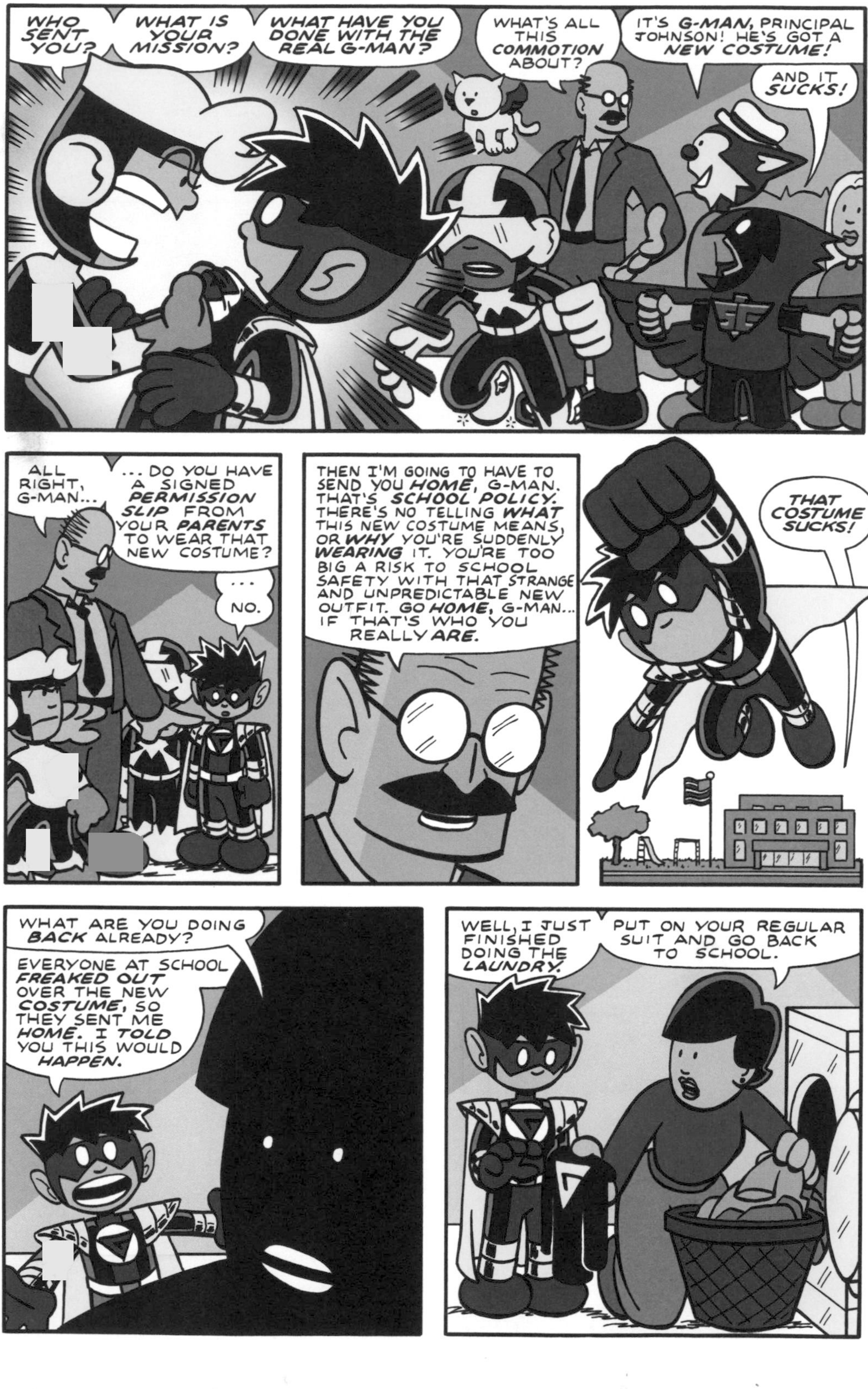
WHO SENT YOU?
WHAT IS YOUR MISSION?
WHAT HAVE YOU DONE WITH THE REAL G-MAN?
WHAT'S ALL THIS COMMOTION ABOUT?
IT'S G-MAN, PRINCIPAL JOHNSON! HE'S GOT A NEW COSTUME!
AND IT SUCKS!
ALL RIGHT, G-MAN...
... DO YOU HAVE A SIGNED PERMISSION SLIP FROM YOUR PARENTS TO WEAR THAT NEW COSTUME?
... NO.
THEN I'M GOING TO HAVE TO SEND YOU HOME, G-MAN. THAT'S SCHOOL POLICY. THERE'S NO TELLING WHAT THIS NEW COSTUME MEANS, OR WHY YOU'RE SUDDENLY WEARING IT. YOU'RE TOO BIG A RISK TO SCHOOL SAFETY WITH THAT STRANGE AND UNPREDICTABLE NEW OUTFIT. GO HOME, G-MAN... IF THAT'S WHO YOU REALLY ARE.
THAT COSTUME SUCKS!
WHAT ARE YOU DOING BACK ALREADY?
EVERYONE AT SCHOOL FREAKED OUT OVER THE NEW COSTUME, SO THEY SENT ME HOME. I TOLD YOU THIS WOULD HAPPEN.
WELL, I JUST FINISHED DOING THE LAUNDRY.
PUT ON YOUR REGULAR SUIT AND GO BACK TO SCHOOL.

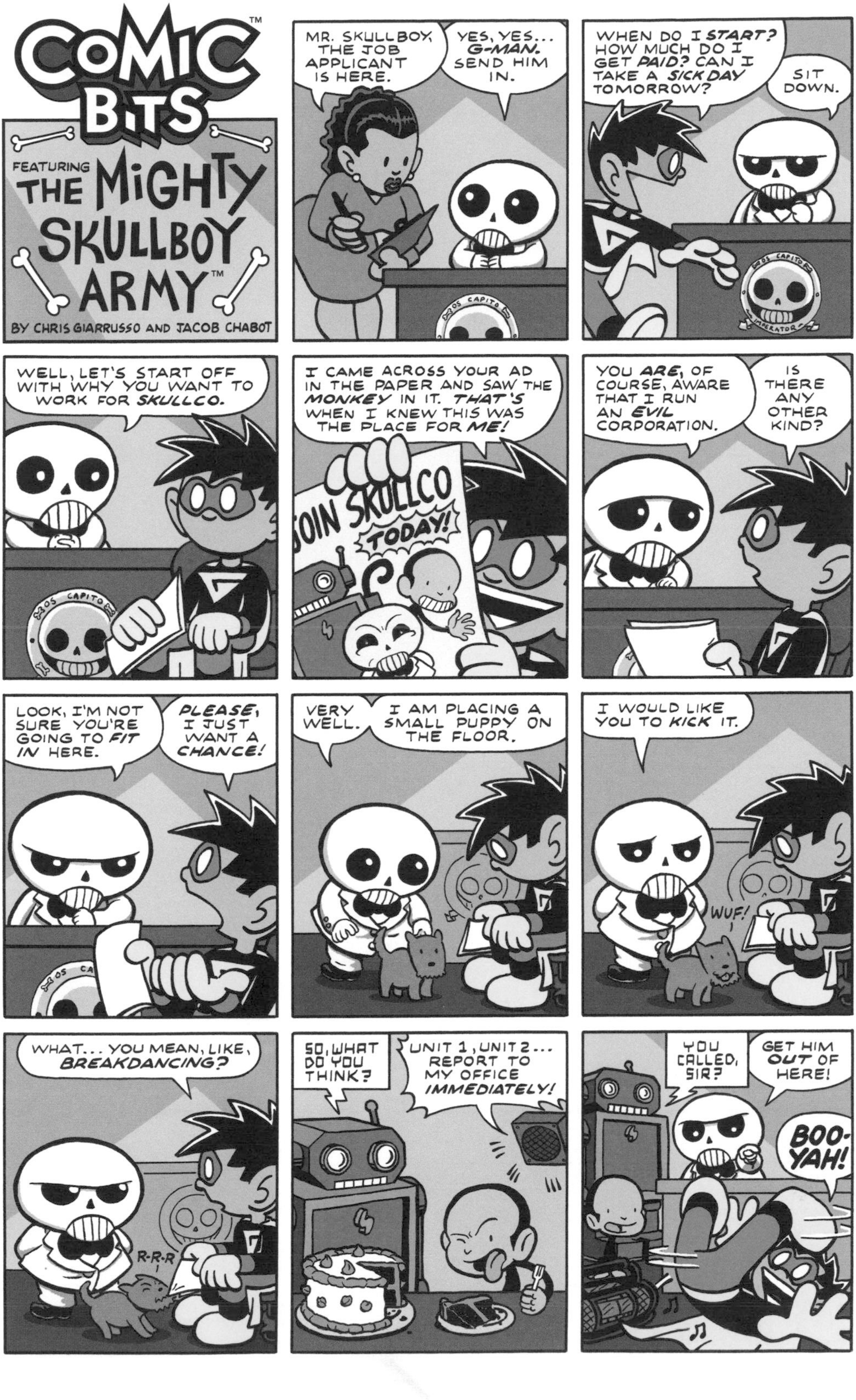

COMIC BITS
FEATURING THE MIGHTY SKULLBOY ARMY™
BY CHRIS GIARRUSSO AND JACOB CHABOT
MR. SKULLBOY, THE JOB APPLICANT IS HERE.
YES, YES... G-MAN. SEND HIM IN.
OS CAPITO
WHEN DO I START? HOW MUCH DO I GET PAID? CAN I TAKE A SICK DAY TOMORROW?
SIT DOWN.
OS CAPITO IMPERATOR
WELL, LET'S START OFF WITH WHY YOU WANT TO WORK FOR SKULLCO.
OS CAPITO
I CAME ACROSS YOUR AD IN THE PAPER AND SAW THE MONKEY IN IT. THAT'S WHEN I KNEW THIS WAS THE PLACE FOR ME!
JOIN SKULLCO TODAY!
YOU ARE, OF COURSE, AWARE THAT I RUN AN EVIL CORPORATION.
IS THERE ANY OTHER KIND?
LOOK, I'M NOT SURE YOU'RE GOING TO FIT IN HERE.
PLEASE, I JUST WANT A CHANCE!
VERY WELL.
I AM PLACING A SMALL PUPPY ON THE FLOOR.
I WOULD LIKE YOU TO KICK IT.
WUF!
WHAT... YOU MEAN, LIKE, BREAKDANCING?
R-R-R
SO, WHAT DO YOU THINK?
UNIT 1, UNIT 2... REPORT TO MY OFFICE IMMEDIATELY!
YOU CALLED, SIR?
GET HIM OUT OF HERE!
BOO-YAH!

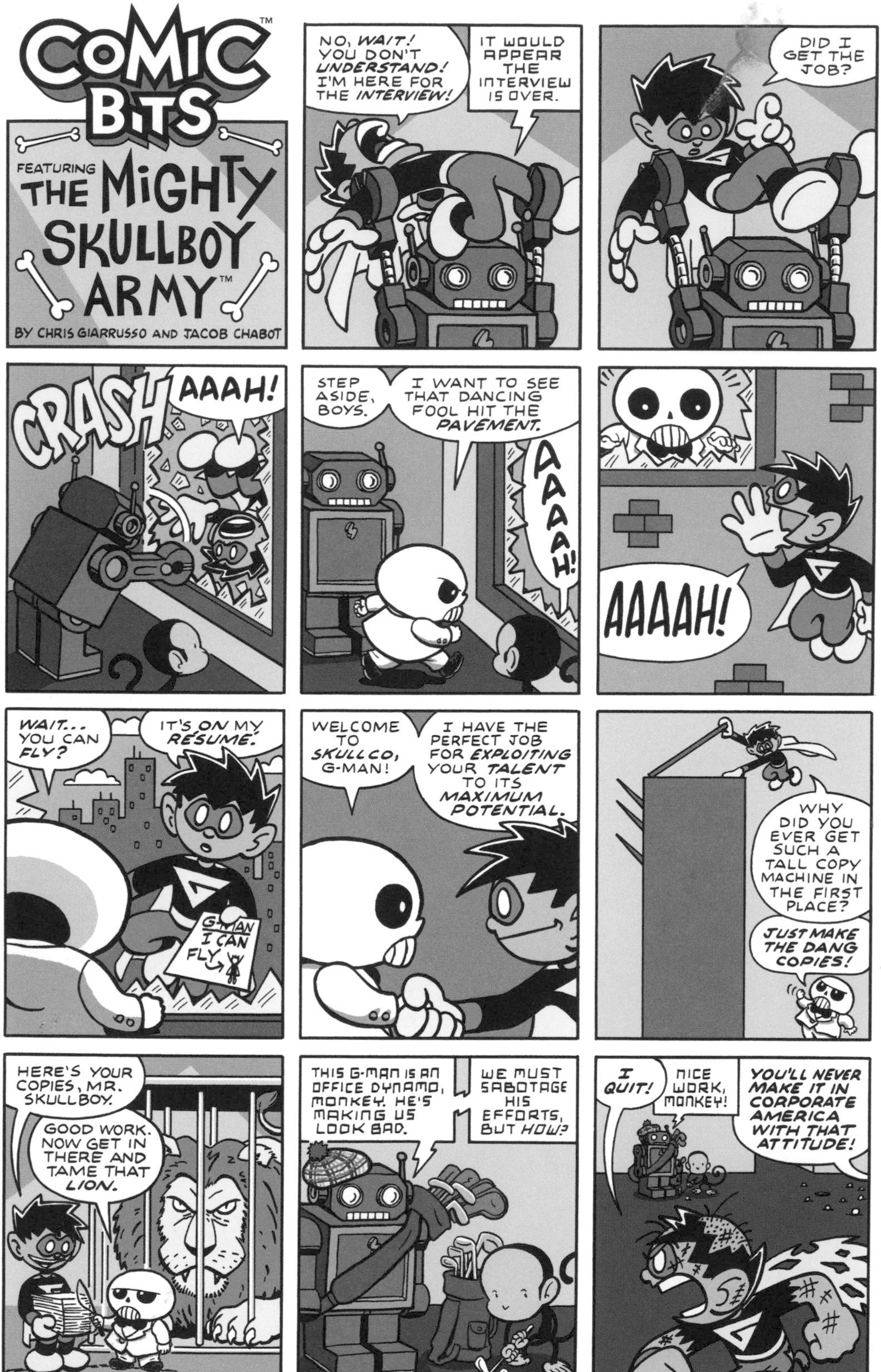

COMIC BITS™
FEATURING THE MIGHTY SKULLBOY ARMY™
BY CHRIS GIARRUSSO AND JACOB CHABOT
NO, WAIT! YOU DON'T UNDERSTAND! I'M HERE FOR THE INTERVIEW!
IT WOULD APPEAR THE INTERVIEW IS OVER.
DID I GET THE JOB?
CRASH
AAAH!
STEP ASIDE, BOYS.
I WANT TO SEE THAT DANCING FOOL HIT THE PAVEMENT.
AAAAH!
AAAAH!
WAIT... YOU CAN FLY?
IT'S ON MY RÉSUMÉ.
G-MAN I CAN FLY
WELCOME TO SKULLCO, G-MAN!
I HAVE THE PERFECT JOB FOR EXPLOITING YOUR TALENT TO ITS MAXIMUM POTENTIAL.
WHY DID YOU EVER GET SUCH A TALL COPY MACHINE IN THE FIRST PLACE?
JUST MAKE THE DANG COPIES!
HERE'S YOUR COPIES, MR. SKULLBOY.
GOOD WORK. NOW GET IN THERE AND TAME THAT LION.
THIS G-MAN IS AN OFFICE DYNAMO, MONKEY. HE'S MAKING US LOOK BAD.
WE MUST SABOTAGE HIS EFFORTS, BUT HOW?
I QUIT!
NICE WORK, MONKEY!
YOU'LL NEVER MAKE IT IN CORPORATE AMERICA WITH THAT ATTITUDE!

COMIC BITS™ featuring G-MAN™
by chris giarrusso

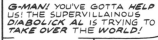

G-MAN! YOU'VE GOTTA *HELP* US! THE SUPERVILLAINOUS *DIABOLICK AL* IS TRYING TO *TAKE OVER* THE *WORLD!*

HE'S STARTING *HERE* IN OUR *NEIGHBORHOOD!*

WE NEED YOUR HELP TO *STOP* HIM!

SORRY, GUYS.

MY MOM SAYS I HAVE TO EAT *DINNER* FIRST.

MOM, *DIABOLICK AL* IS A *MURDERING PSYCHOTIC VILLAIN!* HE LOVES TO CAUSE *MASS DESTRUCTION* AND *CHAOS* FOR *NO REASON!* HE WANTS TO *TAKE OVER* THE *WORLD* AND *ENSLAVE HUMANITY!*

HE'S NOT GOING TO WAIT FOR US TO EAT OUR *VEGETABLES* BEFORE HE STARTS *KILLING INNOCENT PEOPLE!*

DON'T BE *RIDICULOUS.* THAT WOULDN'T BE *FAIR.*

MOM, OUR FRIENDS *NEED* US! THEY'RE BATTLING FOR THEIR *LIVES...* RIGHT OUTSIDE OUR *WINDOW!*

OH, STOP *EXAGGERATING,* MICHAEL.

CRASH

HEY MOM, DO YOU WANT THE DEMON BOY ON OUR TABLE TO STOP EXAGGERATING TOO?

WAITER, THERE'S A FLY IN MY SOUP.

OKAY, MY MOM SAYS WE CAN SKIP THE BRUSSELS SPROUTS TO SAVE THE *WORLD!*

LET'S *STOP* THIS *RUTHLESS VILLAIN!*

TOO LATE, GUYS! IT'S *OVER!* WE *STOPPED* HIM!

IN A *LAST-DITCH EFFORT,* WE PREVENTED *CERTAIN DOOM* FOR US *ALL!* WE *SAVED* THE *WORLD!*

OF ALL THE *ROTTEN LUCK!*

BLEH.

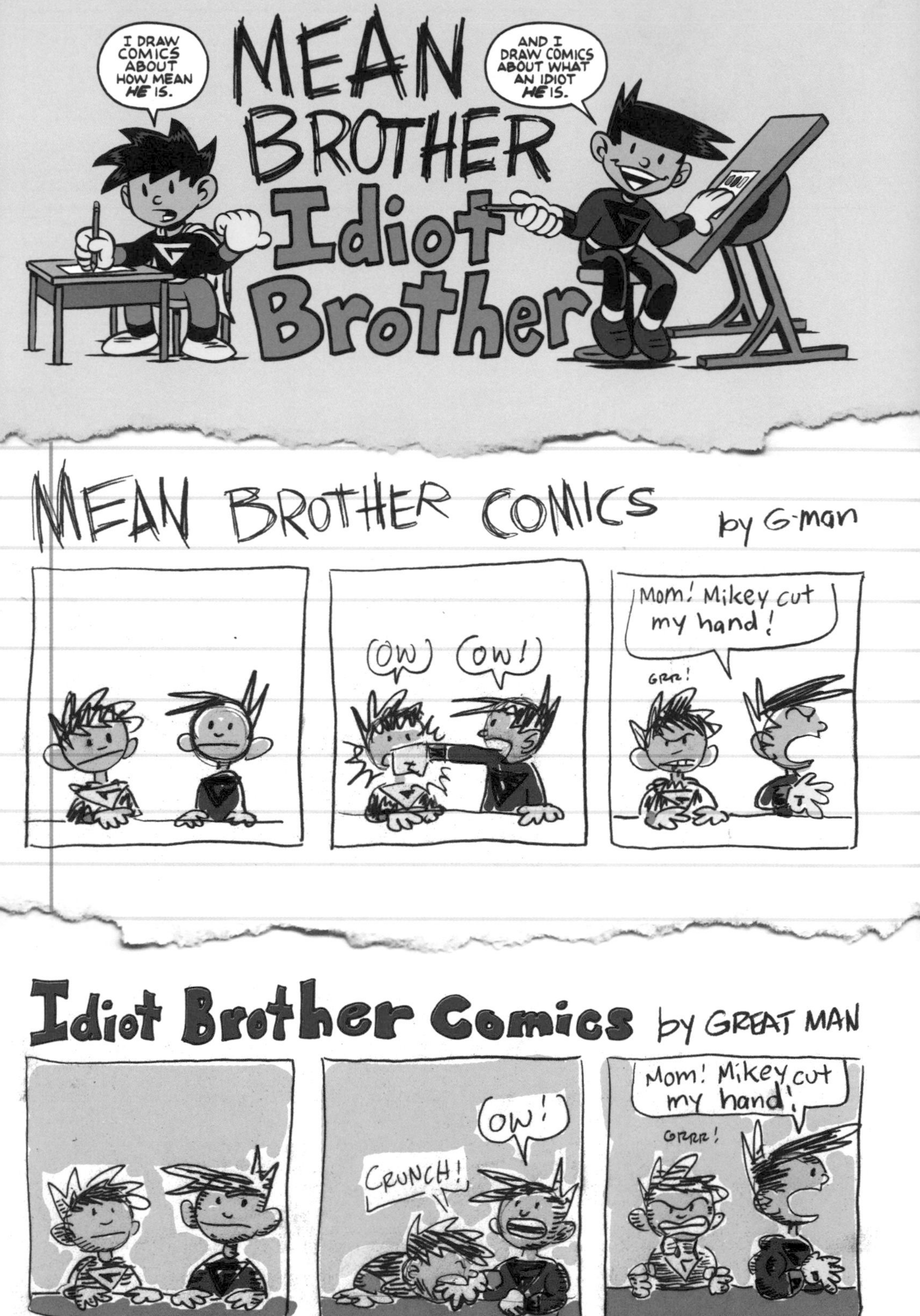
I DRAW COMICS ABOUT HOW MEAN HE IS.
MEAN BROTHER Idiot Brother
AND I DRAW COMICS ABOUT WHAT AN IDIOT HE IS.
MEAN BROTHER COMICS
by G-man
OW
OW!
Mom! Mikey cut my hand!
GRR!
Idiot Brother Comics
by GREAT MAN
CRUNCH!
OW!
Mom! Mikey cut my hand!
GRRR!

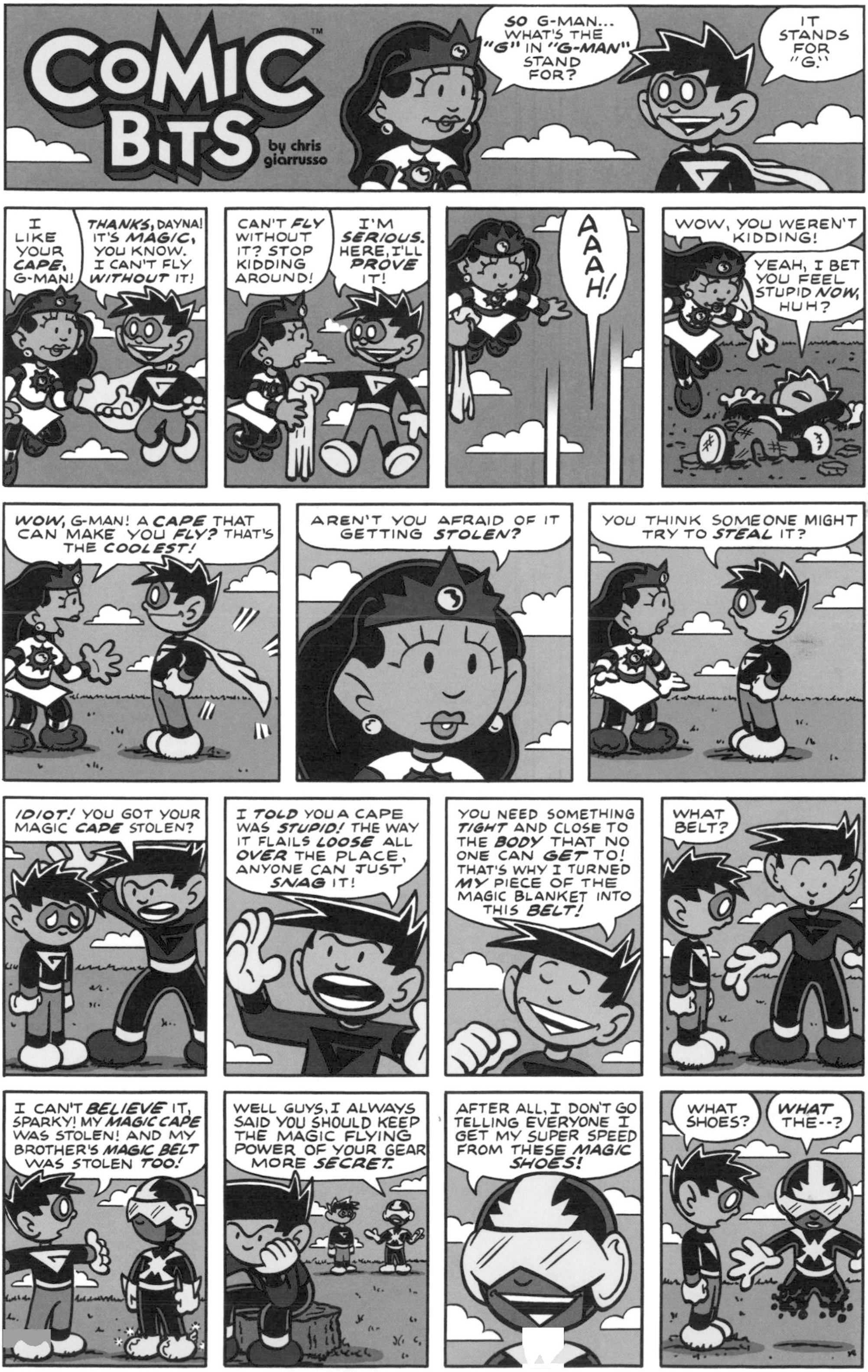
COMIC BITS
by chris giarrusso
SO G-MAN... WHAT'S THE "G" IN "G-MAN" STAND FOR?
IT STANDS FOR "G."
I LIKE YOUR CAPE, G-MAN!
THANKS, DAYNA! IT'S MAGIC, YOU KNOW. I CAN'T FLY WITHOUT IT!
CAN'T FLY WITHOUT IT? STOP KIDDING AROUND!
I'M SERIOUS. HERE, I'LL PROVE IT!
AAAH!
WOW, YOU WEREN'T KIDDING!
YEAH, I BET YOU FEEL STUPID NOW, HUH?
WOW, G-MAN! A CAPE THAT CAN MAKE YOU FLY? THAT'S THE COOLEST!
AREN'T YOU AFRAID OF IT GETTING STOLEN?
YOU THINK SOMEONE MIGHT TRY TO STEAL IT?
IDIOT! YOU GOT YOUR MAGIC CAPE STOLEN?
I TOLD YOU A CAPE WAS STUPID! THE WAY IT FLAILS LOOSE ALL OVER THE PLACE, ANYONE CAN JUST SNAG IT!
YOU NEED SOMETHING TIGHT AND CLOSE TO THE BODY THAT NO ONE CAN GET TO! THAT'S WHY I TURNED MY PIECE OF THE MAGIC BLANKET INTO THIS BELT!
WHAT BELT?
I CAN'T BELIEVE IT, SPARKY! MY MAGIC CAPE WAS STOLEN! AND MY BROTHER'S MAGIC BELT WAS STOLEN TOO!
WELL GUYS, I ALWAYS SAID YOU SHOULD KEEP THE MAGIC FLYING POWER OF YOUR GEAR MORE SECRET.
AFTER ALL, I DON'T GO TELLING EVERYONE I GET MY SUPER SPEED FROM THESE MAGIC SHOES!
WHAT SHOES?
WHAT THE--?

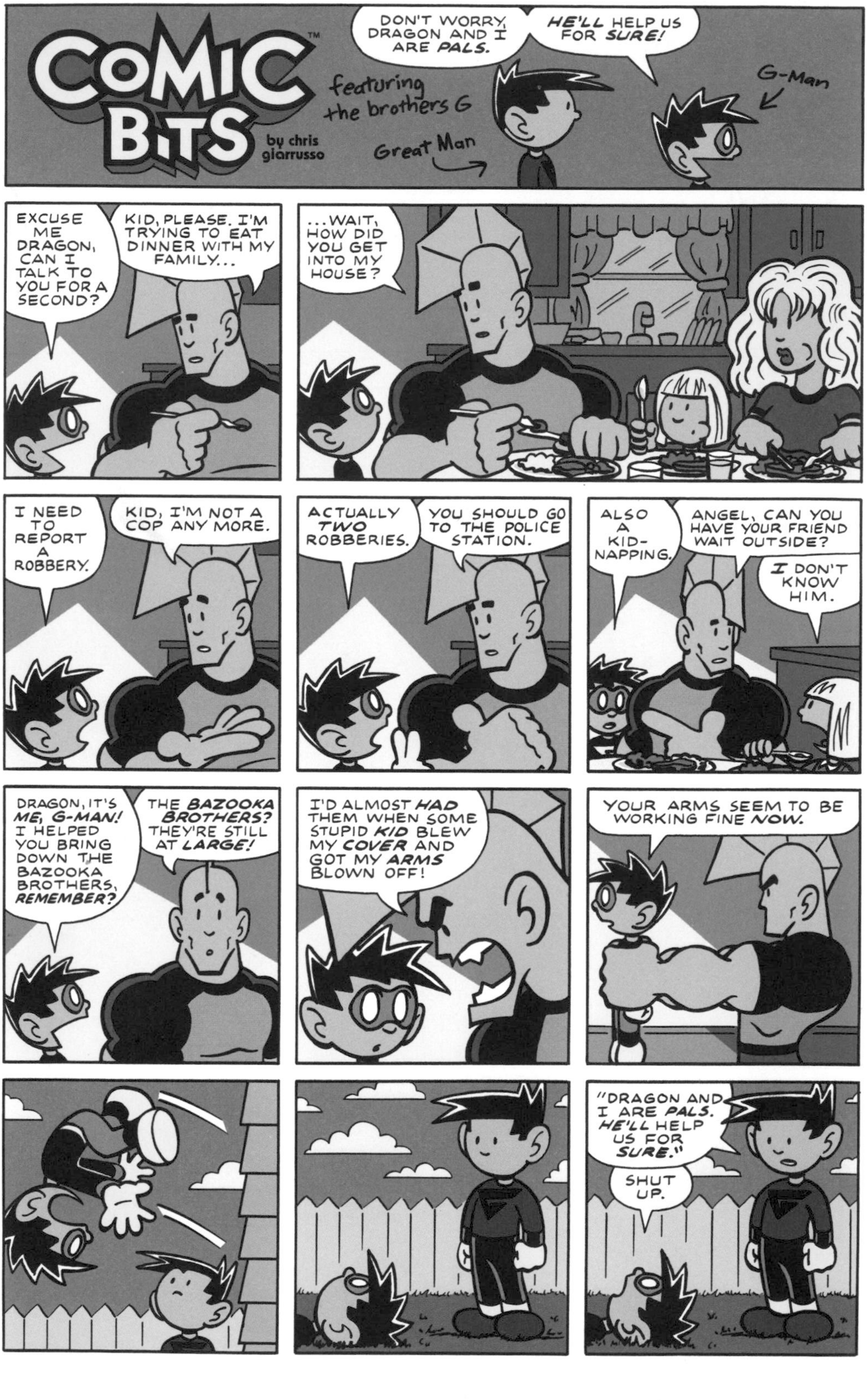
COMIC BITS™
featuring the brothers G
by chris giarrusso
Great Man
G-Man
DON'T WORRY, DRAGON AND I ARE PALS.
HE'LL HELP US FOR SURE!
EXCUSE ME DRAGON, CAN I TALK TO YOU FOR A SECOND?
KID, PLEASE. I'M TRYING TO EAT DINNER WITH MY FAMILY...
...WAIT, HOW DID YOU GET INTO MY HOUSE?
I NEED TO REPORT A ROBBERY.
KID, I'M NOT A COP ANY MORE.
ACTUALLY TWO ROBBERIES.
YOU SHOULD GO TO THE POLICE STATION.
ALSO A KID-NAPPING.
ANGEL, CAN YOU HAVE YOUR FRIEND WAIT OUTSIDE?
I DON'T KNOW HIM.
DRAGON, IT'S ME, G-MAN! I HELPED YOU BRING DOWN THE BAZOOKA BROTHERS, REMEMBER?
THE BAZOOKA BROTHERS? THEY'RE STILL AT LARGE!
I'D ALMOST HAD THEM WHEN SOME STUPID KID BLEW MY COVER AND GOT MY ARMS BLOWN OFF!
YOUR ARMS SEEM TO BE WORKING FINE NOW.
"DRAGON AND I ARE PALS. HE'LL HELP US FOR SURE."
SHUT UP.

THE G-MAN SKULLBOY FUN HOUR*!

BY CHRIS GIARRUSSO AND JACOB CHABOT

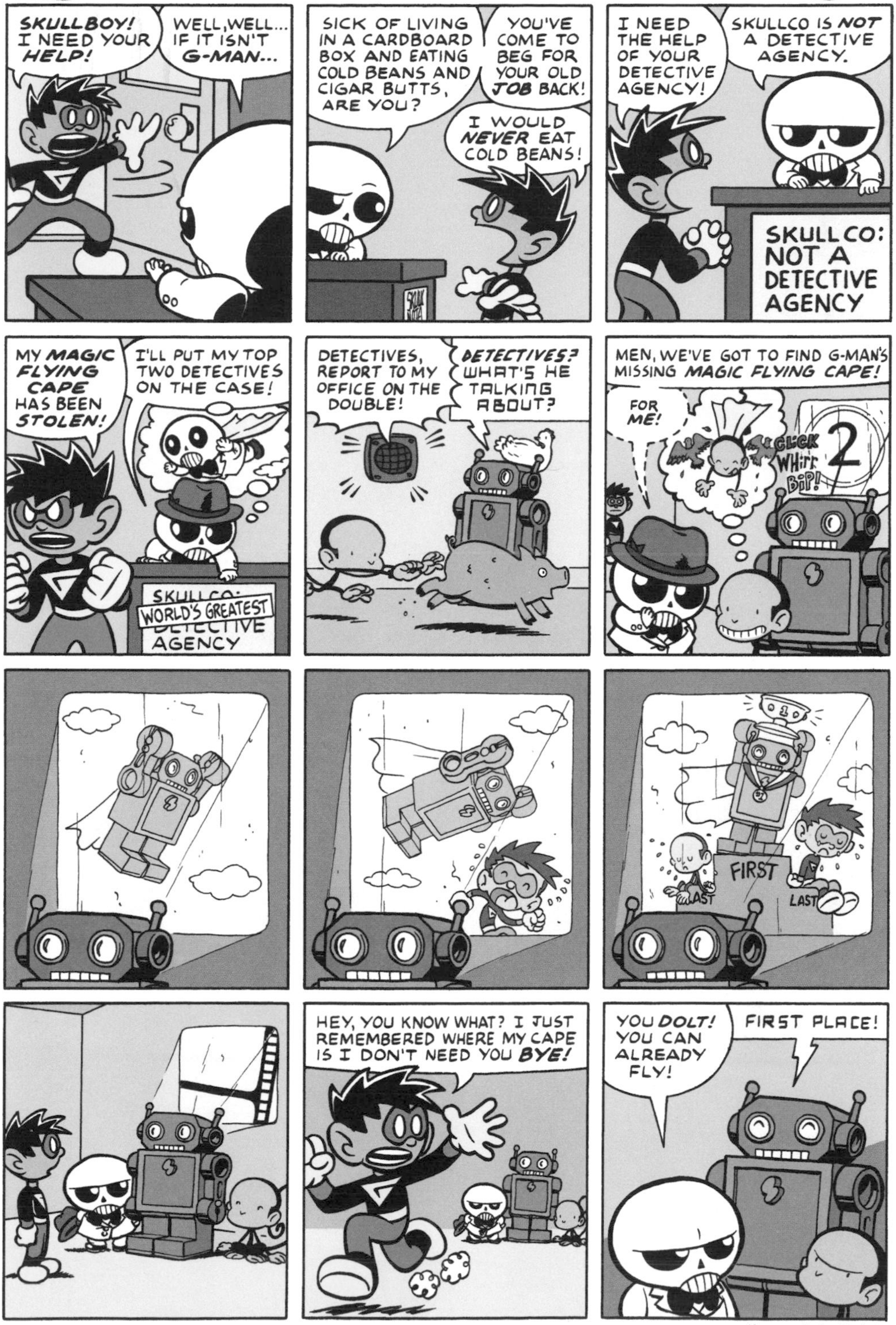
SKULLBOY! I NEED YOUR HELP!
WELL, WELL... IF IT ISN'T G-MAN...
SICK OF LIVING IN A CARDBOARD BOX AND EATING COLD BEANS AND CIGAR BUTTS, ARE YOU?
YOU'VE COME TO BEG FOR YOUR OLD JOB BACK!
I WOULD NEVER EAT COLD BEANS!
I NEED THE HELP OF YOUR DETECTIVE AGENCY!
SKULLCO IS NOT A DETECTIVE AGENCY.
SKULLCO: NOT A DETECTIVE AGENCY
MY MAGIC FLYING CAPE HAS BEEN STOLEN!
I'LL PUT MY TOP TWO DETECTIVES ON THE CASE!
SKULLCO: WORLD'S GREATEST DETECTIVE AGENCY
DETECTIVES, REPORT TO MY OFFICE ON THE DOUBLE!
DETECTIVES? WHAT'S HE TALKING ABOUT?
MEN, WE'VE GOT TO FIND G-MAN'S MISSING MAGIC FLYING CAPE!
FOR ME!
CLICK WHirr BIP!
2
FIRST
LAST
LAST
HEY, YOU KNOW WHAT? I JUST REMEMBERED WHERE MY CAPE IS I DON'T NEED YOU BYE!
YOU DOLT! YOU CAN ALREADY FLY!
FIRST PLACE!

*Average reading time: 58 minutes.

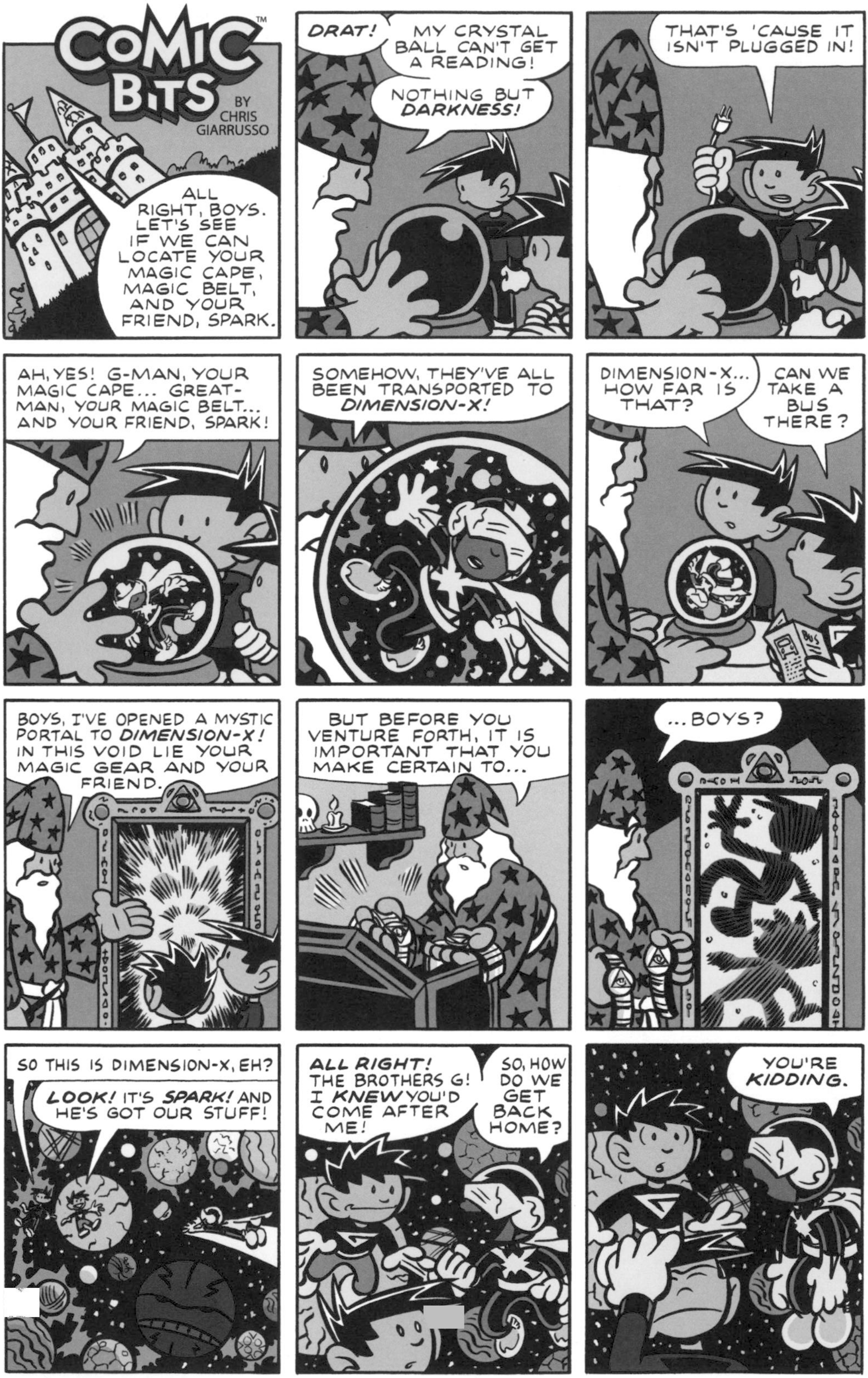
COMIC BITS™
BY CHRIS GIARRUSSO
ALL RIGHT, BOYS. LET'S SEE IF WE CAN LOCATE YOUR MAGIC CAPE, MAGIC BELT, AND YOUR FRIEND, SPARK.
DRAT!
MY CRYSTAL BALL CAN'T GET A READING!
NOTHING BUT DARKNESS!
THAT'S 'CAUSE IT ISN'T PLUGGED IN!
AH, YES! G-MAN, YOUR MAGIC CAPE... GREAT-MAN, YOUR MAGIC BELT... AND YOUR FRIEND, SPARK!
SOMEHOW, THEY'VE ALL BEEN TRANSPORTED TO DIMENSION-X!
DIMENSION-X... HOW FAR IS THAT?
CAN WE TAKE A BUS THERE?
BUS
BOYS, I'VE OPENED A MYSTIC PORTAL TO DIMENSION-X! IN THIS VOID LIE YOUR MAGIC GEAR AND YOUR FRIEND.
BUT BEFORE YOU VENTURE FORTH, IT IS IMPORTANT THAT YOU MAKE CERTAIN TO...
...BOYS?
SO THIS IS DIMENSION-X, EH?
LOOK! IT'S SPARK! AND HE'S GOT OUR STUFF!
ALL RIGHT! THE BROTHERS G! I KNEW YOU'D COME AFTER ME!
SO, HOW DO WE GET BACK HOME?
YOU'RE KIDDING.

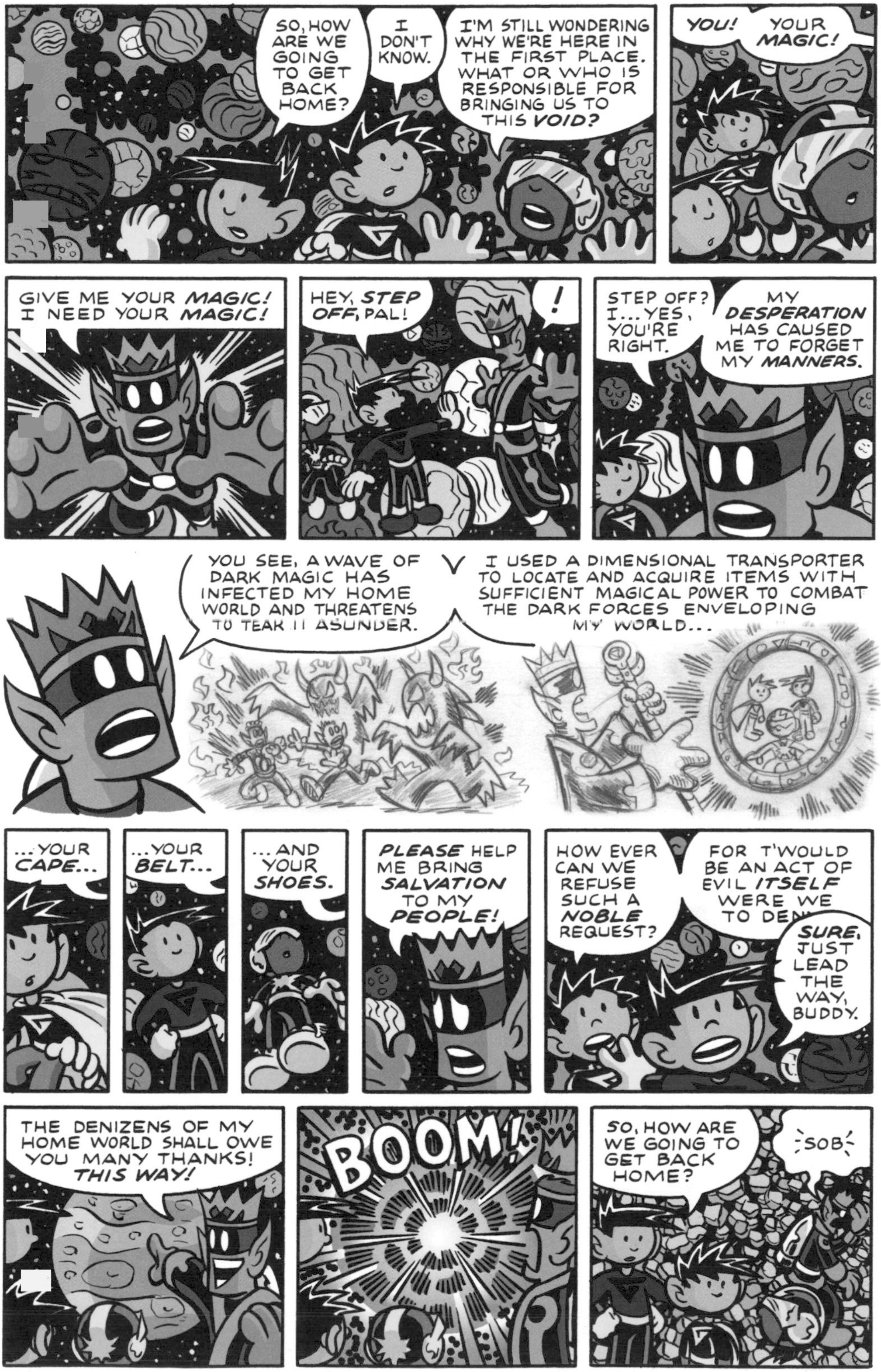
SO, HOW ARE WE GOING TO GET BACK HOME?
I DON'T KNOW.
I'M STILL WONDERING WHY WE'RE HERE IN THE FIRST PLACE. WHAT OR WHO IS RESPONSIBLE FOR BRINGING US TO THIS VOID?
YOU!
YOUR MAGIC!
GIVE ME YOUR MAGIC! I NEED YOUR MAGIC!
HEY, STEP OFF, PAL!
!
STEP OFF? I... YES, YOU'RE RIGHT.
MY DESPERATION HAS CAUSED ME TO FORGET MY MANNERS.
YOU SEE, A WAVE OF DARK MAGIC HAS INFECTED MY HOME WORLD AND THREATENS TO TEAR IT ASUNDER.
I USED A DIMENSIONAL TRANSPORTER TO LOCATE AND ACQUIRE ITEMS WITH SUFFICIENT MAGICAL POWER TO COMBAT THE DARK FORCES ENVELOPING MY WORLD...
...YOUR CAPE...
...YOUR BELT...
...AND YOUR SHOES.
PLEASE HELP ME BRING SALVATION TO MY PEOPLE!
HOW EVER CAN WE REFUSE SUCH A NOBLE REQUEST?
FOR T'WOULD BE AN ACT OF EVIL ITSELF WERE WE TO DEN
SURE. JUST LEAD THE WAY, BUDDY.
THE DENIZENS OF MY HOME WORLD SHALL OWE YOU MANY THANKS! THIS WAY!
BOOM!
SO, HOW ARE WE GOING TO GET BACK HOME?
SOB

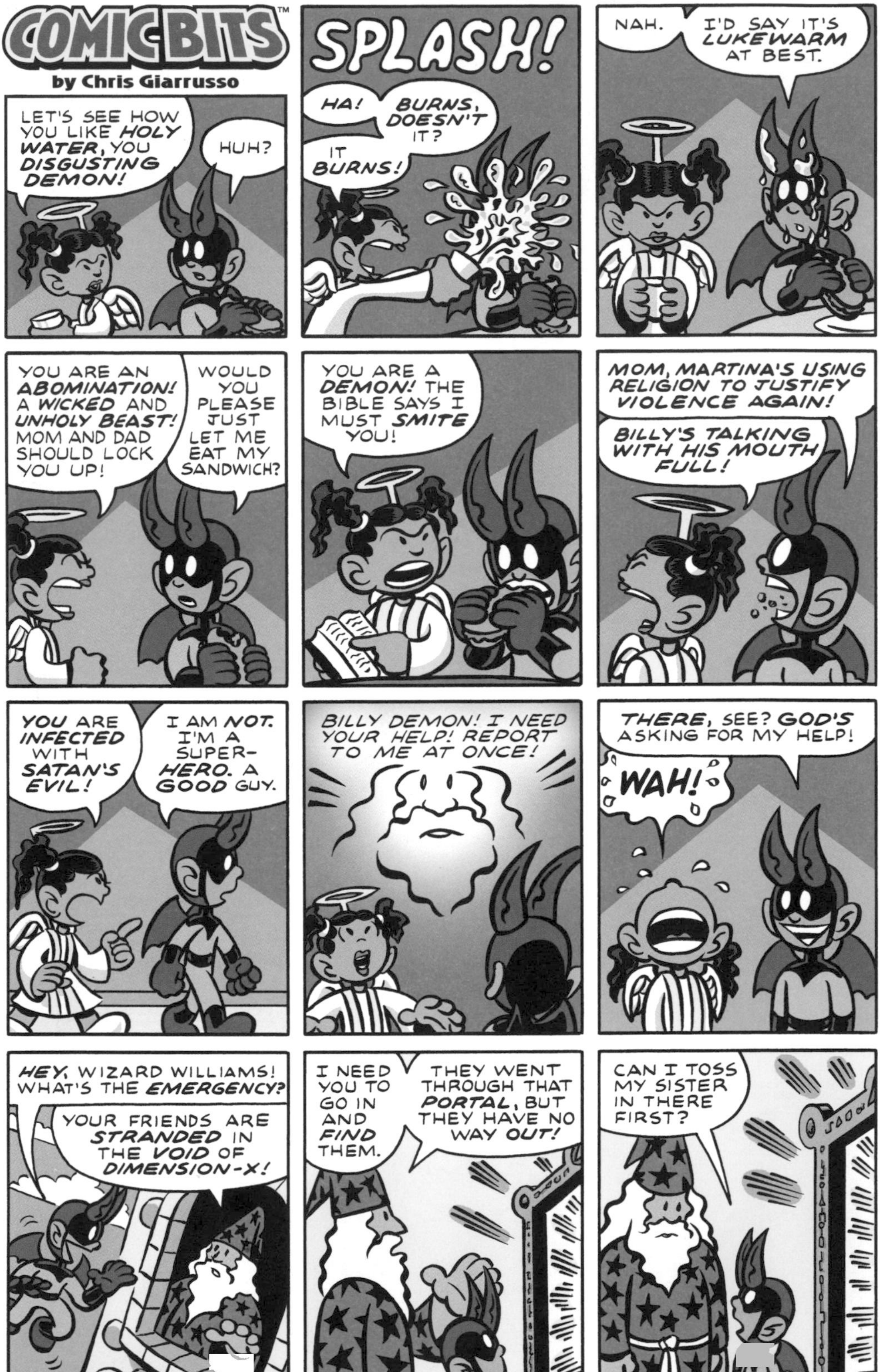
COMIC BITS™
by Chris Giarrusso
LET'S SEE HOW YOU LIKE HOLY WATER, YOU DISGUSTING DEMON!
HUH?
SPLASH!
HA!
BURNS, DOESN'T IT?
IT BURNS!
NAH.
I'D SAY IT'S LUKEWARM AT BEST.
YOU ARE AN ABOMINATION! A WICKED AND UNHOLY BEAST! MOM AND DAD SHOULD LOCK YOU UP!
WOULD YOU PLEASE JUST LET ME EAT MY SANDWICH?
YOU ARE A DEMON! THE BIBLE SAYS I MUST SMITE YOU!
MOM, MARTINA'S USING RELIGION TO JUSTIFY VIOLENCE AGAIN!
BILLY'S TALKING WITH HIS MOUTH FULL!
YOU ARE INFECTED WITH SATAN'S EVIL!
I AM NOT. I'M A SUPER-HERO. A GOOD GUY.
BILLY DEMON! I NEED YOUR HELP! REPORT TO ME AT ONCE!
THERE, SEE? GOD'S ASKING FOR MY HELP!
WAH!
HEY, WIZARD WILLIAMS! WHAT'S THE EMERGENCY?
YOUR FRIENDS ARE STRANDED IN THE VOID OF DIMENSION-X!
I NEED YOU TO GO IN AND FIND THEM.
THEY WENT THROUGH THAT PORTAL, BUT THEY HAVE NO WAY OUT!
CAN I TOSS MY SISTER IN THERE FIRST?

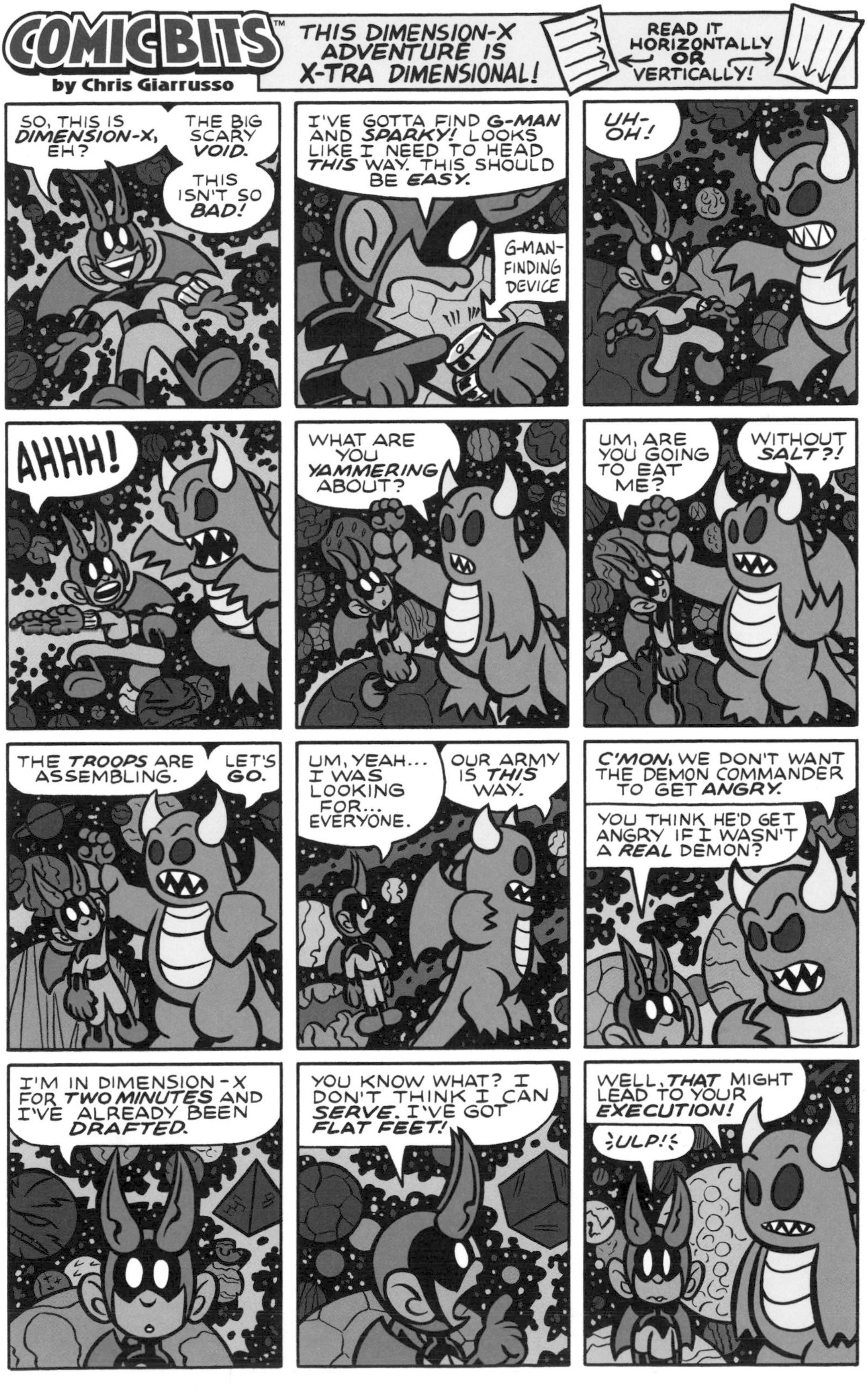
COMIC BITS™
by Chris Giarrusso
THIS DIMENSION-X ADVENTURE IS X-TRA DIMENSIONAL!
READ IT HORIZONTALLY OR VERTICALLY!
SO, THIS IS DIMENSION-X, EH?
THE BIG SCARY VOID.
THIS ISN'T SO BAD!
I'VE GOTTA FIND G-MAN AND SPARKY! LOOKS LIKE I NEED TO HEAD THIS WAY. THIS SHOULD BE EASY.
G-MAN-FINDING DEVICE
UH-OH!
AHHH!
WHAT ARE YOU YAMMERING ABOUT?
UM, ARE YOU GOING TO EAT ME?
WITHOUT SALT?!
THE TROOPS ARE ASSEMBLING.
LET'S GO.
UM, YEAH... I WAS LOOKING FOR... EVERYONE.
OUR ARMY IS THIS WAY.
C'MON, WE DON'T WANT THE DEMON COMMANDER TO GET ANGRY.
YOU THINK HE'D GET ANGRY IF I WASN'T A REAL DEMON?
I'M IN DIMENSION-X FOR TWO MINUTES AND I'VE ALREADY BEEN DRAFTED.
YOU KNOW WHAT? I DON'T THINK I CAN SERVE. I'VE GOT FLAT FEET!
WELL, THAT MIGHT LEAD TO YOUR EXECUTION!
ULP!

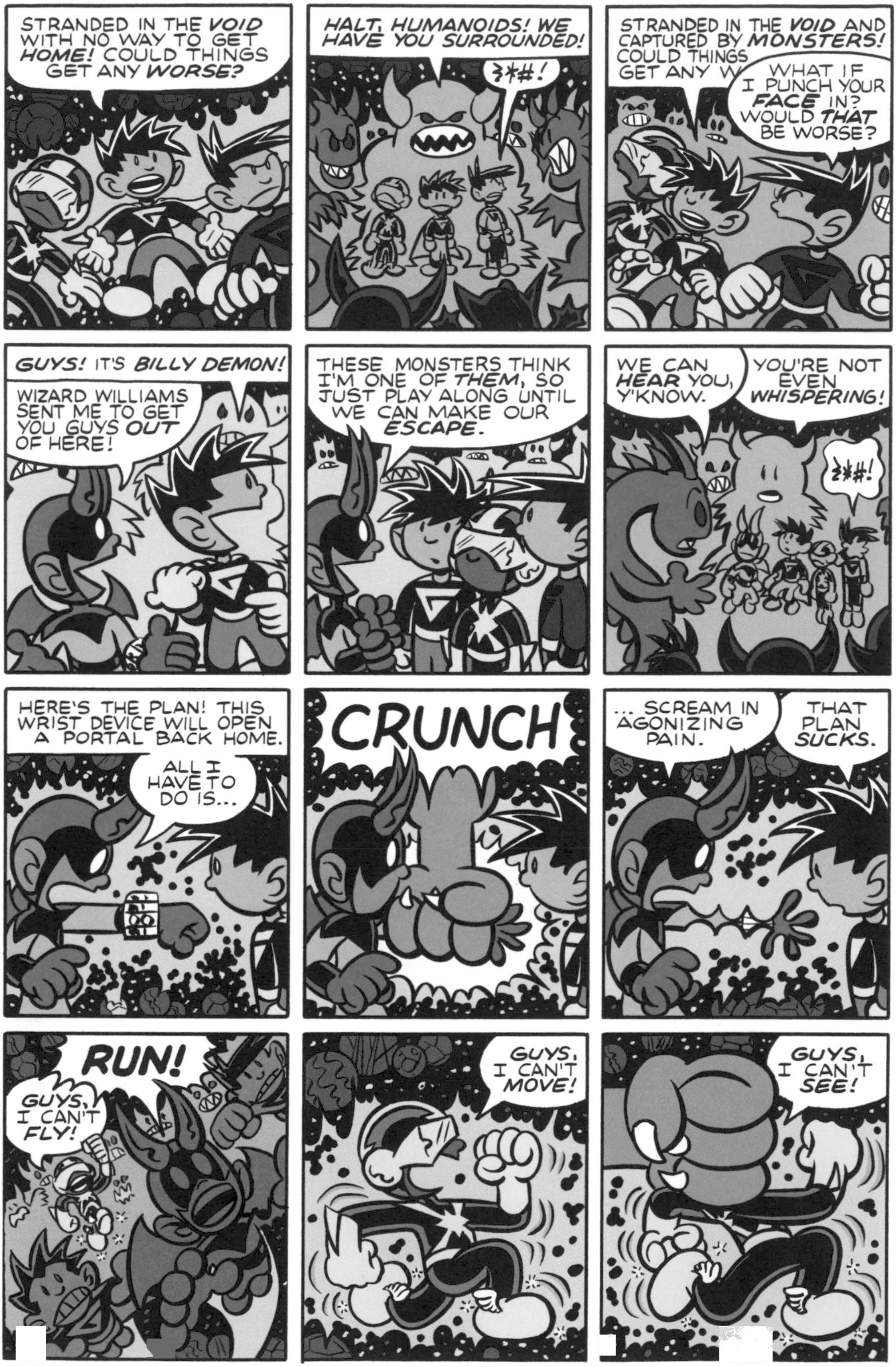
STRANDED IN THE VOID WITH NO WAY TO GET HOME! COULD THINGS GET ANY WORSE?
HALT, HUMANOIDS! WE HAVE YOU SURROUNDED!
ᛘ*#!
STRANDED IN THE VOID AND CAPTURED BY MONSTERS! COULD THINGS GET ANY W
WHAT IF I PUNCH YOUR FACE IN? WOULD THAT BE WORSE?
GUYS! IT'S BILLY DEMON!
WIZARD WILLIAMS SENT ME TO GET YOU GUYS OUT OF HERE!
THESE MONSTERS THINK I'M ONE OF THEM, SO JUST PLAY ALONG UNTIL WE CAN MAKE OUR ESCAPE.
WE CAN HEAR YOU, Y'KNOW.
YOU'RE NOT EVEN WHISPERING!
ᛘ*#!
HERE'S THE PLAN! THIS WRIST DEVICE WILL OPEN A PORTAL BACK HOME.
ALL I HAVE TO DO IS...
CRUNCH
... SCREAM IN AGONIZING PAIN.
THAT PLAN SUCKS.
RUN!
GUYS, I CAN'T FLY!
GUYS, I CAN'T MOVE!
GUYS, I CAN'T SEE!

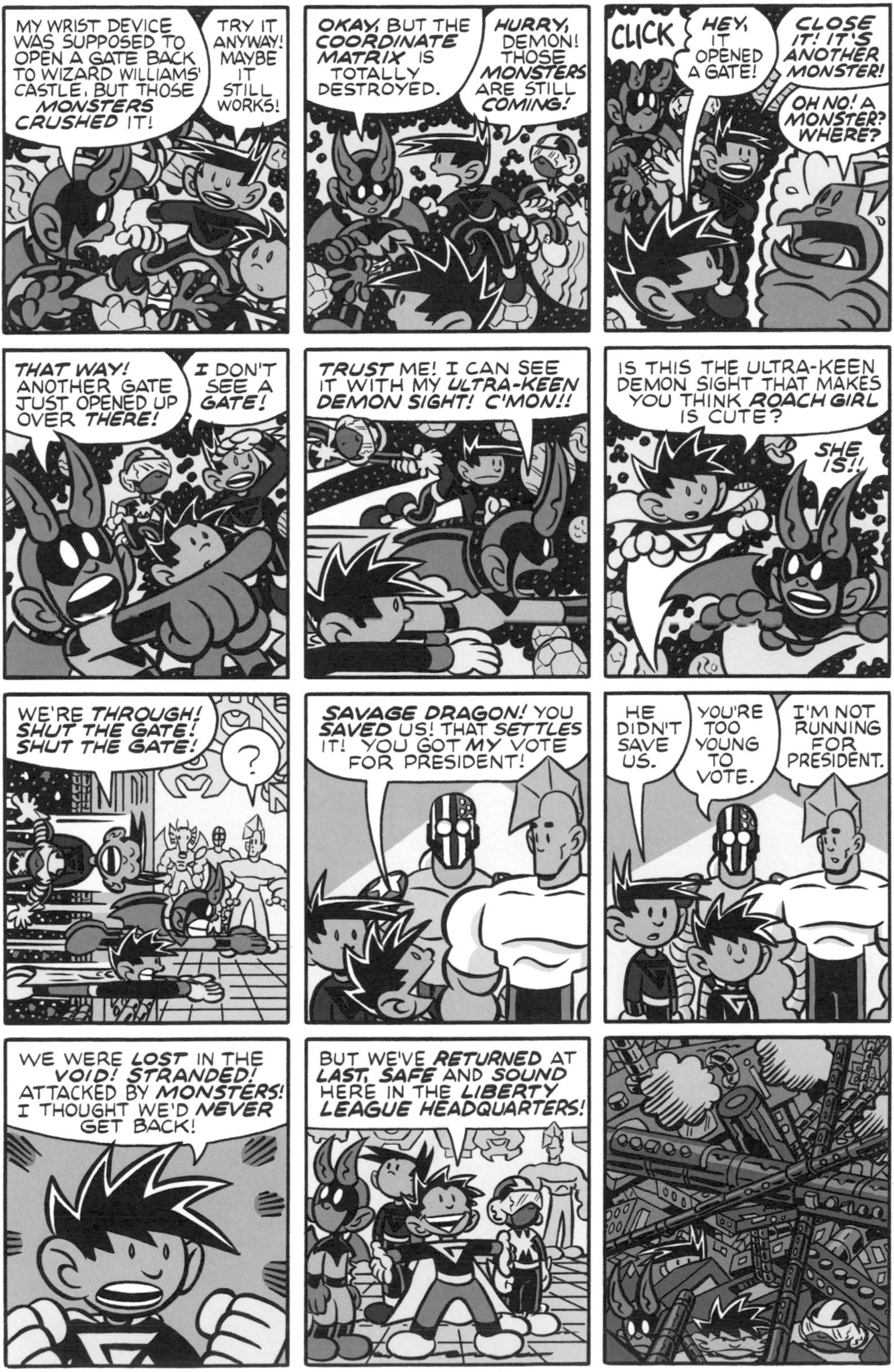
MY WRIST DEVICE WAS SUPPOSED TO OPEN A GATE BACK TO WIZARD WILLIAMS' CASTLE, BUT THOSE MONSTERS CRUSHED IT!
TRY IT ANYWAY! MAYBE IT STILL WORKS!
OKAY, BUT THE COORDINATE MATRIX IS TOTALLY DESTROYED.
HURRY, DEMON! THOSE MONSTERS ARE STILL COMING!
CLICK
HEY, IT OPENED A GATE!
CLOSE IT! IT'S ANOTHER MONSTER!
OH NO! A MONSTER? WHERE?
THAT WAY! ANOTHER GATE JUST OPENED UP OVER THERE!
I DON'T SEE A GATE!
TRUST ME! I CAN SEE IT WITH MY ULTRA-KEEN DEMON SIGHT! C'MON!!
IS THIS THE ULTRA-KEEN DEMON SIGHT THAT MAKES YOU THINK ROACH GIRL IS CUTE?
SHE IS!!
WE'RE THROUGH! SHUT THE GATE! SHUT THE GATE!
?
SAVAGE DRAGON! YOU SAVED US! THAT SETTLES IT! YOU GOT MY VOTE FOR PRESIDENT!
HE DIDN'T SAVE US.
YOU'RE TOO YOUNG TO VOTE.
I'M NOT RUNNING FOR PRESIDENT.
WE WERE LOST IN THE VOID! STRANDED! ATTACKED BY MONSTERS! I THOUGHT WE'D NEVER GET BACK!
BUT WE'VE RETURNED AT LAST, SAFE AND SOUND HERE IN THE LIBERTY LEAGUE HEADQUARTERS!

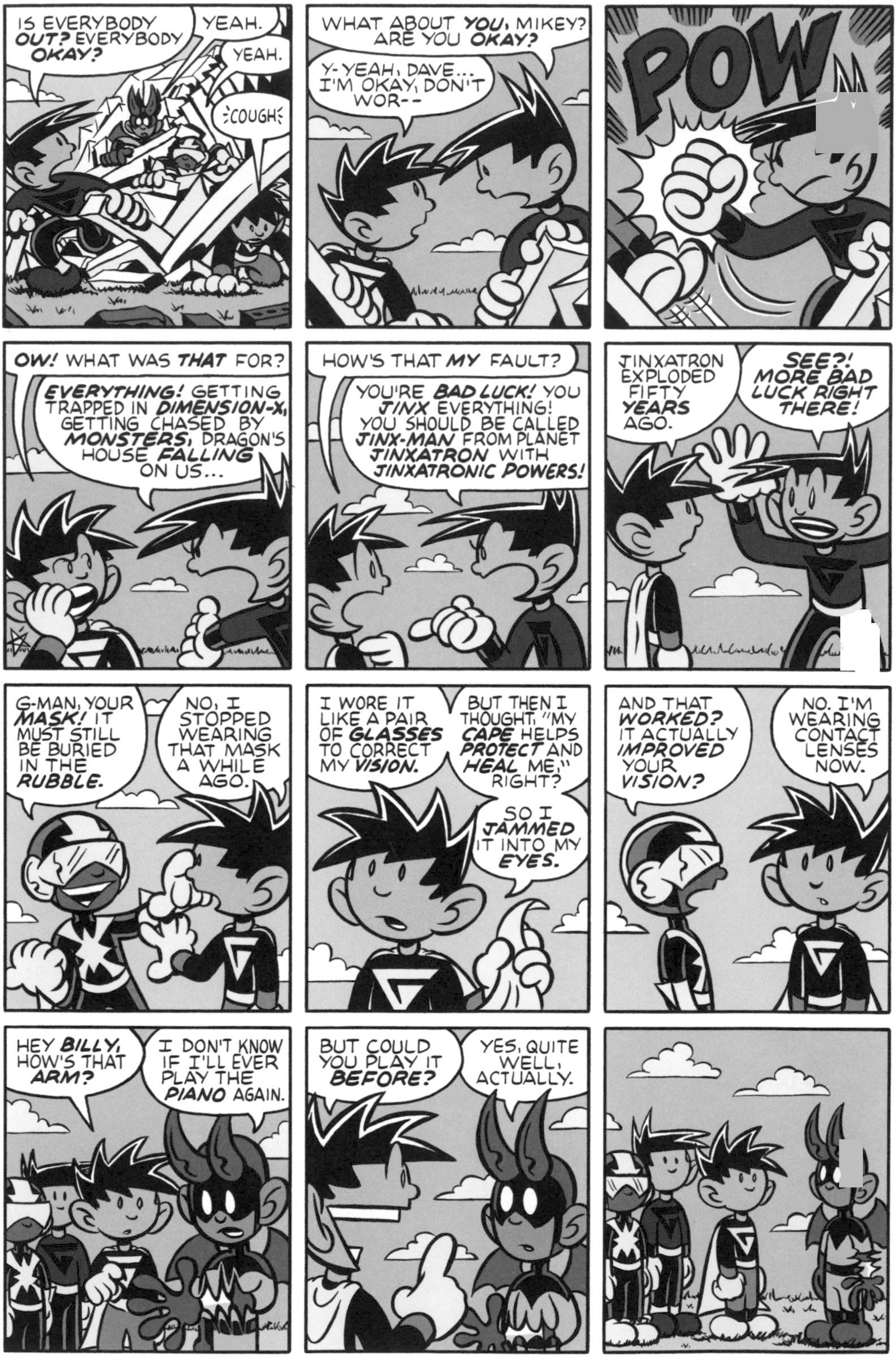
IS EVERYBODY OUT? EVERYBODY OKAY?
YEAH.
YEAH.
COUGH
WHAT ABOUT YOU, MIKEY? ARE YOU OKAY?
Y-YEAH, DAVE... I'M OKAY, DON'T WOR--
POW
OW! WHAT WAS THAT FOR?
EVERYTHING! GETTING TRAPPED IN DIMENSION-X, GETTING CHASED BY MONSTERS, DRAGON'S HOUSE FALLING ON US...
HOW'S THAT MY FAULT?
YOU'RE BAD LUCK! YOU JINX EVERYTHING! YOU SHOULD BE CALLED JINX-MAN FROM PLANET JINXATRON WITH JINXATRONIC POWERS!
JINXATRON EXPLODED FIFTY YEARS AGO.
SEE?! MORE BAD LUCK RIGHT THERE!
G-MAN, YOUR MASK! IT MUST STILL BE BURIED IN THE RUBBLE.
NO, I STOPPED WEARING THAT MASK A WHILE AGO.
I WORE IT LIKE A PAIR OF GLASSES TO CORRECT MY VISION.
BUT THEN I THOUGHT, "MY CAPE HELPS PROTECT AND HEAL ME," RIGHT?
SO I JAMMED IT INTO MY EYES.
AND THAT WORKED? IT ACTUALLY IMPROVED YOUR VISION?
NO. I'M WEARING CONTACT LENSES NOW.
HEY BILLY, HOW'S THAT ARM?
I DON'T KNOW IF I'LL EVER PLAY THE PIANO AGAIN.
BUT COULD YOU PLAY IT BEFORE?
YES, QUITE WELL, ACTUALLY.

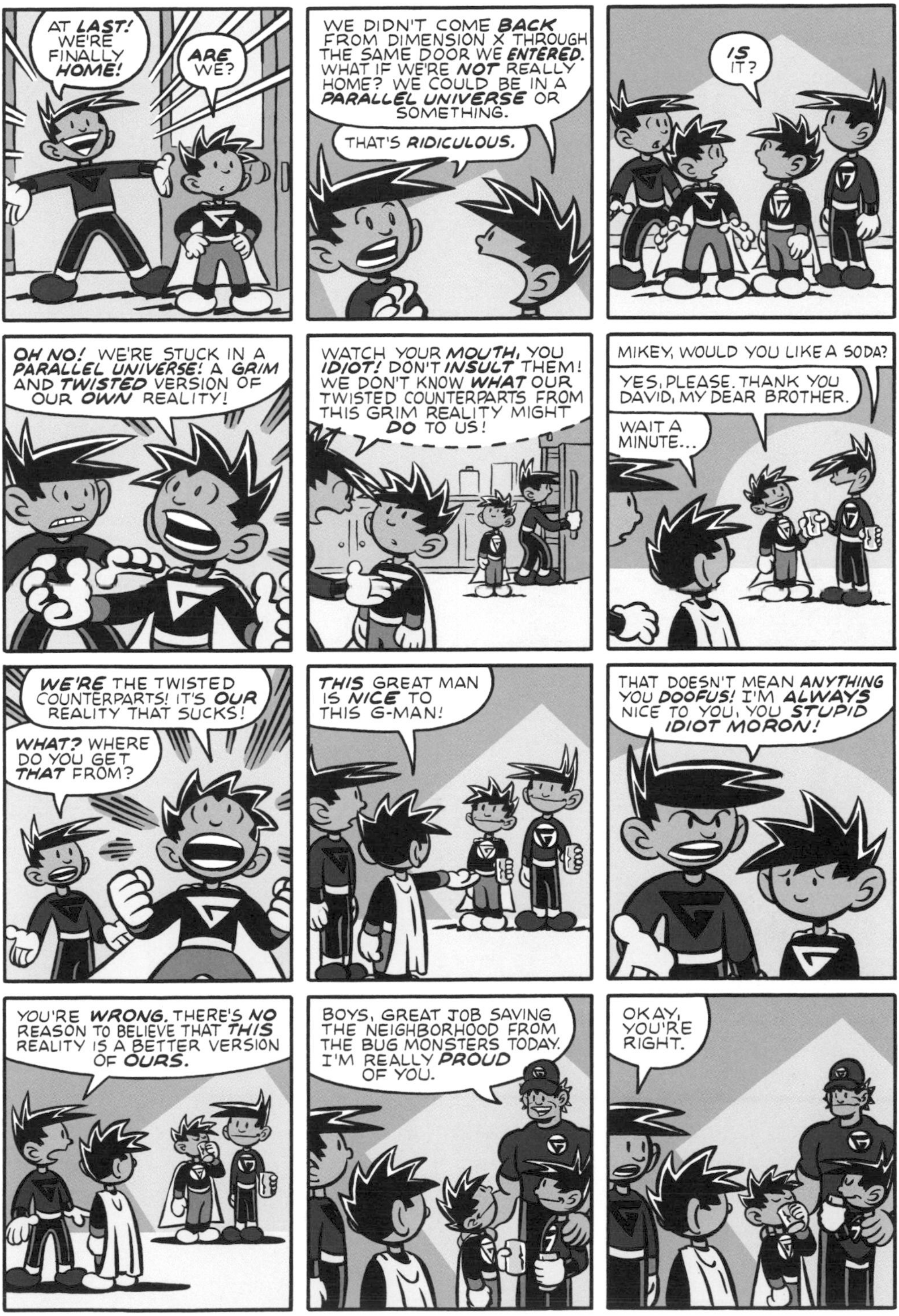

AT LAST! WE'RE FINALLY HOME!
ARE WE?
WE DIDN'T COME BACK FROM DIMENSION X THROUGH THE SAME DOOR WE ENTERED. WHAT IF WE'RE NOT REALLY HOME? WE COULD BE IN A PARALLEL UNIVERSE OR SOMETHING.
THAT'S RIDICULOUS.
IS IT?
OH NO! WE'RE STUCK IN A PARALLEL UNIVERSE! A GRIM AND TWISTED VERSION OF OUR OWN REALITY!
WATCH YOUR MOUTH, YOU IDIOT! DON'T INSULT THEM! WE DON'T KNOW WHAT OUR TWISTED COUNTERPARTS FROM THIS GRIM REALITY MIGHT DO TO US!
MIKEY, WOULD YOU LIKE A SODA?
YES, PLEASE. THANK YOU DAVID, MY DEAR BROTHER.
WAIT A MINUTE...
WE'RE THE TWISTED COUNTERPARTS! IT'S OUR REALITY THAT SUCKS!
WHAT? WHERE DO YOU GET THAT FROM?
THIS GREAT MAN IS NICE TO THIS G-MAN!
THAT DOESN'T MEAN ANYTHING YOU DOOFUS! I'M ALWAYS NICE TO YOU, YOU STUPID IDIOT MORON!
YOU'RE WRONG. THERE'S NO REASON TO BELIEVE THAT THIS REALITY IS A BETTER VERSION OF OURS.
BOYS, GREAT JOB SAVING THE NEIGHBORHOOD FROM THE BUG MONSTERS TODAY. I'M REALLY PROUD OF YOU.
OKAY, YOU'RE RIGHT.

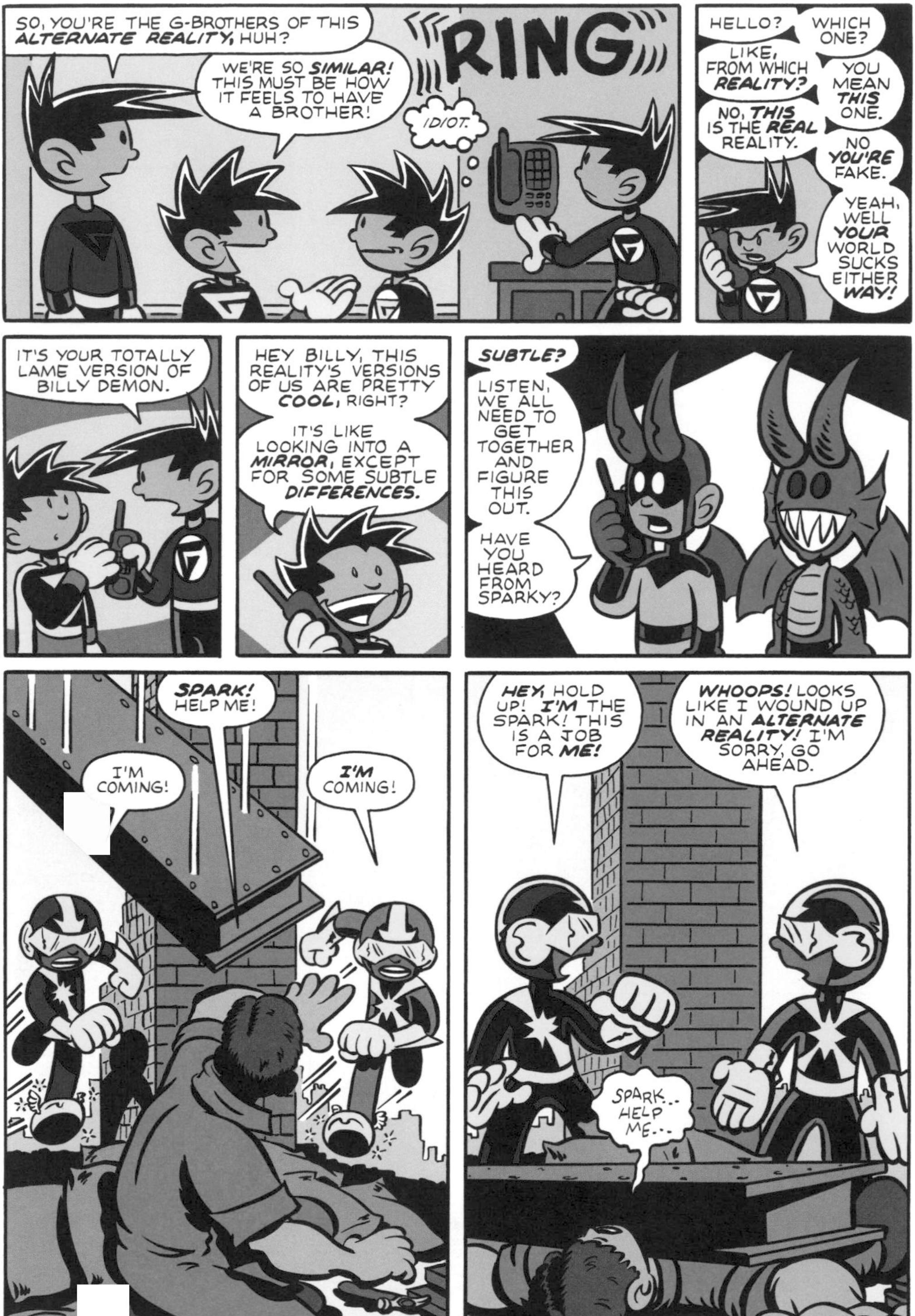
SO, YOU'RE THE G-BROTHERS OF THIS ALTERNATE REALITY, HUH?
WE'RE SO SIMILAR! THIS MUST BE HOW IT FEELS TO HAVE A BROTHER!
RING
IDIOT.
HELLO?
WHICH ONE?
LIKE, FROM WHICH REALITY?
YOU MEAN THIS ONE.
NO, THIS IS THE REAL REALITY.
NO YOU'RE FAKE.
YEAH, WELL YOUR WORLD SUCKS EITHER WAY!
IT'S YOUR TOTALLY LAME VERSION OF BILLY DEMON.
HEY BILLY, THIS REALITY'S VERSIONS OF US ARE PRETTY COOL, RIGHT?
IT'S LIKE LOOKING INTO A MIRROR, EXCEPT FOR SOME SUBTLE DIFFERENCES.
SUBTLE?
LISTEN, WE ALL NEED TO GET TOGETHER AND FIGURE THIS OUT.
HAVE YOU HEARD FROM SPARKY?
SPARK! HELP ME!
I'M COMING!
I'M COMING!
HEY, HOLD UP! I'M THE SPARK! THIS IS A JOB FOR ME!
WHOOPS! LOOKS LIKE I WOUND UP IN AN ALTERNATE REALITY! I'M SORRY, GO AHEAD.
SPARK... HELP ME...

SAVAGE COMIC BITS™

by Chris Giarrusso

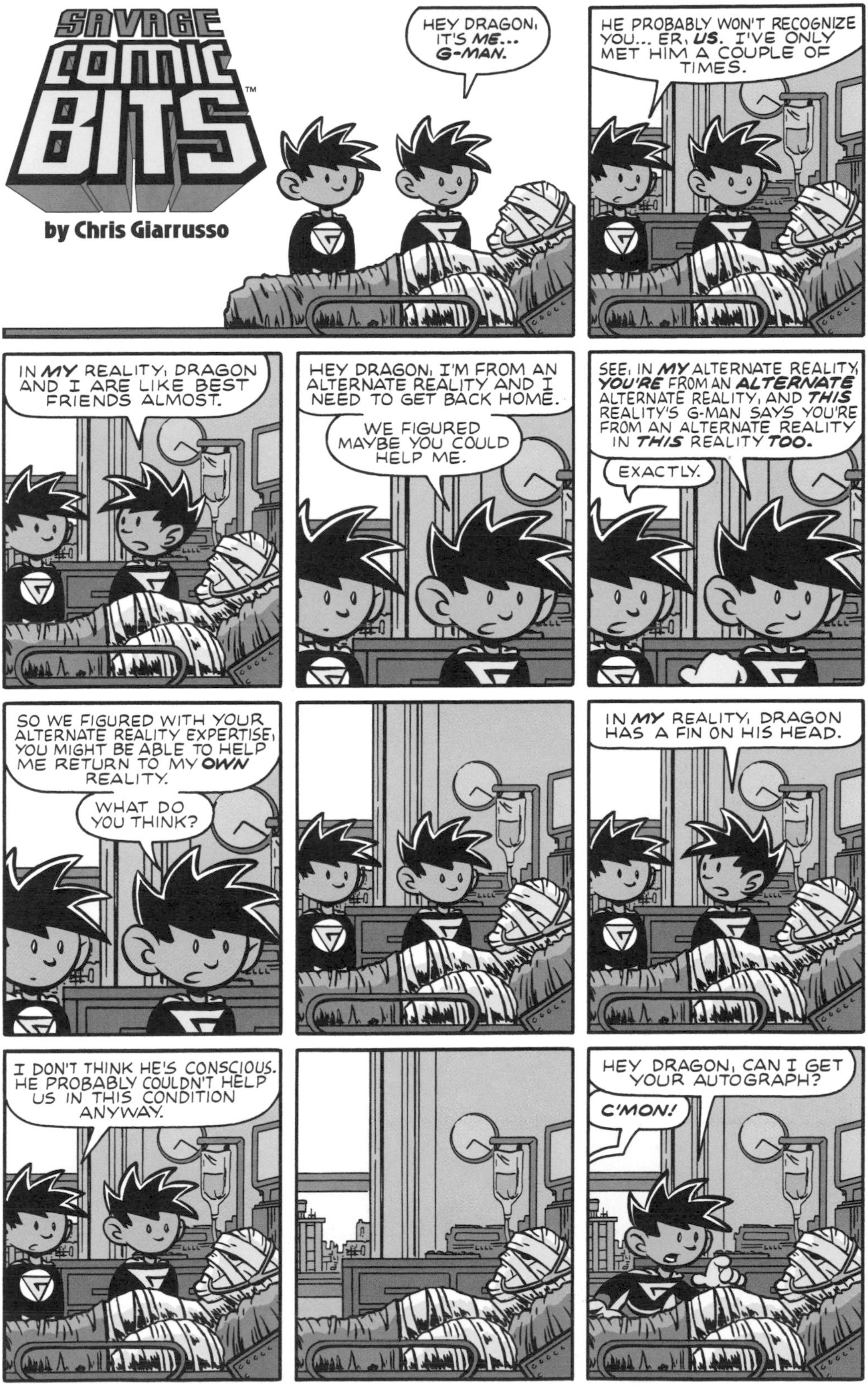
HEY DRAGON, IT'S ME... G-MAN.
HE PROBABLY WON'T RECOGNIZE YOU... ER, US. I'VE ONLY MET HIM A COUPLE OF TIMES.
IN MY REALITY, DRAGON AND I ARE LIKE BEST FRIENDS ALMOST.
HEY DRAGON, I'M FROM AN ALTERNATE REALITY AND I NEED TO GET BACK HOME.
WE FIGURED MAYBE YOU COULD HELP ME.
SEE, IN MY ALTERNATE REALITY, YOU'RE FROM AN ALTERNATE ALTERNATE REALITY, AND THIS REALITY'S G-MAN SAYS YOU'RE FROM AN ALTERNATE REALITY IN THIS REALITY TOO.
EXACTLY.
SO WE FIGURED WITH YOUR ALTERNATE REALITY EXPERTISE, YOU MIGHT BE ABLE TO HELP ME RETURN TO MY OWN REALITY.
WHAT DO YOU THINK?
IN MY REALITY, DRAGON HAS A FIN ON HIS HEAD.
I DON'T THINK HE'S CONSCIOUS. HE PROBABLY COULDN'T HELP US IN THIS CONDITION ANYWAY.
HEY DRAGON, CAN I GET YOUR AUTOGRAPH?
C'MON!

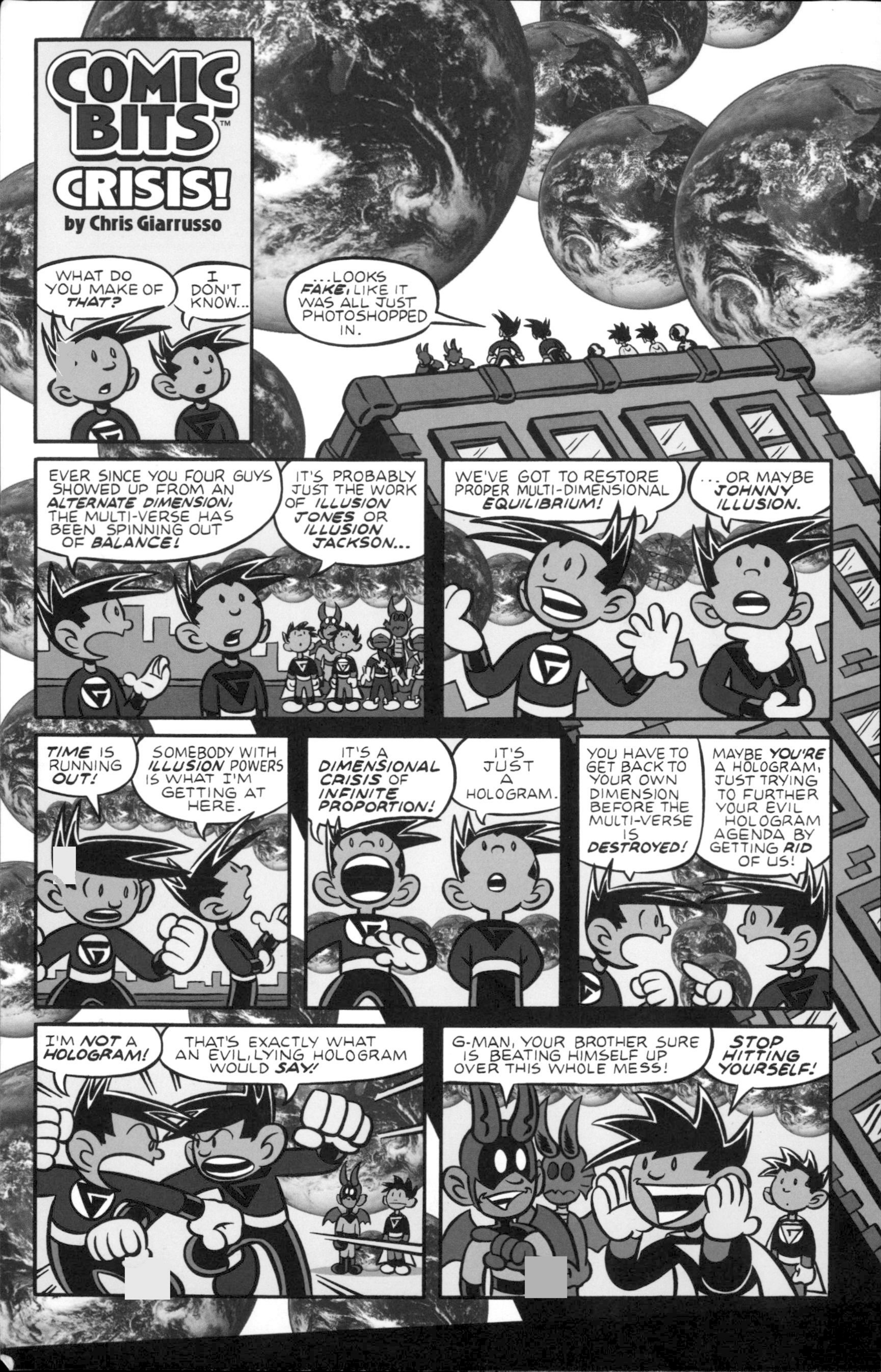
COMIC BITS™
CRISIS!
by Chris Giarrusso
WHAT DO YOU MAKE OF THAT?
I DON'T KNOW...
...LOOKS FAKE, LIKE IT WAS ALL JUST PHOTOSHOPPED IN.
EVER SINCE YOU FOUR GUYS SHOWED UP FROM AN ALTERNATE DIMENSION, THE MULTI-VERSE HAS BEEN SPINNING OUT OF BALANCE!
IT'S PROBABLY JUST THE WORK OF ILLUSION JONES OR ILLUSION JACKSON...
WE'VE GOT TO RESTORE PROPER MULTI-DIMENSIONAL EQUILIBRIUM!
...OR MAYBE JOHNNY ILLUSION.
TIME IS RUNNING OUT!
SOMEBODY WITH ILLUSION POWERS IS WHAT I'M GETTING AT HERE.
IT'S A DIMENSIONAL CRISIS OF INFINITE PROPORTION!
IT'S JUST A HOLOGRAM.
YOU HAVE TO GET BACK TO YOUR OWN DIMENSION BEFORE THE MULTI-VERSE IS DESTROYED!
MAYBE YOU'RE A HOLOGRAM, JUST TRYING TO FURTHER YOUR EVIL HOLOGRAM AGENDA BY GETTING RID OF US!
I'M NOT A HOLOGRAM!
THAT'S EXACTLY WHAT AN EVIL, LYING HOLOGRAM WOULD SAY!
G-MAN, YOUR BROTHER SURE IS BEATING HIMSELF UP OVER THIS WHOLE MESS!
STOP HITTING YOURSELF!

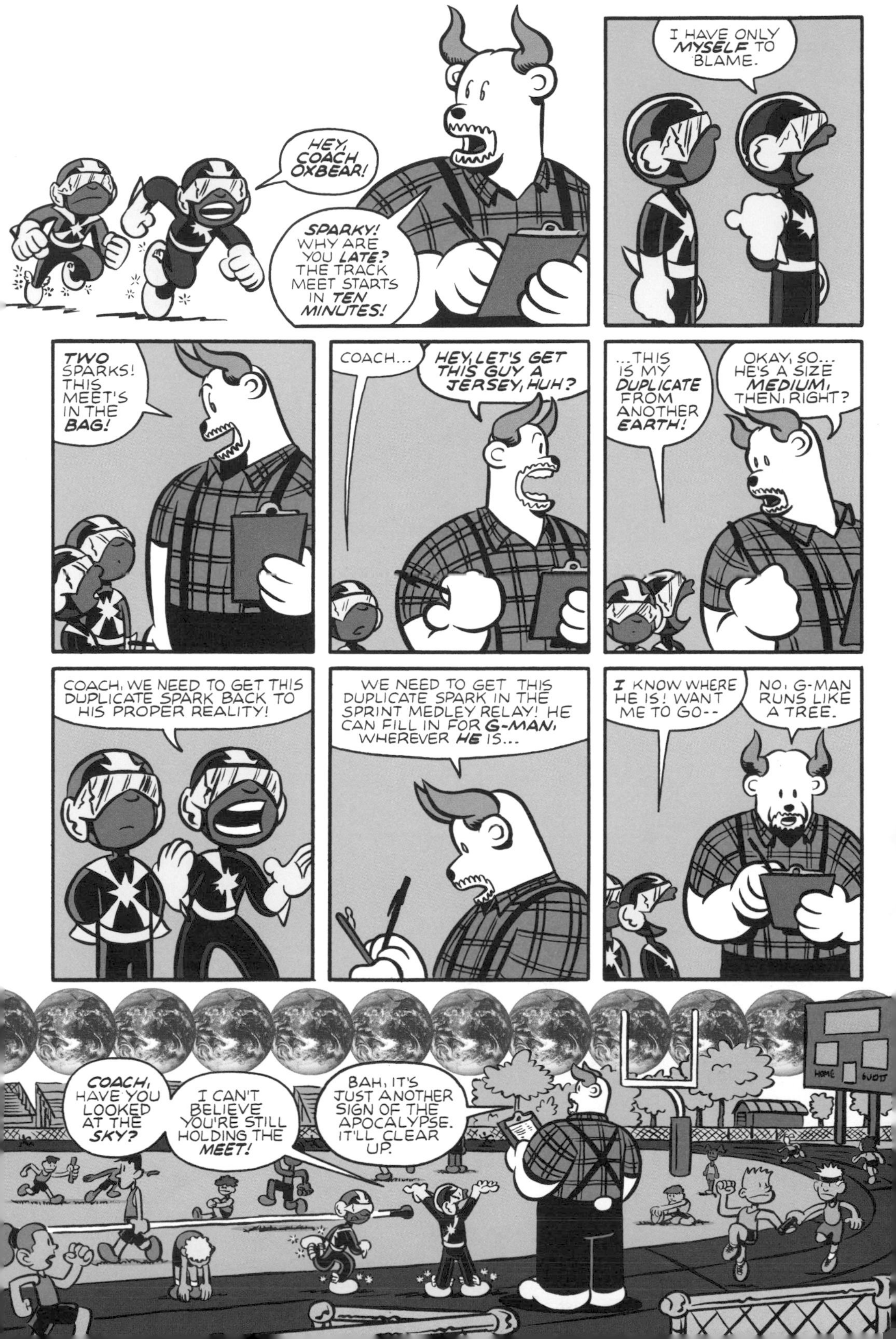
HEY, COACH OXBEAR!
SPARKY! WHY ARE YOU LATE? THE TRACK MEET STARTS IN TEN MINUTES!
I HAVE ONLY MYSELF TO BLAME.
TWO SPARKS! THIS MEET'S IN THE BAG!
COACH...
HEY, LET'S GET THIS GUY A JERSEY, HUH?
...THIS IS MY DUPLICATE FROM ANOTHER EARTH!
OKAY, SO... HE'S A SIZE MEDIUM, THEN, RIGHT?
COACH, WE NEED TO GET THIS DUPLICATE SPARK BACK TO HIS PROPER REALITY!
WE NEED TO GET THIS DUPLICATE SPARK IN THE SPRINT MEDLEY RELAY! HE CAN FILL IN FOR G-MAN, WHEREVER HE IS...
I KNOW WHERE HE IS! WANT ME TO GO--
NO, G-MAN RUNS LIKE A TREE.
COACH, HAVE YOU LOOKED AT THE SKY?
I CAN'T BELIEVE YOU'RE STILL HOLDING THE MEET!
BAH, IT'S JUST ANOTHER SIGN OF THE APOCALYPSE. IT'LL CLEAR UP.
HOME
GUEST

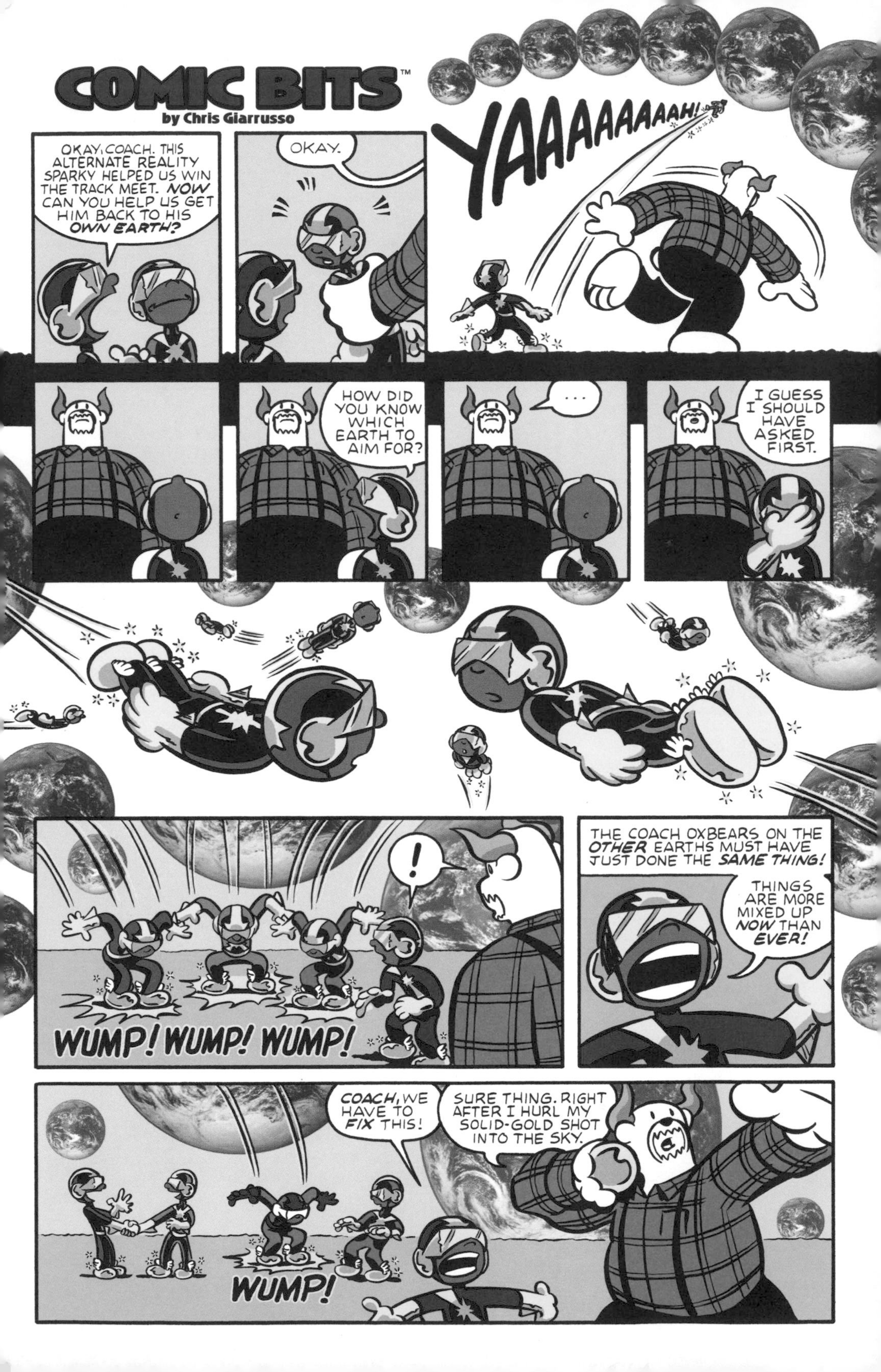
COMIC BITS™
by Chris Giarrusso
OKAY, COACH. THIS ALTERNATE REALITY SPARKY HELPED US WIN THE TRACK MEET. NOW CAN YOU HELP US GET HIM BACK TO HIS OWN EARTH?
OKAY.
YAAAAAAAAH!
HOW DID YOU KNOW WHICH EARTH TO AIM FOR?
...
I GUESS I SHOULD HAVE ASKED FIRST.
!
WUMP! WUMP! WUMP!
THE COACH OXBEARS ON THE OTHER EARTHS MUST HAVE JUST DONE THE SAME THING!
THINGS ARE MORE MIXED UP NOW THAN EVER!
COACH, WE HAVE TO FIX THIS!
SURE THING. RIGHT AFTER I HURL MY SOLID-GOLD SHOT INTO THE SKY.
WUMP!

Wrote by Chris Giarrusso & Jacob Chabot   Drawed by Jacob Chabot

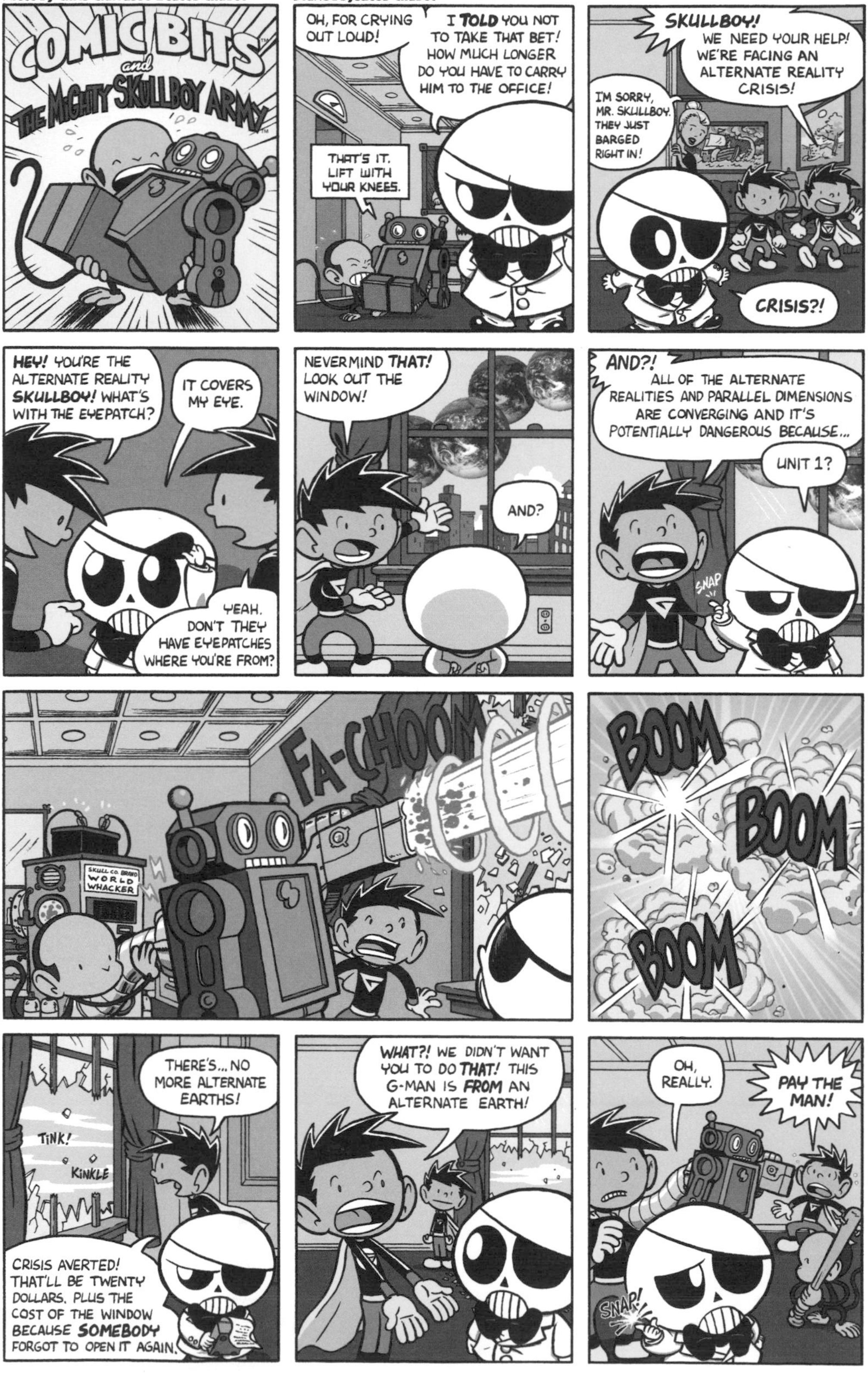
COMIC BITS
and
THE MIGHTY SKULLBOY ARMY
OH, FOR CRYING OUT LOUD!
I TOLD YOU NOT TO TAKE THAT BET! HOW MUCH LONGER DO YOU HAVE TO CARRY HIM TO THE OFFICE!
THAT'S IT. LIFT WITH YOUR KNEES.
SKULLBOY! WE NEED YOUR HELP! WE'RE FACING AN ALTERNATE REALITY CRISIS!
I'M SORRY, MR. SKULLBOY. THEY JUST BARGED RIGHT IN!
CRISIS?!
HEY! YOU'RE THE ALTERNATE REALITY SKULLBOY! WHAT'S WITH THE EYEPATCH?
IT COVERS MY EYE.
YEAH. DON'T THEY HAVE EYEPATCHES WHERE YOU'RE FROM?
NEVERMIND THAT! LOOK OUT THE WINDOW!
AND?
AND?! ALL OF THE ALTERNATE REALITIES AND PARALLEL DIMENSIONS ARE CONVERGING AND IT'S POTENTIALLY DANGEROUS BECAUSE...
UNIT 1?
SNAP
FA-CHOOM
SKULL CO. BRAND WORLD WHACKER
BOOM
BOOM
BOOM
THERE'S... NO MORE ALTERNATE EARTHS!
TINK!
KINKLE
CRISIS AVERTED! THAT'LL BE TWENTY DOLLARS. PLUS THE COST OF THE WINDOW BECAUSE SOMEBODY FORGOT TO OPEN IT AGAIN.
WHAT?! WE DIDN'T WANT YOU TO DO THAT! THIS G-MAN IS FROM AN ALTERNATE EARTH!
OH, REALLY.
PAY THE MAN!
SNAP!

Comic Bits™ and The Mighty Skullboy Army™

Wrote by Chris Giarrusso & Jacob Chabot

Drawed by Chris Giarrusso

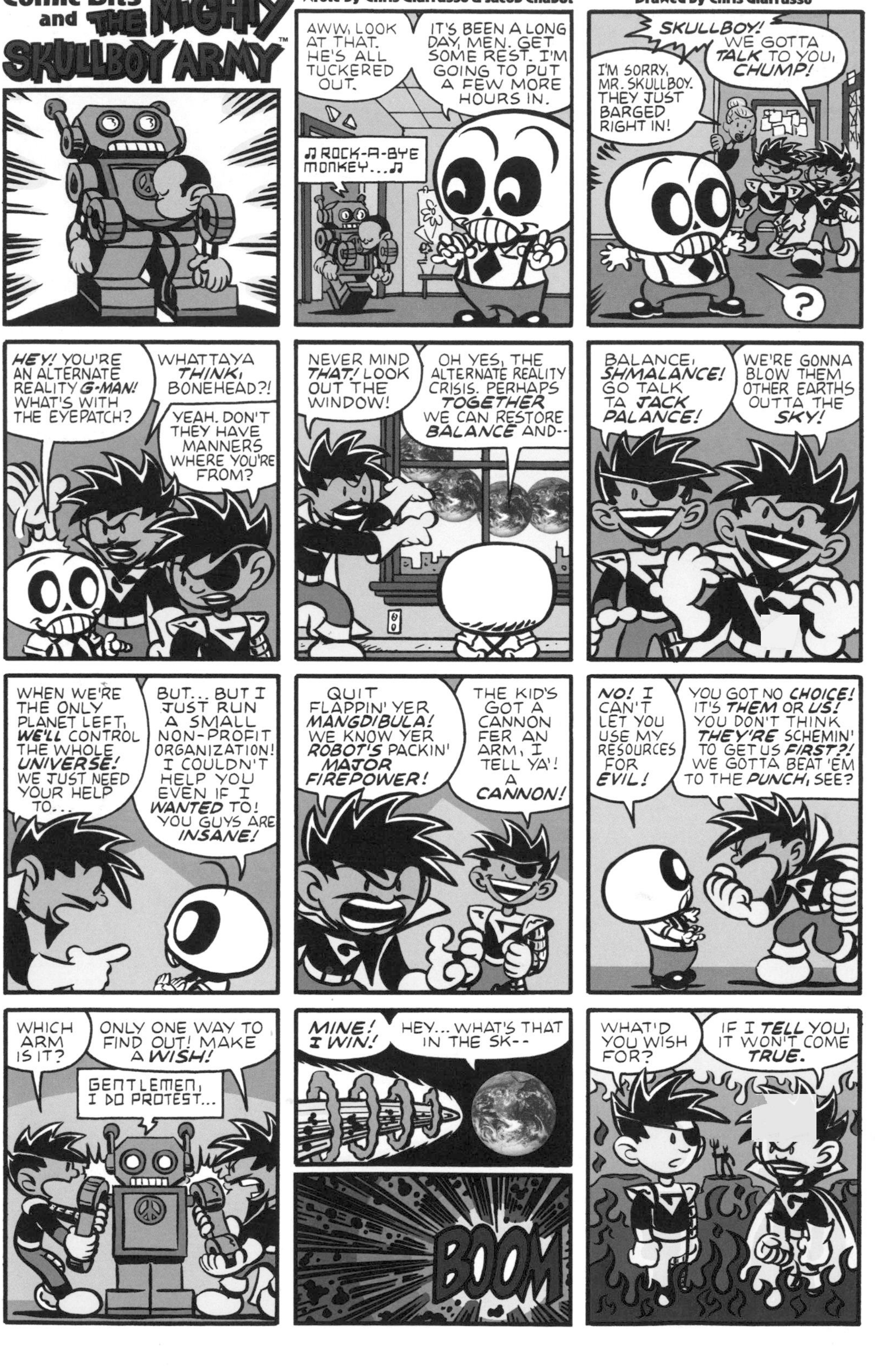
AWW, LOOK AT THAT. HE'S ALL TUCKERED OUT.
IT'S BEEN A LONG DAY, MEN. GET SOME REST. I'M GOING TO PUT A FEW MORE HOURS IN.
♫ROCK-A-BYE MONKEY...♫
SKULLBOY!
WE GOTTA TALK TO YOU, CHUMP!
I'M SORRY, MR. SKULLBOY. THEY JUST BARGED RIGHT IN!
?
HEY! YOU'RE AN ALTERNATE REALITY G-MAN! WHAT'S WITH THE EYEPATCH?
WHATTAYA THINK, BONEHEAD?!
YEAH. DON'T THEY HAVE MANNERS WHERE YOU'RE FROM?
NEVER MIND THAT! LOOK OUT THE WINDOW!
OH YES, THE ALTERNATE REALITY CRISIS. PERHAPS TOGETHER WE CAN RESTORE BALANCE AND--
BALANCE, SHMALANCE! GO TALK TA JACK PALANCE!
WE'RE GONNA BLOW THEM OTHER EARTHS OUTTA THE SKY!
WHEN WE'RE THE ONLY PLANET LEFT, WE'LL CONTROL THE WHOLE UNIVERSE! WE JUST NEED YOUR HELP TO...
BUT... BUT I JUST RUN A SMALL NON-PROFIT ORGANIZATION! I COULDN'T HELP YOU EVEN IF I WANTED TO! YOU GUYS ARE INSANE!
QUIT FLAPPIN' YER MANGDIBULA! WE KNOW YER ROBOT'S PACKIN' MAJOR FIREPOWER!
THE KID'S GOT A CANNON FER AN ARM, I TELL YA'! A CANNON!
NO! I CAN'T LET YOU USE MY RESOURCES FOR EVIL!
YOU GOT NO CHOICE! IT'S THEM OR US! YOU DON'T THINK THEY'RE SCHEMIN' TO GET US FIRST?! WE GOTTA BEAT 'EM TO THE PUNCH, SEE?
WHICH ARM IS IT?
ONLY ONE WAY TO FIND OUT! MAKE A WISH!
GENTLEMEN, I DO PROTEST...
MINE! I WIN!
HEY... WHAT'S THAT IN THE SK--
BOOM
WHAT'D YOU WISH FOR?
IF I TELL YOU, IT WON'T COME TRUE.

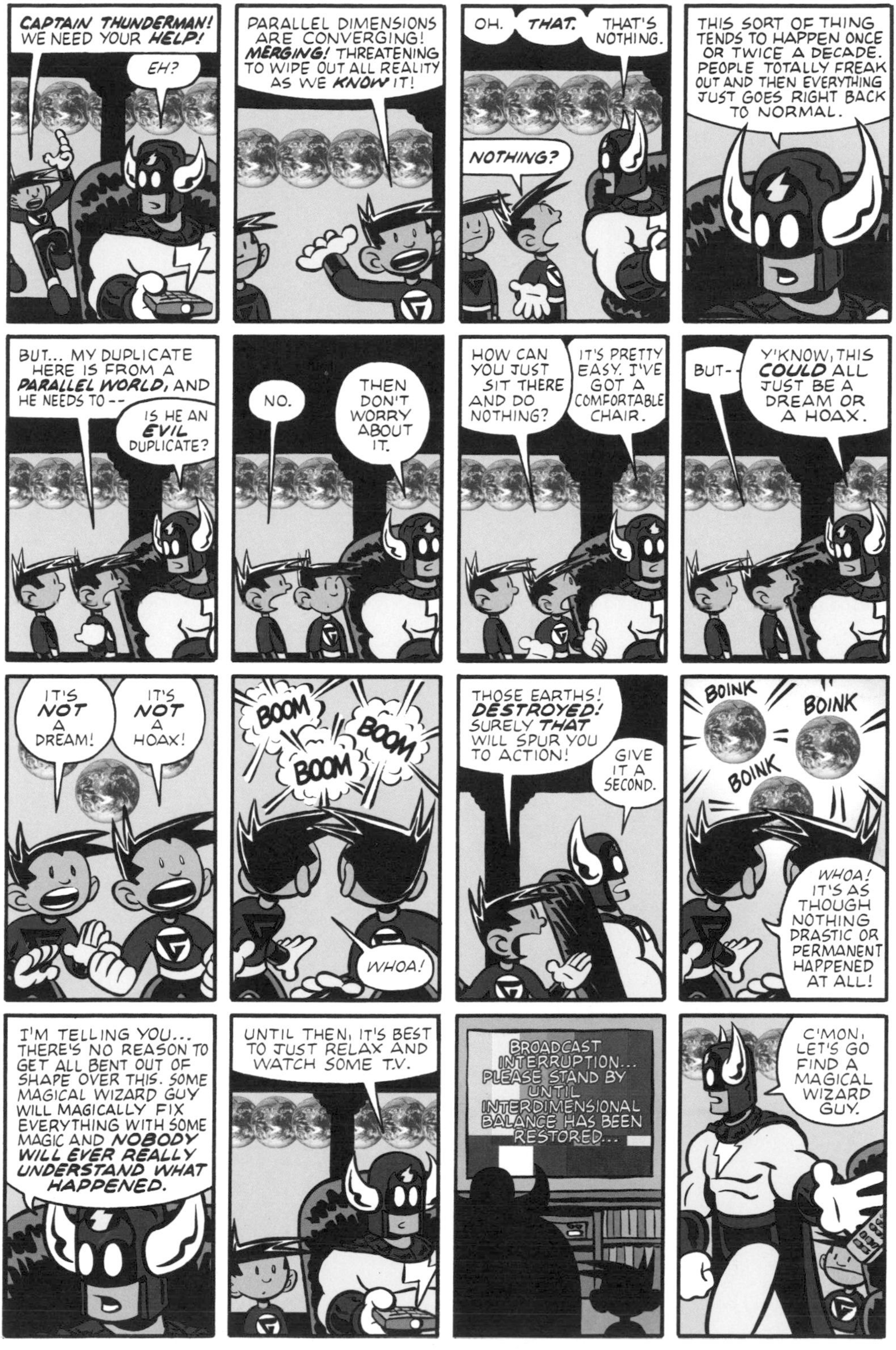
CAPTAIN THUNDERMAN! WE NEED YOUR HELP!
EH?
PARALLEL DIMENSIONS ARE CONVERGING! MERGING! THREATENING TO WIPE OUT ALL REALITY AS WE KNOW IT!
OH.
THAT.
THAT'S NOTHING.
NOTHING?
THIS SORT OF THING TENDS TO HAPPEN ONCE OR TWICE A DECADE. PEOPLE TOTALLY FREAK OUT AND THEN EVERYTHING JUST GOES RIGHT BACK TO NORMAL.
BUT... MY DUPLICATE HERE IS FROM A PARALLEL WORLD, AND HE NEEDS TO --
IS HE AN EVIL DUPLICATE?
NO.
THEN DON'T WORRY ABOUT IT.
HOW CAN YOU JUST SIT THERE AND DO NOTHING?
IT'S PRETTY EASY. I'VE GOT A COMFORTABLE CHAIR.
BUT--
Y'KNOW, THIS COULD ALL JUST BE A DREAM OR A HOAX.
IT'S NOT A DREAM!
IT'S NOT A HOAX!
BOOM
BOOM
BOOM
WHOA!
THOSE EARTHS! DESTROYED! SURELY THAT WILL SPUR YOU TO ACTION!
GIVE IT A SECOND.
BOINK
BOINK
BOINK
WHOA! IT'S AS THOUGH NOTHING DRASTIC OR PERMANENT HAPPENED AT ALL!
I'M TELLING YOU... THERE'S NO REASON TO GET ALL BENT OUT OF SHAPE OVER THIS. SOME MAGICAL WIZARD GUY WILL MAGICALLY FIX EVERYTHING WITH SOME MAGIC AND NOBODY WILL EVER REALLY UNDERSTAND WHAT HAPPENED.
UNTIL THEN, IT'S BEST TO JUST RELAX AND WATCH SOME T.V.
BROADCAST INTERRUPTION... PLEASE STAND BY UNTIL INTERDIMENSIONAL BALANCE HAS BEEN RESTORED...
C'MON, LET'S GO FIND A MAGICAL WIZARD GUY.

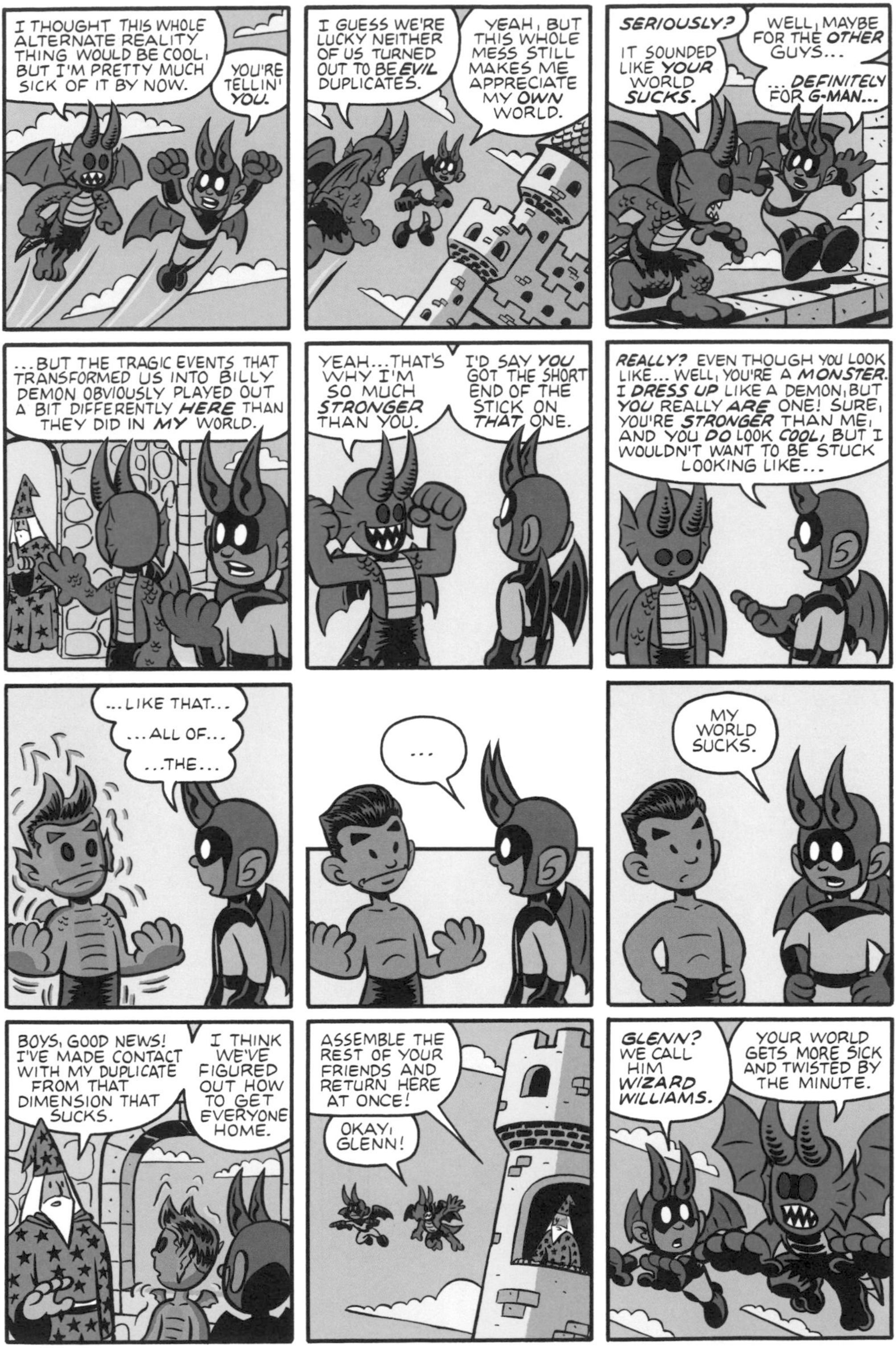
I THOUGHT THIS WHOLE ALTERNATE REALITY THING WOULD BE COOL, BUT I'M PRETTY MUCH SICK OF IT BY NOW.
YOU'RE TELLIN' YOU.
I GUESS WE'RE LUCKY NEITHER OF US TURNED OUT TO BE EVIL DUPLICATES.
YEAH, BUT THIS WHOLE MESS STILL MAKES ME APPRECIATE MY OWN WORLD.
SERIOUSLY?
IT SOUNDED LIKE YOUR WORLD SUCKS.
WELL, MAYBE FOR THE OTHER GUYS...
...DEFINITELY FOR G-MAN...
...BUT THE TRAGIC EVENTS THAT TRANSFORMED US INTO BILLY DEMON OBVIOUSLY PLAYED OUT A BIT DIFFERENTLY HERE THAN THEY DID IN MY WORLD.
YEAH...THAT'S WHY I'M SO MUCH STRONGER THAN YOU.
I'D SAY YOU GOT THE SHORT END OF THE STICK ON THAT ONE.
REALLY? EVEN THOUGH YOU LOOK LIKE... WELL, YOU'RE A MONSTER. I DRESS UP LIKE A DEMON, BUT YOU REALLY ARE ONE! SURE, YOU'RE STRONGER THAN ME, AND YOU DO LOOK COOL, BUT I WOULDN'T WANT TO BE STUCK LOOKING LIKE...
...LIKE THAT...
...ALL OF...
...THE...
...
MY WORLD SUCKS.
BOYS, GOOD NEWS! I'VE MADE CONTACT WITH MY DUPLICATE FROM THAT DIMENSION THAT SUCKS.
I THINK WE'VE FIGURED OUT HOW TO GET EVERYONE HOME.
ASSEMBLE THE REST OF YOUR FRIENDS AND RETURN HERE AT ONCE!
OKAY, GLENN!
GLENN? WE CALL HIM WIZARD WILLIAMS.
YOUR WORLD GETS MORE SICK AND TWISTED BY THE MINUTE.

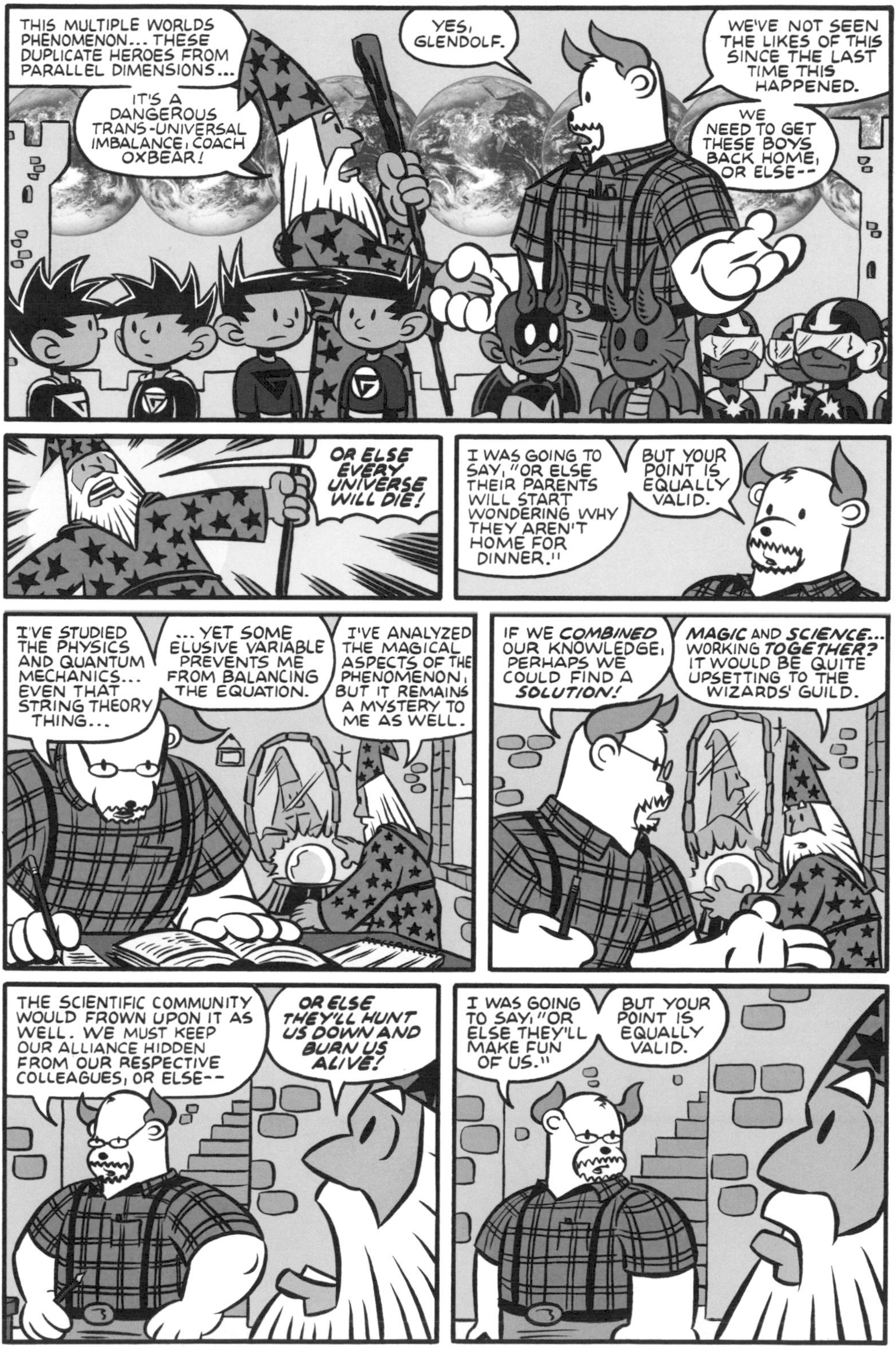
THIS MULTIPLE WORLDS PHENOMENON... THESE DUPLICATE HEROES FROM PARALLEL DIMENSIONS...
IT'S A DANGEROUS TRANS-UNIVERSAL IMBALANCE, COACH OXBEAR!
YES, GLENDOLF.
WE'VE NOT SEEN THE LIKES OF THIS SINCE THE LAST TIME THIS HAPPENED.
WE NEED TO GET THESE BOYS BACK HOME, OR ELSE--
OR ELSE EVERY UNIVERSE WILL DIE!
I WAS GOING TO SAY, "OR ELSE THEIR PARENTS WILL START WONDERING WHY THEY AREN'T HOME FOR DINNER."
BUT YOUR POINT IS EQUALLY VALID.
I'VE STUDIED THE PHYSICS AND QUANTUM MECHANICS... EVEN THAT STRING THEORY THING...
...YET SOME ELUSIVE VARIABLE PREVENTS ME FROM BALANCING THE EQUATION.
I'VE ANALYZED THE MAGICAL ASPECTS OF THE PHENOMENON, BUT IT REMAINS A MYSTERY TO ME AS WELL.
IF WE COMBINED OUR KNOWLEDGE, PERHAPS WE COULD FIND A SOLUTION!
MAGIC AND SCIENCE... WORKING TOGETHER? IT WOULD BE QUITE UPSETTING TO THE WIZARDS' GUILD.
THE SCIENTIFIC COMMUNITY WOULD FROWN UPON IT AS WELL. WE MUST KEEP OUR ALLIANCE HIDDEN FROM OUR RESPECTIVE COLLEAGUES, OR ELSE--
OR ELSE THEY'LL HUNT US DOWN AND BURN US ALIVE!
I WAS GOING TO SAY, "OR ELSE THEY'LL MAKE FUN OF US."
BUT YOUR POINT IS EQUALLY VALID.

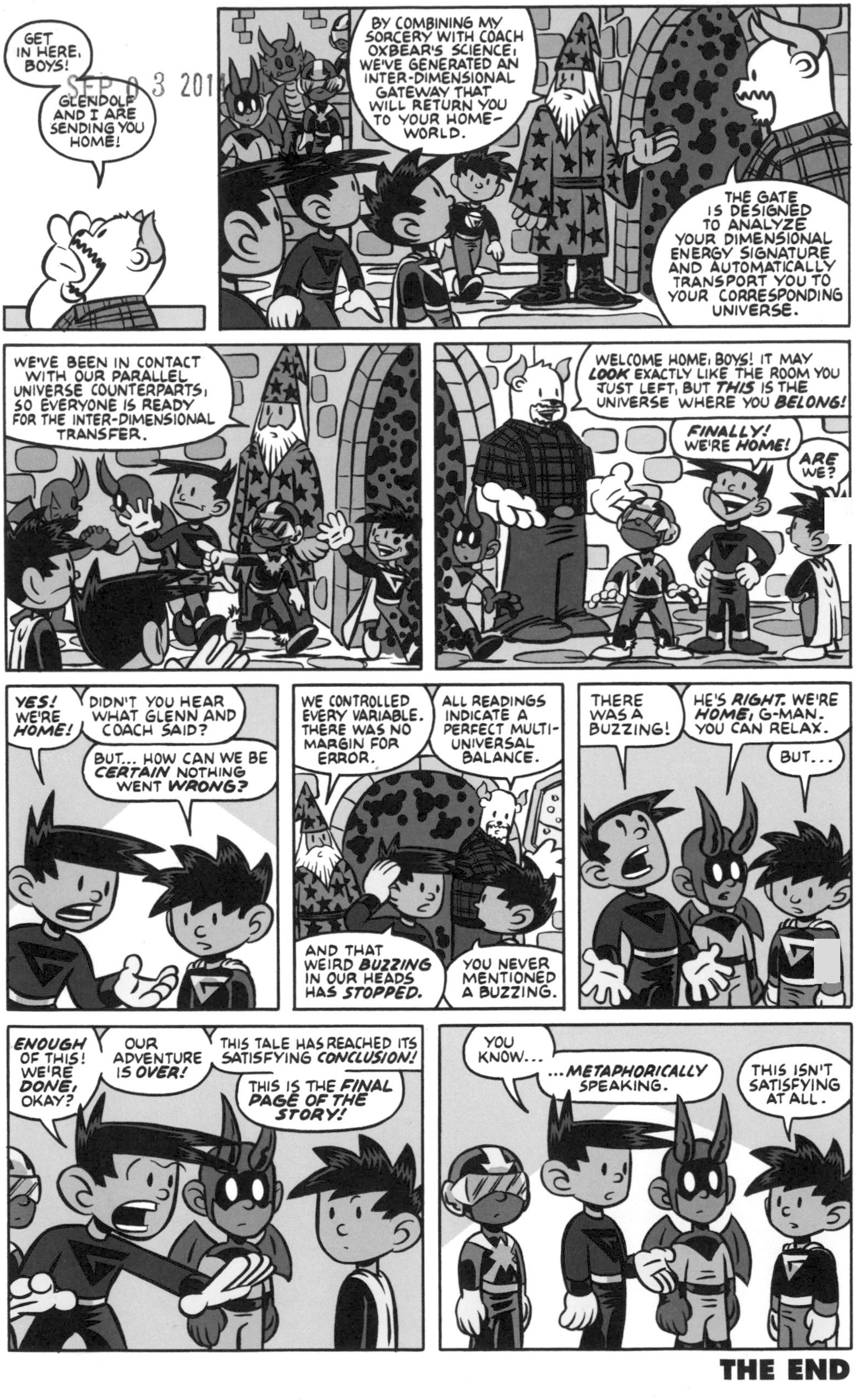
GET IN HERE, BOYS!
GLENDOLF AND I ARE SENDING YOU HOME!
BY COMBINING MY SORCERY WITH COACH OXBEAR'S SCIENCE, WE'VE GENERATED AN INTER-DIMENSIONAL GATEWAY THAT WILL RETURN YOU TO YOUR HOME-WORLD.
THE GATE IS DESIGNED TO ANALYZE YOUR DIMENSIONAL ENERGY SIGNATURE AND AUTOMATICALLY TRANSPORT YOU TO YOUR CORRESPONDING UNIVERSE.
WE'VE BEEN IN CONTACT WITH OUR PARALLEL UNIVERSE COUNTERPARTS, SO EVERYONE IS READY FOR THE INTER-DIMENSIONAL TRANSFER.
WELCOME HOME, BOYS! IT MAY LOOK EXACTLY LIKE THE ROOM YOU JUST LEFT, BUT THIS IS THE UNIVERSE WHERE YOU BELONG!
FINALLY! WE'RE HOME!
ARE WE?
YES! WE'RE HOME!
DIDN'T YOU HEAR WHAT GLENN AND COACH SAID?
BUT... HOW CAN WE BE CERTAIN NOTHING WENT WRONG?
WE CONTROLLED EVERY VARIABLE. THERE WAS NO MARGIN FOR ERROR.
ALL READINGS INDICATE A PERFECT MULTI-UNIVERSAL BALANCE.
AND THAT WEIRD BUZZING IN OUR HEADS HAS STOPPED.
YOU NEVER MENTIONED A BUZZING.
THERE WAS A BUZZING!
HE'S RIGHT. WE'RE HOME, G-MAN. YOU CAN RELAX.
BUT...
ENOUGH OF THIS! WE'RE DONE, OKAY?
OUR ADVENTURE IS OVER!
THIS TALE HAS REACHED ITS SATISFYING CONCLUSION!
THIS IS THE FINAL PAGE OF THE STORY!
YOU KNOW...
...METAPHORICALLY SPEAKING.
THIS ISN'T SATISFYING AT ALL.
THE END